Helen felt Alice's thigh pressing up against hers, felt her scrawny arm slip around the back of the sofa. "Been a long time since I had someone come over." Alice sighed. She put her head down on Helen's shoulder. "I spotted you right away, sitting there all by yourself at the bar. I couldn't remember seeing you before."

Helen managed to keep from flinching at the feel of Alice's body snuggled close. God, how the hell did she get into this? "Yeah, well, I don't go to the White Horse too much."

"Then I guess it was my lucky night, huh?" Alice leaned in for a kiss. "Usually it's just guys there, you know? Not someone as cute as you." She breathed into Helen's ear and grazed her lips across Helen's neck.

A Time to Cast Away

A Helen Black Mystery

Pat Welch

2005

Bella Books, Inc.
P.O. Box 10543
Tallahassee, FL 32302

Printed in the United States of America on acid-free paper
First Edition

Editor: Christi Cassidy
Cover designer: Sandy Knowles

ISBN 1-59493-036-8

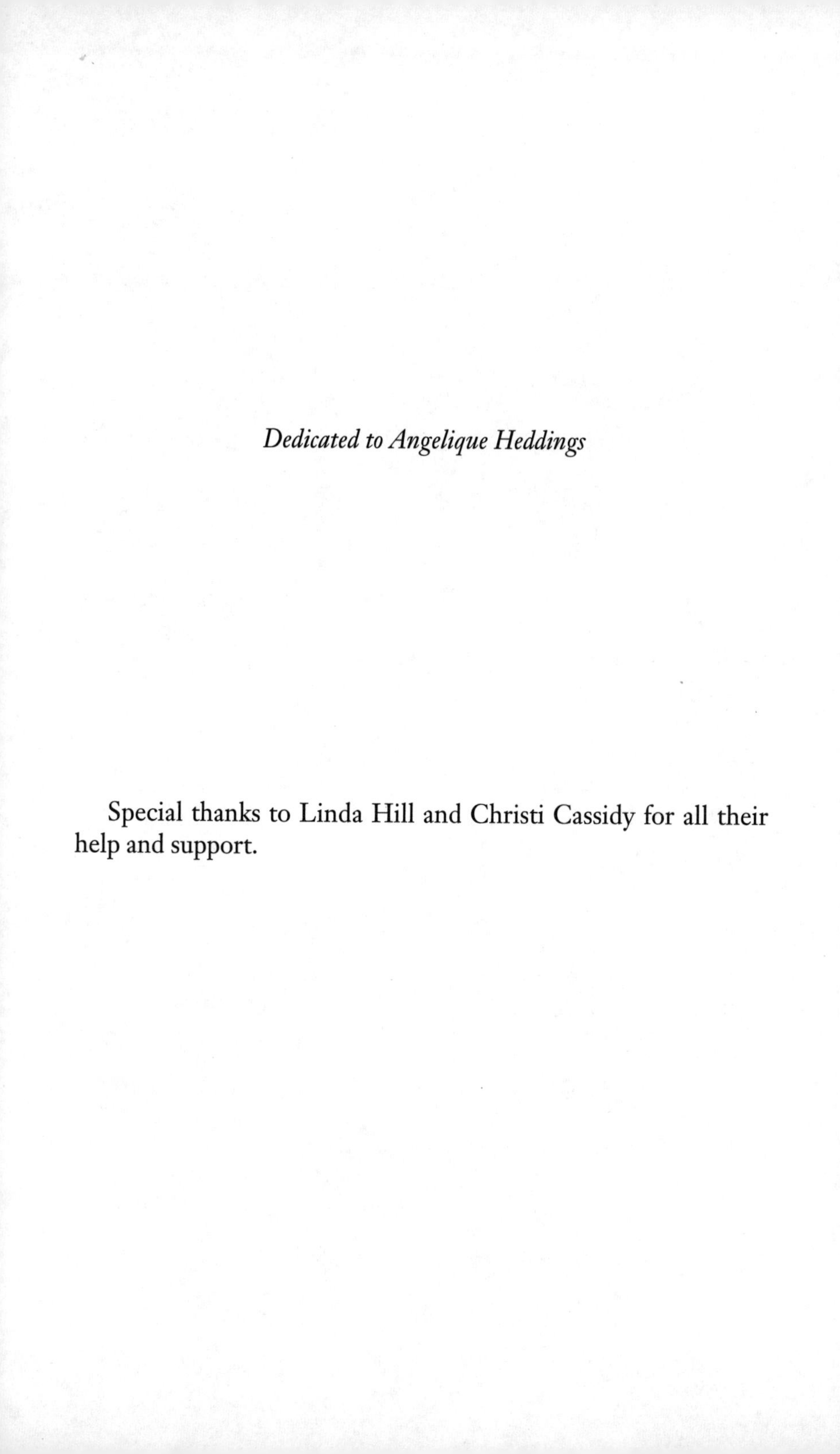

Dedicated to Angelique Heddings

Special thanks to Linda Hill and Christi Cassidy for all their help and support.

Chapter One

"So this is all I have left of her. Some pictures in a photo album."

Helen nodded. Jesus, the apartment was hot. It was making her head hurt. Well, the heat and maybe a couple more drinks than had been wise. She put her drink down on the battered coffee table, pushing aside the stained mugs and aging *TV Guides*, and gave a longing glance at the window. If only she could open it for a few minutes, take in deep breaths of cold January air. It had started to rain when Helen and Alice left the White Horse for Alice's apartment. The thin drizzle had turned into a downpour during the last half-hour. Dirt streaked in gray runnels down the bay window overlooking Telegraph Avenue in Oakland. Outside a car thumped out a deep heavy beat as it moved slowly down the street toward Berkeley. Murmurs from the floor above ascended into angry yelling, followed by the sound of breaking glass. Then silence. Helen stifled a sigh. Alice was probably too drunk to notice

Helen's discomfort. She'd been on the verge of a crying jag when they'd left the bar. While digging out her spare key from under the potted plant resting in the hallway by the front door, Alice had nearly upset all the potting soil onto the stained carpet.

"She was the best woman I ever knew. Smart, educated, all that shit. Hot, too. You know? Don't know what she saw in me, but damn, she was hot."

Helen sat back down gingerly on the sagging sofa, trying to ignore the crunching sounds coming from beneath the cushion. "So, you haven't heard from her in a long time?"

"Been almost a year now. Never thought she'd do it. Leave, I mean. You know?"

Helen tried not to think about what she was sitting on. She shifted on the sofa and heard a definite crunch. Maybe a bag of potato chips left over from the last binge. Maybe a newspaper. She looked over at Alice, who was leaning forward on the sofa, elbows on knees and head in hands. Shit, the woman had tears running down her face. "Wow, that's a long time, all right. You have no idea where she lives now?"

"Nope. Just wish she'd call sometimes, you know?"

No, Helen thought, I don't know. I don't know why I offered to take you home when the bartender refused to give you anything else to drink. I don't know why for a moment you looked appealing in that dim lighting. I don't know who you are or what the hell you're talking about. Some poor girl who dumped you that you're still crying over. And if you say "you know" one more time I will leave.

"Every night, same thing. Just waitin' around for her to call." Alice sniffled loudly, ran a shaky hand over her face. "I keep taking out this paper and lookin' at it, trying to understand her. Trying to make sense out of the way she left."

Helen picked up her drink and finished it quickly, welcoming the burning heat in her throat. This was the first night in months she'd had enough cash left to take herself out for a drink. Just a drink after work on a Friday night, that's all she'd planned for.

Alice had looked all right when she'd sat down on the barstool next to Helen. It had all begun when Alice commented on the cute young dykes playing pool in the corner. The jokes and smiles had pierced Helen with the sharp clear pain of loneliness. Lonely for the company of other lesbians, lonely for women's voices.

Rain pounded hard against the walls of the building. Great slashes of water sluiced against the window. The streetlight outside shone in through the warped blinds. Somewhere a cat yowled. Alice's cat? There had been a faint odor of aging kitty litter wafting out the door when they entered, but it was hard to distinguish one smell from all the rest. Maybe Jenny—that was the name, right?—had left the cat behind, too, and it was in its own way still grieving for the loss.

"See here, look, I keep it in this photo album." Alice pulled at Helen's arm, forcing her to lean in closer. "She used to go through it all the time, telling me all about her family." Helen watched Alice turn the pages. It seemed to calm her, and she even smiled as she studied the pictures. "I don't have anything like this, you know? Nothing of my own family. My dad left us when I was just a baby, and my mom was always working. I had to take care of my baby sister. Didn't have a camera."

It was hard to see the photographs in the dim light. Curiosity crowded out disgust and Helen moved closer on the couch so she could see. Interesting—the pictures went back several generations. She ran her hands over the album. Old cracked leather, some kind of pattern embossed in it. It must have been in the ex-girlfriend's family for a couple of generations.

Helen felt Alice's thigh pressing up against hers, felt her scrawny arm slip around the back of the sofa. "Been a long time since I had someone come over." Alice sighed. She put her head down on Helen's shoulder. "I spotted you right away, sitting there all by yourself at the bar. I couldn't remember seeing you before."

Helen managed to keep from flinching at the feel of Alice's body snuggled close. God, how the hell did she get into this? "Yeah, well, I don't go to the White Horse too much."

"Then I guess it was my lucky night, huh?" Alice leaned in for a kiss. "Usually it's just guys there, you know? Not someone as cute as you." She breathed into Helen's ear and grazed her lips across Helen's neck.

"Look—" Helen struggled up from the sofa and out of Alice's arms. "I think I ought to be going now. I mean, you're home safe and sound, you can get your car tomorrow." Please let me find my keys, Helen prayed. There they were, next to her wallet on the television set.

"You're leaving?" Alice splayed across the sofa, her face tear-stained, the photo album falling off her lap onto the floor. "But you just got here."

"It's a school night for me, Alice. I have to get home and go to bed. Early morning," Helen lied. Well, maybe it was true—maybe the temp agency would have a job for her on a Saturday. Right. "I think you might want to go to bed soon, too."

But Alice's face had set like concrete into a sullen stare. "Sure. Whatever." She picked up her beer and took a long swallow. "Guess it's pretty late, huh?"

Helen sighed under the weight of guilt. Great. Another stray. "Look, what's your number? I'll give you a call tomorrow, see how you're doing."

Alice peered up at her. "I don't know. If you're working and all, maybe you'll be too busy."

"Got a pen?"

"Maybe in the kitchen." Alice disappeared, and Helen heard drawers slamming and papers shuffling. A couple of muttered curses revealed that Alice was having trouble finding pen and paper. Helen began to follow her but was stopped in her tracks by a glimpse of herself in the watery mirror hanging in the dimly lit foyer of the small apartment. Dark brown hair liberally streaked with gray came down to her chin. Her mouth and eyes, ringed with lines, carried anger and suspicion. She was thinner than she had been in years, almost gaunt, in fact. But she'd lost her appetite since coming back to California from Mississippi. Helen watched herself grinning wryly. She looked as bad as when she came out of prison a few years ago. The few pounds she'd put on while getting her life back together had melted away since her return to Oakland. Helen pushed her hair behind her ears and made herself look long and hard. She looked tired, angry, beaten. She looked a lot like Alice, in fact.

"Here we go." Alice scribbled on a notepad, tore off a sheet and handed it over. "Tomorrow is my day off, so call anytime."

Helen tucked the paper in her wallet without looking at it. "Thanks. Get some sleep now, okay?"

"Hey, you can come over, too, if you want. We don't have to talk about Jenny, you know? I mean, we can talk about anything you like."

Helen fussed with her keys and avoided looking at Alice. The eager note in the other woman's voice made her cringe. "I'll call you." At least she could do that, even if she couldn't bring herself to visit.

Helen walked quickly down the empty hallway to the staircase, knowing that Alice was watching her as she left. She almost ran down the stairs into the street, grateful for the rain and cold wind after the stifling heat of Alice's apartment. Helen stood for a moment, disoriented, looking at the row of cars gleaming wetly under the street lamp. Then she spotted the old sedan. She'd only had the car for a month, and it still didn't feel right.

In fact, most of her life didn't feel right at the moment. Alice was just the latest episode in a lengthening line of odd events that didn't seem to fit anywhere. Helen had been back in the East Bay of San Francisco for almost six months. Six months of looking for a job and settling for temp jobs lined up by a friend of an ex-lover who worked at an agency in Berkeley. Six months of spending Aunt Edna's gift of money to make ends meet. Six months of praying her old car wouldn't break down altogether.

"And I can't even remember where my apartment is anymore," Helen muttered aloud as she missed her street. The visit with Alice—the embarrassment of fending off her feeble sexual advances, the realization that Alice was not so very different from herself—had shaken her more than she cared to acknowledge. Her stomach sank even further when she realized what she'd done. Without thinking, her body had followed patterns years old and taken her to a location she'd been trying hard to forget.

Of course, the lease on her old office on Shattuck had run out a long time ago. The sign reading "Helen Black, Private Investigator" had been gone for a long, long time. A coffee shop had taken over the ground floor. What had it been when she worked there? Oh, yes, a florist. She stared at the stacked chairs and tables, shiny with rain, until the driver behind her tapped impatiently on the horn.

It seemed to take a very long time to get turned around toward her street, and her head started to hurt again. She cracked the window a couple of inches and felt rain on her face. The ancient windshield wipers did little to help her vision, merely smeared rain and dirt around the window. She drove slowly around her block, unable to see anything clearly outside the fuzzy yellow glow of the streetlights. As usual, there was no parking near her building. She finally eased her car between a motorcycle and the rusted VW van that had been sitting there acquiring tickets since she'd moved to the neighborhood.

"Of course no umbrella. Shit." The rain was pouring again, hammering like fists on her car. Helen pulled her coat up over her head and walked carefully in the street, stepping around the detritus washed up against the curb. In the doorway of the building next to hers someone had arranged plastic sheeting into a makeshift shelter. Black plastic garbage bags pushed up against the length of plastic, and Helen could see a pair of legs extended beyond the edge. The legs shifted, stirred in the wind and cold, then drew up behind the tenuous protection of the plastic.

A heavy gust of rain riding on icy wind tore at Helen as she got inside her building. Grateful for the relative warmth of the lobby she climbed slowly up the stairs—the elevator was still out of order, and she didn't trust it anyway—taking in the sounds and smells of the building as she went up to the third floor. She had never seen the baby in the first-floor apartment, but the crying hadn't stopped since she'd moved in. And the elderly man just below her on the second floor still had the volume cranked up on his television set. Helen had tried politely asking him to turn the sound down after a couple of weeks of sleepless nights. Her request had resulted only in a stare filled with hatred that would have rivaled anything she'd experienced in prison.

Overcome with sudden weariness, her head splitting, Helen made it into her own apartment and leaned against the door. She surveyed the small square living room with a growing sense of depression. A few boxes of clothes and books leaned against a few pieces of rickety furniture she'd picked up from the Salvation Army. The door to the bedroom was open. She didn't have to turn on lights to see—the yellow glow of a street lamp filtered through the crooked blinds. Canned laughter from the old man's television reverberated against her feet. Not for the first time she wondered if the sour smell that persisted in the little apartment came from the dumpsters in the alley below. "Move," she told herself. Pushing away from the door she saw the red light blinking on her answering machine. Maybe a job for tomorrow? Three messages this time, hopefully at least one with good news.

"Hi, Helen, it's Brenda with the agency. Just letting you know that job in San Francisco isn't available yet but they do want someone starting next month, on the first. Give me a call and let me know if you still want it, okay?"

The first of the month. Helen glanced at the wall calendar from a local drugstore pinned over the phone. Today was Friday, January twenty-third. It would be tight but she could make it for another couple of weeks. No more drinks at the White Horse, but after tonight she could do without that. She hit the button to move on to the next message and listened for a couple of moments to the sales pitch of someone trying to interest her in a mortgage. Helen choked off a laugh. She'd most likely never have the money to consider buying her own home, certainly not in California, and being a convicted murderer hadn't helped her credit rating any. She erased the message with a brief curiosity about where they'd gotten her name.

There was one more message. "Hi, it's Katy. It's about—oh, I think seven-thirty? Jan and I are in the city and we're going to grab some food. We were thinking of stopping by later with your stuff. We'll call you once we're back over the bridge, see if you're at home. What—oh, Jan says hi and hopes you're settling in all right. Hopefully see you later."

Helen jabbed the button to erase the message, fighting down an unreasonable anger. Katy had been helpful, generous, understanding toward her since her return to California—in fact, all the things the rest of her ex-lovers had never been. The affair had lasted only six months and they'd never considered living together. Maybe that's why, Helen mused. Fast and fierce, with the emphasis on lots of sex. In the end Helen had gotten tired of being treated like a prize and dropped Katy. She'd felt like a kind of trophy wife, a lover with the added fillip of excitement because she was a private eye. It had taken a lot for her to build up the courage to approach Katy, sleek and successful in her closeted life, for help. And she still couldn't completely understand why Katy had decided to help her get resettled into her new life. As a charity project? Some kind of write-off? Out of the goodness of her heart? Recalling the narrowed eyes and cool gaze Katy had given her at their initial meeting a couple of months ago, when Helen was desperate for work and a place to live, she doubted all Katy's motives were kind. Most likely there would be some payback involved. Katy hadn't taken kindly to Helen's rejection. But Helen was in no position to question anyone's kindness. Rather, it was her role at the moment to be grateful.

Grateful. Something sour twisted in Helen's stomach, and she stumbled over a box and into the tiny kitchen. Water helped. She looked out the window over the sink without seeing the brick wall opposite. She was fucking sick of being grateful. Grateful to her Aunt Edna for fronting her the cash to get out of Mississippi.

Grateful to people like Katy, who was able to get her a temp job with a single phone call. Grateful to Brenda at the agency, who clearly saw her as a "problem" to be solved. And now, tonight, grateful to the likes of poor old Alice for helping her kill some time and fight off the black claw of depression that threatened to rip off the carefully composed shell she lived in these days. And even grateful, she realized, that Alice had provided her with a moment of feeling a cut above. Despite the fact that Helen had a criminal record and had lost everything she'd built up over the years—home, friends, lovers, career—she could still feel superior to Alice, who sat weeping in bars trapped in a melodrama of her own making.

Helen put the empty glass on the counter when the phone rang again. It was Katy. "We're a couple of blocks from your place," she said over the crackling line of her cell phone. "Is it okay to stop by with those boxes? Or is it too late? I realize it's about ten o'clock. We were at the restaurant longer than we thought."

"No, come on up. It's the yellow building on the corner of Mason and Telegraph, number forty-two-oh-seven. I'm apartment number eighteen." Might as well get it over with. Helen braced herself for the abrasive buzz of the doorbell, pushed the button that would open the front door, then hurried down the stairs to meet Katy.

"Hey," Katy said breathlessly. "God, did you get caught in the rain? We have weeks of sunshine in the winter then all of a sudden this."

"I'll take that." Easier to grab the box than to do a lot of talking or worm one's way through some form of greeting. It wasn't very heavy, Helen thought, just a bit awkward because of its size. "Is Jan waiting outside?"

"No, she's just parking the car. She should be right behind—oh, there she is. Come on in, Jan. Meet Helen."

"Hey. Need any help?"

"No, thanks, I got it." Helen looked over the box at the young, strong, olive-skinned woman. Something Mediterranean there, maybe. Short dark hair crowned a sharp-featured face, and the simple, tailored white shirt was silk. Jan's deep-set dark eyes and hawk nose made her look interesting rather than ugly. Between Katy's well-groomed corporate look of navy blue suit and Jan's striking appearance Helen knew she cut a poor figure. Thank God for the box to cover her. "So you found parking?"

Jan smiled, and Helen caught her breath at the sudden beauty of the younger woman's face. She saw Katy reach out to touch her lover on the arm—just enough to show possesiveness, no more, but it was a recognizable territorial move.

Jan said, "Got lucky. Some guy in a pickup truck right out front pulled away just as we got here. I guess parking is terrible in this neighborhood?"

"Yeah, it's difficult." Helen began to feel a strain on her arms and realized they'd been standing still in the hallway for a few minutes now. "Would you—do you want to come up for a minute?"

To her surprise Katy nodded. "I wouldn't mind using your bathroom. That was a long drive over the bridge, a lot of traffic." Helen led the way and did a mental inventory—yes, there was toilet paper and a couple of fresh towels in the bathroom. It was clean and functional, although the bathtub could use some extra scrubbing.

"Here, I'll hold that for you." Jan grabbed the box while Helen fumbled at the door. She let Katy and Jan go in ahead of her and wondered what they would think of the place. Katy glanced around the room without comment, then sped off to the bathroom. Jan set the box carefully on top of another box next to the sofa, then straightened up and stared at Helen. No words, just an unreadable look in her eyes.

"Thanks for doing this. I've told my aunt to send things to me here, now that I've moved in, so I hope Katy won't be getting any more boxes from Mississippi. It was really nice of you to come out in the rain and deliver this." Helen caught herself babbling nervously. Christ, what was Katy doing in there, taking a shower? "I'd forgotten I had all this stuff in storage back there."

She felt the bile rise up in her throat again as she realized that the box contained paperwork from her days as an investigator. Why had she kept that? She didn't need any reminders of the old Helen Black.

"Lots of loose ends to tie up," she said, glancing up again.

"Yeah, well, it's a lot of work starting over." Jan looked down at her shoes, her mouth twisting in what might pass for a wry smile. Some kind of history there, Helen thought. For a second Jan looked old—much older than Katy, older maybe than Helen. The moment passed. "It must be strange, coming back to California."

How much had Katy told her? "Yes, it is," she finally said. Probably Jan knew the whole story. "I'm lucky to have friends like Katy. I owe her a lot."

"Friendship matters, sometimes more than lovers or family." Again that odd expression. What the hell was going on? Helen remembered the hint of ownership in Katy's behavior in the hallway. Maybe Jan, like Helen several years ago, was starting to feel uneasy with being one of Katy's possessions. Sure, she got nice clothes out of it—that shirt must have cost a couple hundred, easy—got to drive a great car, got a good-looking woman to squire around for a while. "I've had friends who lasted longer than any lovers."

"Me, too."

"So, how are you settling in?" Katy sailed across the room, looking around at the boxes and sagging sofa and peeling paint. "Still in boxes?" Her brow wrinkled and she seemed to be sniffing the air, taking in the sour stench from the dumpsters. "You've been here a couple of months, I think."

"I'm not sure how long I'll be staying here. And besides, I don't have a lot of stuff to pack or unpack."

Katy's little smile seemed to pick out the lie in her words. She gave Helen a pat on the arm. "You'll let me know if there's anything else I can do for you, won't you? You only have to call," and with a sweep of perfume and clicking heels they were gone.

Helen waited until she heard the front door shut and looked

out of the bedroom window to the street below. A small dark expensive car roared to life and pulled away toward Telegraph and the freeway. Helen watched it go before collapsing on the bed.

Another week before the job opened up, Helen reminded herself. Two weeks until another check, but Brenda had sounded hopeful. So at least work was possible. Helen tried to think about that, tried to focus on where the job would be and what kind of work she'd be asked to do. Answer phones? Type up invoices? But Alice's face kept intruding, superimposing itself on the image of Katy's eyes sweeping across the ugly apartment, of Jan's stare that could have been contempt or pity. Helen fell asleep thinking about the rain-soaked office building where she'd once created a life. In her dreams something—or someone—cried for hours and hours and hours.

Chapter Two

Helen surveyed her sandwich with some misgivings. She was starting to get a little tired of tuna. At least tuna had been on sale at the grocery store. Maybe this weekend they'd have chicken at a reduced price. And it was certainly a lot cheaper than buying a seven-dollar sandwich loaded with sprouts and low-fat mayonnaise at the café on the first floor. Fortunately the coffee in this particular office was free. Tasted like it, Helen grumbled to herself as she sipped at the bitter burned stuff poured from the bottom of the pot. But free is good, she reminded herself. She sighed and took a bite of the sandwich, leafing through the copy of that morning's paper someone had left in the lunchroom. Free paper, too. Can't beat that.

The headlines for this Tuesday in February were just as dismal as they had been for months. Depressed by the latest disasters in the Middle East—a dismal repetition of cruelty and ignorance played out on a grand scale—and disgusted with the commander-in-chief's most recent bungled speech, Helen dropped the paper and surveyed the lunchroom. It was almost identical to all the other lunchrooms in all the other offices she'd worked in since returning to Oakland. How many temp jobs now? This made six. At least it was going to last for two full weeks. Between that and the last of Aunt Edna's loan and scrupulous shopping at the discount grocery, she should make it until the end of the month. And Brenda had hinted at a long-term temp assignment the following month. Helen took a pen from her backpack and scribbled a few numbers on a corner of the newspaper. Yes, she'd just be all right. The memory took her by surprise, making her hand freeze over the paper. She had a glimpse of herself doing just this, making a careful list of expenses and figuring out just how far she could go, when she was starting out as a private investigator. Suddenly the figures blurred on the paper as her eyes filled with unexpected tears. She coughed a couple of times, willing the memory to go back to the dead past where it belonged.

Over her coughing she could hear voices in the hallway, coming from the region of the soft-drink machines. For a moment the familiar clatter of a soda can dropping down covered the words, then she made out her own name. Two women discussing her. They must not know I'm here, Helen thought with dread. She sat still and silent. Maybe they'll go away, she hoped.

"Yeah, Helen, that's her name."

"Well, she's only going to be here a couple of weeks, I think. Just until Marian gets back."

"Right. Hope she's not looking to get Marian's job."

"I doubt it, although it's not like it's tough to sit there and enter sales figures. If Marian can do it, even some dumb-ass temp can do it, I guess."

"I know, but you also have to put up with Harvey. How do you think Hot-hands Harvey got his name?"

"Well, this one is pretty much bow-wow. I think Harvey goes for the dumb blonde type, not a dog like this Helen."

The two female voices faded down the hallway to the nether

regions of the office. Helen kept sitting there, emptiness opening out in her gut. Should she laugh? Cry? Get mad? Or just not give a flying fuck what these idiots thought of her? The last response seemed best. The corridor was silent now, safe to go back to her desk and fend off Hot-hands Harvey, or at least take a look at the guy and see if he was worth all the excitement. She walked slowly past the soft-drink and candy machines, glancing at herself as she made her way. Yes, she did look pretty drab and dreary, with a tear in her stockings and plain blouse and skirt. Basic thrift store couture. Thank God for small favors—Hot-hands would probably not even notice.

But something else nagged at her as she sat down at her desk and switched on her computer terminal. Some faint memory, something she had done—or not done. The memory surfaced when she stuffed her backpack under the desk and noticed a slip of paper sticking out of the front pocket. With a sinking feeling Helen gently pulled the paper out and read Alice's name and phone number. That was it. The discussion of Helen's plainness, the clarity of just how unwanted she was, had jogged her thoughts in Alice's direction. Helen and Alice, two dogs set loose and barking in a world that didn't really want them, except maybe to fetch once in a while. Yes, those comments along with her own observation of the dull blouse and skirt and flat shoes in beige tones. Alice's life was even more beige than Helen's, sitting around waiting for some ex-lover to call, letting her filthy apartment slide further and further into decay.

Helen set the slip of paper aside and entered numbers into the computer for a couple of hours, hoping for numbness to set in so she wouldn't think about Alice. No good. She worked her way through a pile of invoices, completing the work with about an hour to go before she could leave for the day. Hot-hands Harvey had stopped by a couple of times, making sure she really was working and not painting her nails. He had bad breath and little flecks of white toilet paper where he'd cut himself shaving. She forced a perky smile on her face when he inquired as to her progress, let herself slump when he bounced away in the wake of a slim, pretty brunette stalking by the door. Good, he was busy for a few minutes. And she needed a break.

Helen stretched, longing for a window to let her see the real world, and looked down at Alice's phone number again. "Okay, okay. Just to leave a message or say hi," she told herself as she picked up the phone and dialed an outside line. Of course she wasn't supposed to make personal calls. Brenda had been very clear about that, and so had Hot-hands. She grabbed the last invoice and held it ready in case she had to pretend she was calling a customer to confirm a number.

Helen sighed with relief when she got a busy signal and put the note away. "It's a paycheck, just remember that," she muttered as she finished the invoices. A couple of hours later, as she gathered up her backpack and switched off the terminal, she glanced over her shoulder. Everyone else had left for the day, including Hot-hands. One more try, then, before going home.

But Alice's line was still busy. Troubled, Helen replaced the receiver. Maybe she had unplugged the phone in order to sleep off another hangover. Or the ex-lover had called and they were having a long heart-to-heart. Or something was wrong.

"Enough," she scolded herself. She was not her sister's keeper, not this time. She needed to keep off the radar screen, maintain a low profile, anything that would help her get used to this new life. And Alice was most definitely trouble. Helen shook her head and tried to forget the look on Alice's face when she'd taken down her phone number and promised to call. That was a real dog-look—not ugly, not "bow-wow," but desperate for some kindness. For a crumb, a bone, a little compassion.

By the time she'd gotten out to her car, Helen had given up trying to fight the impulse to make sure Alice was okay. She fished a few quarters out of her bag and went to the bank of public phones on the ground floor of the office building.

"Shit," she hissed when she got a busy signal again. The security guard glanced her way as she spoke, then went back to watching his basketball game on the tiny television set shoved up under the counter next to all the video screens showing different views of the parking lot.

Helen drove home slowly, chewing her lip as she went toward Telegraph. Her route took her by the White Horse, and she found herself turning down the side street next to the bar. Sure enough, Alice's caramel-colored van still sat under the half-dead tree. Branches black with too much rain scraped the top of the van as the wind blew through the street. A bright green parking ticket pocked with rain had been tucked under the windshield wiper. It was Tuesday, and the car had been sitting there over a week. Sure enough, there was the red-lettered sign announcing street cleaning every other Tuesday morning. Alice was lucky the car hadn't been towed. But shouldn't she have come back for it by now? Helen kept driving, found an empty parking spot in the next block over. She pulled her jacket closer, shivering in the fresh burst of icy wind, and hurried into the bar.

The same bartender who'd refused to serve Alice that night was polishing the bar, moving a stained white rag around in lazy circles. He glanced at Helen, said something under his breath to the two men seated on barstools and walked toward her as the others giggled at his parting remarks. "Looks like you need a hot toddy, darling," he said, leaning over the counter. "Is it starting to rain again?"

Helen forced a smile. She didn't really want to buy a drink and hoped she wouldn't have to scrape up the money for one just to get a couple of questions answered. "Looks that way. It's getting a lot colder out there."

"Tell me about it. It's keeping all the cuties at home this week."

"Actually I just wanted to ask you something."

He knotted the towel in his hands and Helen watched as the others sitting a few feet away grew quiet. "Ask away, darling, you might get an answer. Just not a straight one."

The others snickered, then went back to their drinks. "I'm sure it'll be straight enough," Helen said lamely. "I'm looking for someone."

"Aren't we all?"

"Too true. But I was in here two Fridays ago and met this woman, Alice. I think she's a regular here? She talked as if she might be. Her last name is"—Helen fumbled for and found the note—"Alice Harmon."

The bartender's face fell, darkened into anger. "Oh, yes, I know her. Honey, you don't want to mess with that one. She's been bad news from the get-go."

The two men were listening intently. Fuck it, Helen thought, and she went on, "I'm actually kind of worried about her. I tried to call her several times today and got a busy signal. And I noticed her van is still parked out where she left it that Friday night. Have you seen her at all since then? Or heard anything from her?"

"Darling, she's eighty-sixed out of here, as far as I'm concerned." His eyes narrowed and straightened as he stared at her. "Hey, wait a minute. You're the one that took her home that night, right?"

The two patrons studied her openly, intrigued at the drama unfolding in the quiet little neighborhood gay bar. "I just took her home, that's all," Helen began, then realized she probably sounded like she was protesting too much. She shook her head, angry at herself for getting involved. It was the last thing she needed. "Anyway, I wondered if she'd been by to get her car."

"It's going to be towed by the end of the week if she doesn't show up for it," one of the guys at the bar offered helpfully. "They don't let cars sit around forever, not in Berkeley."

Terrific. Now, whatever else happened, three different men would remember her very well. With a sigh Helen murmured a thanks to the bartender and quickly headed toward the door. The two men leaning on the bar hooted after her.

"We'll be sure to tell her she has a new girlfriend!"

"Yeah, that'll be a first!"

Helen rolled her eyes and opened the door to find rain pouring down on the sidewalk, sloshing debris around the curb and into the gutter. As she struggled to get her umbrella out of her backpack—thank God she'd remembered to grab it this morning—she saw with surprise that the bartender had followed her out. He stayed under the awning and called out, "Hey, hold on."

"Yeah?" Helen stepped back under the awning. He was older than he'd looked at first, in the dim lighting that flattered everyone who sat down at his bar—age lines crinkled around his eyes and mouth, and Helen was relieved to see his worried expression.

"I meant what I said, about Alice. You seem like a nice person, trying to do the right thing. I just don't want you to get mixed up with her."

"Why?"

He shrugged, looked away, folded his arms across his chest. The white towel flapped in the chill breeze. "Just—be careful around her. She's gotten into things, in the past, you know? Gotten herself into trouble. She could be a real headache."

Helen stared at him, worry tensing her stomach. "What are you trying to tell me?"

Abruptly he turned away and opened the door. Helen got a good look at his lined face, suddenly aged in the weak light of the streetlamps. In the darkness of the bar he could pass for a lot younger. "Just remember what I said." The door flapped behind him and Helen was alone on the street. Ignoring the cold, she stood outside the door while another couple hurried in out of the rain. A passing car nearly drenched her, and she looked down the block toward Alice's car. The rain had been steadily pelting the bright green envelope holding her ticket, pounding the paper into mush against the windshield. Shreds of the envelope slid across the glass and stuck on the windshield wipers. She turned back into the rain, cursing herself for what she knew she was about to do.

"Why the fuck do I get into shit like this?" she muttered as she drove the few blocks to Alice's neighborhood. The rain eased a little, and she leaned over the steering wheel to peer at the rows of dingy apartment buildings, grayish green blocks darkened with rain. Black branches of the denuded trees waved in the wind, spraying her car with water. Eventually, after two false turns, Helen found the block. She remembered the broken chain-link fence on the corner, the empty lot overgrown with tall weeds and mounds of old clothes and wadded newspapers wedged in amongst the rubble. Helen parked the car just past the lot and stared at the buildings beyond. That was it, she decided, the dull yellow two-story building. Another downpour started just as she reached the stairs. Yes, this was it—the over-watered potted plant with brown-edged fronds, the pile of newspapers just around this corner. Helen went up the stairs, careful to avoid suspicious-smelling puddles on the outside staircase. She paused in front of number sixteen. Yes, this looked right. She could see the same dark outline of the strip mall she'd noticed a few nights ago. And that had to be the as-yet-unseen cat yowling inside. Maybe Alice was sick? Passed out? Helen had a fleeting memory of the bartender's warning, then knocked on the door.

Two things happened. First the increase in volume and plaintiveness of the cat, moving near the door at the sound of Helen's knock. No, not plaintive. Angry, or scared. Next the door moved open, just barely ajar, with the pressure of Helen's hand.

Helen could see inside the entryway, just enough to register the darkness and stillness. She felt a rustling at her feet. Something small and white and furry. Alice's cat poked its head out, screeched at Helen, then disappeared again. The cat stayed just on the other side of the door and wailed. Helen stood there—she didn't know for how long, maybe a full minute—and tried to think around the cat's cries and the drumming of rain. There was a package of lunch meat split open on the floor. A few shreds of whatever it was, chicken or turkey or bologna, were stuck in the shredded plastic. She very nearly called Alice's name, but something stopped her. What? Why that sensation in the pit of her stomach? It took another couple of minutes for her to figure it out. The smell, familiar and horrible, drifted up through all the other smells. Memory flooded in, memories of crime scenes and corpses from her past.

Fighting down panic she stepped away from the door and forced herself to walk slowly, almost furtively, to the stairwell. If someone was still in the apartment would the cat be crying?

Wouldn't it be huddled under a dresser or behind a shelf? But Helen didn't want to count on that. She stopped at the head of the stairs and looked down the row of doors, all shut tight, all quiet with the single exception of Alice's door. Maybe one of the neighbors would be at home. Helen shook her head, aware only too well of what her own reaction would be if some strange woman pounded on her door at nine o'clock at night asking for help. Not in this kind of building, not in this section of Oakland.

Maybe the building had a superintendent, probably somewhere on the ground floor. Helen kept looking over her shoulder as she headed down the stairs. Still nothing. She waited at the bottom of the stairwell, straining to hear any other noise coming from the second level. Nothing, just wind and rain and, faintly in the distance, the sound of the cat crying ceaselessly against some unnamed horror. Another minute went by. "Okay, move," Helen ordered herself. She found the super's apartment around the corner of the building, next to a row of doors that looked like storage areas. Some kind of television show was going on inside. Helen heard canned laughter so loud it buzzed through the walls. Shit, how was she going to get his attention?

It took several tries of yelling and pounding before the door opened. A bleary-eyed man with gray stubble and a strong smell of liquor peered at her over the chain. As he leaned against the door she could see his belly bulging over his jeans—once a well-muscled body now sagging with age and neglect. "Yeah? We don't got vacancies right now."

"I don't want an apartment. I need your help. I think one of your tenants is in trouble." Helen was halfway through her explanation when she saw his face freeze over. He muttered something, no doubt a curse on her foolishness, and started to shut the door. She wedged her foot in painfully and pushed with one arm. "Look, I'm not playing around here. Something is wrong and you need to call the cops for me, all right? I don't have a cell phone."

"What the fuck—who the fuck are you?"

"Please just call nine-one-one and get someone over here."

"It's prob'ly just that cat of hers. Been screaming for two days now."

God. Two days. And the car sitting there for over a week. Helen kept the door open while the man disappeared. Apparently he switched off the television or muted the sound. Silence rang in her ears and she could hear the cat again. Then she heard his voice. She sighed with relief as she caught a word here and there. At least something was happening now. Then he reappeared. She stepped back as he closed the door to unchain it. When he came out his stained plaid shirt flapped in the breeze, revealing a wife-beater T-shirt and khaki pants that could have stood a few cycles in the washing machine. A big ring of keys dangled from his hand. The crew cut, the rigid walk, the cold stare—no doubt military once upon a time.

"Wait a minute—I think we ought to wait for the police to get here."

"Wait?" He turned to look at her as he led the way to the stairs. "What the fuck do you think this is, *Cops* or something? They ain't gonna get here till they get good and ready. Not to this neighborhood." He ambled on, keys jangling by his side.

"What's your name?"

He stopped and turned around again just as he reached the stairwell. "George W. Bush. What the hell is your name, Princess Elizabeth?"

"I'm Helen Black." She extended her hand. He looked down at it with puzzlement, then took her hand. She was surprised at the strong steady grip. Maybe he could have cleaned up a bit but that was a lot of muscle along those arms and shoulders. She wondered what he did before he was an apartment building super. "What's your name?"

"Walt. Walt Greeley."

"Listen, Mr. Greeley. I really think we should wait. I meant what I said. Something is very wrong up there."

She held Walt's gaze for a moment, then his eyes cut to the

small parking lot. "I ain't seen her or heard her for a long time now. Week or so. I thought maybe she went to visit that lezzie girlfriend someplace or something—forgot about her cat."

Helen decided not to tell him about the car. That was for the police, if they decided to show up. "You're the boss here, Mr. Greeley, but I think we should hold on."

He twisted his mouth. Helen watched him, taking in the crew cut, the narrowed eyes studying her, the sense of wasted strength in his body. He wasn't drunk or stupid—maybe a bit down and out, but still paying attention. Maybe someone who used to go to the gym? Helen had a strange feeling of recognition. It took her a moment to understand—Walt Greeley had the same buffed look lots of ex-cons had, the ones who spent their time inside working out. "Let's just go up the stairs, then. See if we can get that cat to shut the fuck up." He started up the stairs. Helen sighed and followed. "I been tellin' her she ain't supposed to have that cat and she kept promising me—" He stopped a few feet from the door still standing ajar. "Jesus fucking Christ."

Helen almost bumped into him. The keys shook once at his side as he controlled his trembling arm. She stared around him but couldn't see anything different. "That smell. Goddammit."

Helen moved to where she could see his face. His eyes were clear and cold, his features rigid.

Through stiff lips he said, "I haven't smelled that since I left the Persian Gulf almost fifteen years ago."

Ex-military, then. Helen had a fleeting moment of curiosity about what had happened to Walt Greeley since the first round of insanity in Iraq. Then she touched his arm. It felt like a slab of marble under her fingers, cold and smooth and unyielding. "Come on, Mr. Greeley. Let's wait downstairs."

Something dark and hard passed over his face. He turned away as if he didn't see her and walked into the apartment. Helen swallowed hard and stood in the doorway. A blur of white and gray darted by her feet and disappeared toward the stairwell. Just a few feet ahead, silhoutted in the bleak light of the day, Walt Greeley looked down at the body in the foyer. "Fuck," he said through clenched teeth. "Fuck."

"Yeah." Helen turned away and looked out over the cars lined up along the sodden street. At the end of the street, where it intersected Telegraph, Helen saw the black-and-white turn the corner.

Chapter Three

Helen sat in Walt's apartment and watched a *Jeopardy* rerun on some game show network. She was surrounded by piles of magazines with oddly varying subjects. One pile was devoted to recent developments in the study of UFOs. Another told her more than she ever wanted to know about horses. Still another revealed various building schemes for cabins. Other than the sofa where she now sat, and the television that occupied one wall, there was nothing of interest in the room. No photographs or posters or little objects that most people generally clustered around themselves—not even a beer can collection. There was, to her surprise, a police scanner mounted on a kind of entertainment center that also housed the television. But that was the sum total of how Walt spent his days, apparently, except for taking out the garbage and doing odd jobs in the apartment building. Walt, Helen decided, was a man looking for distraction. From what? From whatever demons haunted him as a result of his previous military experience?

After pronouncing his profanity over Alice's dead body, Walt Greeley had gone into high military mode. Practically securing the perimeter, Helen thought, as she tried to concentrate on the questions the cute skinny starlet was being asked by a toothy game-show host. Walt had ordered her out of the way and stood like a sentinel at the door of Alice's apartment, in a stance similar to some kind of at-ease position. Helen, knowing she'd be called to talk to the police soon enough, had meekly submitted. She didn't want to venture inside Alice's place, didn't want to go near the body that had most likely been dead for a couple of days. Thank God it had been cold for the past week.

A sudden wave of nausea passed through her and she got up in search of the kitchen for a glass of water. She stumbled through a dark hallway filled with a jumble of items. Her shin bumped against a box and knocked something down, something that cracked on the floor. A picture frame. She picked it up carefully, wincing at the sight of an elderly woman's face staring solemnly back under broken glass. "Sorry," Helen muttered as she nestled it back amongst a pile of bric-a-brac perched on top of a large packing box. The hallway presented an obstacle course of such odds and ends, leaning in disarray against the walls. Daunted at the thought of maneuvering through the mess, she gave up and went back to the living room. She heard a thud overhead and had a sudden image of Alice getting off the floor, looking around in confusion—

Helen tried to shut off that line of thought. She shifted on the uncomfortable couch, crinkling the plastic sheeting Walt had tucked over the cushions. The commercial about hair conditioner wasn't enough, however, to drown out the sound of footsteps above her. Alice's apartment was situated almost exactly above Walt's. The constant tread of heavy shoes tramped an uneven beat that pounded into her mind as deeply as the image of Alice lying dead on the floor.

Twenty years—nearly twenty years since Helen had had the right to work alongside the officers who were walking around above her. She could picture the scene vividly: bright yellow tape stretching across the door, flashbulbs and camcorders recording every object and every position, the sound and feel of the rubber gloves they'd all be wearing. Blood samples. Baggies marked with the flotsam and jetsam that made up evidence. Flat even voices discussing the details of death.

She'd had her share of crime scenes before Aunt Josephine's money had let her buy her way out into the related but more controlled world of private investigation. Enough bodies had come with that one, but on a much smaller scale, with a lot fewer corpses. Then, for several years, Helen had been on the other side of the process. Convicted of manslaughter, five years in prison before being let out on good behavior, then up to her ears in yet another murder. Now she was here again, up to her eyeballs in death. It didn't matter whether she had done her time or not, it didn't matter that she was doing all she could to stay below the radar and make a new life for herself.

"The doctor who invented the polio vaccine. Connie, yours for six hundred."

"Who was Salk? Jonas Salk," Helen muttered to the TV screen.

Then she heard it again, the voice she hadn't heard in over ten years. Helen tried to make out the words—she couldn't, too far away—but she knew the voice as if she'd spoken with him yesterday. Seeing her old homicide partner, Manny Hernandez, arrive on the scene had almost been too much for her. It had almost been too much for Manny, too. They'd stared at each other like statues across the corridor outside Alice's door, both too stunned to speak for a while. Helen had barely heard Walt say that she'd been the one to alert him to trouble. And the little red-headed guy, Manny's current partner, had nudged Manny more than once in his now-ample gut before Manny had responded with a gruff command for Helen to go wait somewhere to be questioned.

Then she heard a shift overhead. Still a lot of tramping around, still a lot of talking—but something moved in a different direction. They're coming down, she realized with a jolt. She felt a vibration on the floor, most likely several people going down the stairs. Then the door opened and Walt came in.

"They wanna talk to you now," he said. His pale face was still set like stone, still rigid with duty to cover his shock.

"Okay. Thanks for letting me sit here, Walt. By the way, I knocked over a picture in your hallway. I was heading to the kitchen and bumped against the box. The glass in the frame broke." She let her words drift off before she could offer to get a new frame, taken aback by the look on his face. Fear? Some kind of tension hunched his shoulders, clenched his hands into fists for a moment.

"Forget it. The cops want to see you. Now."

Helen couldn't tell if he was angry or upset or much of anything. It felt like she'd been told "dismissed," so she simply turned and left. As soon as she got out Manny and his partner were waiting for her.

"This is Lieutenant Barry Jordan." Manny lit up a cigarette and kept talking. He paused after a long drag, narrowed his eyes and looked at her through the smoke. "You mind if we talk out here? I think Mr. Greeley"—he glanced over her shoulder at Walt's door—"could use a break from this."

"No problem." And since when did you start smoking? Helen wanted to ask him. And not taking care of yourself, she added internally, noting his belly straining against his waistband, the heavy jowls. But of course she was no one to cast stones. God only knew what she must look like to Manny right now. Old and gray and tired. Used up. She folded her arms and leaned against the wall, for the moment not caring about the damp concrete at her back, turning her face up to the sky. The rain had stopped during the last game show, and a sliver of moonlight poured down over the grimy street, bathing the rundown buildings in a soft pearly glow. Come on, she begged him silently, let's get this over with.

Jordan did most of the questioning. Helen felt Manny's eyes on her as she spoke. No, she'd only met Alice a week ago last Friday. Felt sorry for the woman, took her home, wanted to check on her.

"And that was the White Horse?"

"Right." Helen couldn't help a quick glance at Manny on that one. Her sexuality had been a struggle for him when they were partners. Would it be now? She couldn't read anything off his face as he stubbed out the cigarette and kept on staring. "I'd promised to call her this week, see how she was doing. She was very depressed and upset that Friday night."

"Nice of you, to look out for her that way." Jordan merely scribbled notes with a blank face and blank voice. "Just friends, then?"

Helen shrugged. Of course it must look like they'd been more than that. "Trying to get some good karma, I guess."

"Something you probably have in short supply. Or maybe you used it all up." The words came out as if pushed by force from Manny's mouth, like he was fighting to keep from talking at all. Helen looked at him until he spoke again. "She didn't exactly look like your type."

"It's nice to see you, too, Manny. Ten years? No, more than that." When he didn't say anything, she pushed on, suddenly wanting very badly for him to say something, anything. Anything besides that cold stare full of hate. "A lot of water under the bridge."

"That's one way of putting it."

"How's your wife?" Wrong question. She watched his face go from white to red to almost purple. He balled his fists in his pockets; his jaw clenched and unclenched. Fuck. Had they split up? How was that connected to her? She watched in awe as Manny fought himself back to icy calm.

Jordan looked over at Manny, back to Helen. The redhead's freckled face froze as he said, "So, you guys done with the reunion now?"

"Yeah, we're done." Jordan waited but Manny seemed disinclined to say anything else. Everyone was saved by the arrival of the ambulance to carry Alice to the morgue. Manny mumbled something and walked away quickly, barking a command at the two men who jumped out of the wagon.

"Lieutenant Jordan—I guess Manny told you something about me."

"Something, yeah," Jordan answered, still wearing his frozen face. It seemed out of place with the freckles. She suddenly had the impression he should be smiling and laughing and telling jokes, not taking a part in this grim drama.

"Something. Well, I don't know what that something was but I'm assuming it includes not only our partnership in homicide several years ago as well as my recent bout with the legal system in Mississippi."

"For killing that girl. Yes, I know all about it."

She sighed and watched the stretcher go up the stairs. She wanted to be out of there before Alice's remains came down. "Tell me what happened to Alice. How she died. You'll find my prints in there because I was here that Friday night. But that's it. I wasn't in there today. Greeley must have told you." As soon as she spoke Helen knew that one was full of holes. Of course she could have visited Alice at any time during the past week. Of course she could have gone in there before she'd roused the building super from his apartment.

And of course Jordan knew it too, as she could tell by the look that passed across his face. "We both know better than that, ma'am. And we both know I can't tell you anything yet."

"Look—" She rubbed her hands on her face for a moment, frustrated and exhausted. "Alice was a very, very depressed woman. I mean, I was worried about her. Seriously. As in suicide worried. Can you tell me if that's what happened?" Can you absolve me of guilt that I didn't come by sooner, that I didn't call or try to find out how she was doing? Can you give me that shred so I can go back out and keep trying to have some kind of life?

Jordan shook his head, never taking his eyes off her. What was that in his expression now—contempt or suspicion? Maybe just pity. Pity for the aging dyke, the one Manny had told him about who had lost it all in one stupid shitty move in the depths of Mississippi. After throwing it all away here in California. "Ms.

Black, go home. Just go home, try to get some rest." He fished a card from his pocket. "Give us a call if you think of anything else. And we'll call you if we have any further questions."

Manny had come up beside his partner now. "They're bringing her out. You go with them, okay? I'm going to stick around and see what else I can dig up."

"Sure thing." Jordan gave them both another glance before heading for the stairs, and for the first time in a decade Helen was alone with Manny.

He looked over his shoulder at the stretcher coming awkwardly down the stairs. One of the men carrying the stretcher bumped against the handrail and Helen could see Alice's body shift inside the body bag. She had a sudden vision of Alice crying on the sofa, holding onto the scrapbook like a sacred relic. Helen remembered the package of lunch meat. That must have been how the cat managed to get through the past few days.

"Go home, Helen. This is not for you."

"How are you, Manny?"

He kept his face turned from her, his jaw rigid in the yellow glare of the streetlights.

Anger, Helen realized. Manny was angry at her. "You are really pissed off with me, aren't you?"

He snorted, wiped his face. "*Pissed* is not exactly the word I'd use, Helen."

"Tell my why."

He finally turned around and glared at her. "You have to ask? Jesus, Helen, you have to fucking ask me?"

"Yeah, Manny, I do." She deliberately turned her back on the ambulance, on the grisly cargo being loaded inside. "I can't just stand there and watch you so full of hate. I didn't expect hearts and flowers, but I didn't expect your hate."

Helen took a step backward as she saw his face crease in pain. "It's you, you stupid fucking bitch," he said in a low flat voice. "You became one of them. You did it to yourself. Fucked yourself over. A goddamm fucking loser who threw it all away."

Shocked, she stared at him. There was hurt and betrayal in his words. It didn't make sense. Anger was certainly better to deal with than pity, but why? Manny blamed her for something. But what?

The ambulance drove off, and the other officers started trooping down the stairs. From the landing Helen heard someone call out, "Hey, Hernandez! You coming or what?"

"Yeah, I'll be right there!" He looked down at Helen, anger drained away into a calm stony contempt. "Go home. Now."

Without a word Helen left, walking down the street in search of her car. In the old days Manny would have asked her if she needed someone to take her home, if she had anyone at home to turn to. It was what any of them would have done. In the old days.

She found her car after what felt like several hours of searching. In the cover of darkness she sat and wept, clutching the steering wheel so hard her knuckles hurt, her chest sore with the racking sobs, her face aching with the strain. The moon was full and heavy, high in the sky, when her tears finally eased. She was about to start the car when she heard a familiar cry.

"Jesus, where the hell are you?" She rolled down the window and looked around for the cat. It had darted away when Walt went into the apartment. She remembered a streak of gray and white and a growl at her feet. She got out of the car. "Come on, cat. It's cold and I'm tired and I've had a hell of a day." She peered into the darkness and shivered against the cold wind. It could be anywhere—under one of the cars lining the street, up in a tree, crouched in a doorway. "Come on, start yelling again so I can find you. You've been yelling all day, why quit now?"

Helen heard a noise to her back. She turned around swiftly, her heart pounding, to see an elderly woman loaded down with plastic grocery bags making her slow way up the front steps of an adjacent building. Late to be shopping, Helen thought. It was after eleven. The woman stopped in her progress to take a look at her, make sure Helen wasn't a major threat. Helen leaned back against her car and almost laughed out loud. She must have looked insane, talking to herself in the street like that. Of course it couldn't be all that unusual a sight in this neighborhood, which had long borne the brunt of the kinder, gentler society that sliced away the underpinnings of stability from all those hanging onto the safety net by their fingertips.

"Just another crazy woman wandered over from Berkeley, that's me." Helen sighed. She was just about to open the car door when she heard the cat.

This time Helen stayed still and listened until she could figure out the source of the cries. Yes, it was coming from the bedraggled shrubs across the street. She crept across the street, taking her time until she spotted it, barely larger than a kitten.

Helen shook her head at the cat's wispy coat and shivering body. "Okay. Let's get out of here, all right?"

The cat let her get close, then lashed out with a snarl. Helen managed to wrestle it into her arms, acquiring a sliced palm for her efforts. For such a small animal its fury seemed boundless. She struggled out of her jacket and wrapped the cat firmly inside. Its mud-caked face glared up at her, its green eyes wide with hatred.

"Fine, we're even. Now just take it easy while I get us home." Thank God the car had automatic transmission. She kept the cat relatively still on her lap with one hand while she drove with the other. By the time she reached her own apartment both hands bore quite a few scratches. The cat's last act of aggression before diving beneath Helen's bed was to swipe at Helen's face, nearly clipping her on the nose.

"You're welcome, cat. What's for dinner?" Helen found the remains of her tuna salad and put it in a plastic bowl. She added another plastic bowl next to that for water. Now, kitty litter. "I am not going out into the cold and rain tonight, cat," she called out. "We'll have to make do with newspaper." She found a box, lined it with a plastic grocery bag and shredded newspaper, then slid it under the bathroom sink.

The cat stayed under the bed throughout Helen's activities. Now and then she got a glimpse of paw, but every time she walked through the bedroom the cat retreated. It didn't matter.

Helen found herself beginning to relax, thinking about cat food and litter boxes. "You're a good distraction, cat. As long as you don't kill me first."

Shit. Wrong word. Helen sank down onto the bed, felt her throat tighten with unshed tears. Alice was dead, maybe at her own hand. Maybe Helen could have done something, maybe not. She'd never know now.

"And you saw it all, didn't you, cat?" she said, lying down. "No wonder you're pissed off. Wish you could talk to me."

The cat muttered a growl of some kind, then subsided into silence again. Helen let her mind open up once again to the brief image she'd had of Alice, lying dead on the floor, face down. Useless to fight this, she realized. She had to think about it, had to get it sloughed off and out of her mind. There was Walt, standing over her, a big shadow hulking over the body. Alice's face was to the floor, no marks visible in that dim light from a distance. Cat screaming, phone on the floor beside her—

Helen's eyes opened and she sat up, surprising another growl from the cat. "The phone. On the floor beside her," she whispered aloud. Was it a last desperate decision to save herself, an attempt to call for help? But how did she die? Just because Helen hadn't been able to see any wounds or blood didn't mean they hadn't been there. And the door was open, too. Would someone leave the door unlocked when they were going to commit suicide? Alice was a heavy drinker. Wouldn't it have made more sense to shut and lock the door, down a bunch of pills and drink a lot of booze, safe in your bed? And the cat. Helen couldn't imagine Alice not taking measures to get the cat safely out of the way. Not when it was all she had left of the woman she was so besotted with. Or—grisly thought—maybe making sure the cat died with her.

As if it could read her thoughts, the cat let out another yelp. She heard it padding out from under the bed, across the bare floor. She got up and followed. Where had it gone? Nothing in the bathroom. Helen moved to the kitchen and switched on the light. The cat blinked in the sudden light, its green eyes still dark and angry, then bent back over the bowl of tuna fish. The mud on its fur had dried to grayish brown. Only a glimpse of white remained.

Helen sat down on the single chair in the kitchen and watched the cat finish its meal. "It doesn't add up, cat," she said. Alice's death did not look like a suicide. Certainly Alice had been depressed, maybe suicidal, but this didn't fit. That left accident—she could have fallen and hit her head—or someone else killed her. "Shit."

The cat looked up again, then proceeded to lick its paws and rub the paws over its face. Murder meant Manny and Jordan would definitely be talking to her again. Murder meant Alice was more than an old drunk. Murder meant all hell was going to break loose in Helen's life. Again.

Nothing else fit the fleeting glimpse Helen had had of Alice dead on the floor. Helen sat up with a start. For all she knew, someone had been in that apartment when she arrived that afternoon. For all she knew Walt had done it. She flashed back to the bartender at the White Horse. He'd warned her not to get mixed up with Alice. What did he know about it?

Then she caught herself. "Stop it." The cat paused, a wet paw on its wet furry face. "No, not you, go ahead. You look like shit." The cat went back to its ablutions while Helen leaned forward and rested her head in her hands. She couldn't do this again. The years in prison, the aftermath of trying to avoid trouble in Mississippi, the subsequent shattering of everything she'd tried to put together—she had to stay out of this. She wouldn't survive another round with death.

Something brushed against her leg. She sat up with a start and looked down to see the cat, still muddy and bedraggled, wrapping itself around the legs of the chair with a sinuous swirl of fur. And was that purring she heard? She reached down to pet it but it shrank away from her hands.

"Okay, no problem." She sat up again and watched as the cat plodded off, its stringy tail held high, toward the bedroom.

So she'd acquired a cat. A cat and God knows what else, now

that she was trying to get her head around Alice's death. She was a suspect, no doubt about it. Just on general principles, because of her record. For tonight, the cat was a much easier problem to think about. She had no idea if it was allowed in her building. Had no idea if she should try to keep it. For now it was probably all right. Besides, where else could it go?

Chapter Four

The coffee tasted bitter, as if it had been sitting in the pot for several hours. Helen took a sip, added more cream and sugar, fiddled with the laminated breakfast menu. The door of the café swung open again, letting in the cool morning air. The breeze washed over the counter, ruffling the napkins. Helen twisted around on her stool—no, not Manny. No sign of him yet. She suppressed a sigh and went back to deciding between an oatmeal with fruit or the scrambled eggs.

The plump dark-skinned waitress topped off Helen's mug of coffee before Helen could protest. "Still waiting?" she asked, taking an order pad from her apron.

"I guess not. I'll have—I'll have the oatmeal." It was the cheapest thing on the menu. Helen glanced over the waitress's shoulder. She had only a half an hour before she had to get to work. She hated Mondays. This week she was subbing for someone else on maternity leave at a different company. Brenda assured her there would be lots of work ahead. Helen drank more coffee and tried to ignore the tension in her stomach. She'd managing to pay her rent for February and put food on the table, but only just. And now she had a cat to be worried about. Cat—Helen hadn't gotten around to naming the critter yet, wasn't sure she wanted to since she was going to have to give it up—seemed to tolerate her well enough. As long as Helen didn't try to coax it out from under the bed. Helen looked ruefully down at the latest wound inflicted on her arm, a scratch running all the way from wrist to elbow. At least it was quiet now, not yowling from under the bed for Alice.

Someone turned on the television tucked behind the counter, and Helen heard a perky anchor start talking about the breaking news for this February Monday morning. Monday. She'd found Alice Tuesday night, six days ago. The local news had made brief mention of her death, making a ridiculous connection to gang activity in Oakland—but of course that was the immediate assumption about any crime in Oakland. And although Helen had no way of confirming this, she was certain Alice had been dead for at least a couple of days before that. That put her death over the final weekend of January, then. The same time she'd been worrying about rent and groceries for February. At least the news reports confirmed her own suspicions. This was being treated as a murder, not a suicide, by the local police.

And speaking of the local police, where the hell was Manny? Helen squirmed around on the barstool, stirring sugar into her oatmeal with sliced apples. She took a bite, hoping its bland texture would calm her stomach.

The door opened again. This time Manny strode in, his bulk blocking out the faint sunlight seeping over the office buildings of downtown Oakland. He sat down on the stool next to Helen and picked up a menu without saying a word. He didn't even look up at the waitress when she stood expectantly before him. Even after ordering sausage and eggs he refused to look at Helen, fixing his gaze instead on the bank of coffeepots and mugs lined up against the wall.

"Thanks for coming down, Manny." Helen took another bite of oatmeal. Maybe, just maybe, away from Jordan and the others Manny would thaw enough to get past whatever was making him so mad. "I appreciate your time."

"Gee, that makes me feel all warm and fuzzy inside." He hunched forward on the stool and played with his fork, tracing the tines along his napkin.

Helen gave up on the oatmeal and leaned on the counter. "Okay, Manny. I get it. I get that there's no love lost here—no hearts and flowers, no happy reunion. You've made your point." She stared at the shiny metal surface of the coffee machines. Her distorted reflection showed an elongated face and strangely tilted eyes. "I'm not looking for hugs and kisses, either."

"What's on your mind, Helen? I got a busy day today."

So it was going to be like that. The oatmeal settled like lead inside her. She swallowed past the lump in her throat and said, "I wanted to talk to you about Alice Harmon."

Manny slurped his coffee, keeping his face firmly set toward the wall. "You know damn well I'm not going to say a thing about that to you."

Okay, let's try again, Helen thought. She swiveled around on the stool and made herself look at him, taking in his rigid posture and stony face, his dark eyes cold and hard. "So I'm a suspect?"

"A suspect." Manny's face shifted into a tight little smile. "Did you do it?"

"Of course not. You know me better than that, Manny."

"Really?" He finally turned to face her. "Once I thought I did. Once I thought we were as close as partners could get. But I don't know you, Helen. I'm starting to wonder if I ever did."

Now Helen looked away. "You know what happened in Mississippi, and you know I never meant for—for anything like that to happen."

"You mean you never meant to kill that girl."

Helen glanced around the room. The waitress was taking orders on the other side of the room, and for the moment they had the counter to themselves. Manny was keeping his voice very low, and Helen matched his tone. "Yeah, Manny. That's exactly what I mean. Shit, you know how it goes. You know how as soon as a gun shows up things can get out of control very, very fast."

The waitress appeared with his eggs and sausage. He waited until she'd hurried away before speaking. "Save it for someone who gives a fuck, Helen." He stabbed his eggs as if they were still alive and posing a threat. "You've been on some kind of downward spiral for years, ever since you quit homicide."

The hurt turned to anger. Helen felt rage flood through her body and she carefully pushed the cold oatmeal aside. "Then what the hell are you doing here this morning, Manny? Why did you come?"

"To get a look at you again. To see what kind of fucking woman you are now." His smile didn't reach his eyes and he leaned in closer. Helen could smell the bitter coffee on his breath. "To watch you squirm like a worm on a hook."

She leaned back. For the first time she was afraid of her old partner. That wasn't just anger in his eyes. Hate gleamed there, hate that was ready to explode. "What the hell happened to you, Manny? What did I do?"

The fire in his eyes flared up. "You tell me. You tell me what you did all those years to my wife. How long were you two muff diving behind my back?" he whispered.

"Shit." For a moment the room froze around her as she took in his words. "You're telling me that your wife—that she—"

"The bitch took the kids and moved in with her. Left me with my dick swinging in the wind and ten years of marriage down the shit hole." Now the sausage came under attack as he continued talking, still barely above a whisper. "My kids call her Mama Janey. Can you fucking believe it? They have two mommies and one daddy. One big happy fucking family."

"Jesus," Helen breathed. "Manny, when did this happen?"

He picked up his coffee and drank it like water. "You tell me, Helen. You're the dyke. As far as I know you two were eating each other out while we were still partners. If you're asking me when Mama Janey took possession of my wife, that was a year ago last week." He set the empty cup down with a clatter that bounced the silverware along the counter.

The waitress—she'd been watching them for a few minutes, Helen realized—moved over with coffeepot in one hand and water pitcher in the other.

"Can I get you folks anything else?" Her voice was calm and cheerful but her eyes took it all in. Uncertain of her voice, Helen smiled and shook her head.

"Just the check, please." Manny dug his wallet out. When Helen tried to put money down for the breakfast she'd been unable to eat he waved her away. Helen tried not to flinch as if she were expecting a blow. "Keep your money, Helen. I just wish it was broken glass in that bowl instead of oatmeal." He tossed a twenty on the counter and left.

Helen saw the waitress breathe a sigh of relief. She came over to take the money. "You okay, honey? I saw how he was talking to you."

"I'm okay. But thanks."

"You want me to call the cops? He looked pretty mean. I know how mean a guy can get."

For one wild moment Helen wanted to laugh hysterically. She looked up at the waitress, reading concern in her dark plump face. "No, it's okay. I doubt I'll be seeing him again. Could I have another glass of water, please?" The water helped, and she left the café. A man sitting in a booth near the door looked up from his paper to watch her exit, no doubt curious about the conversation at the counter. When he noticed her glance he tugged his Yankees baseball cap lower over his face and turned back to his newspaper. Different, she thought, taking in the distinctive blue *NYY* lettering on the beige cloth. In this town you were more likely to see the black-and-silver of the Oakland Raiders. He looked up again when she gently closed the door, relieved to be away from prying eyes and concerned waitresses.

She walked the three blocks to the office, welcoming the cool breeze on her burning cheeks. This news was going to take a little while to digest. Of course Manny would see her as the enemy now—he was too raw from his wife's departure to think rationally. Especially with the kids being gone. Helen winced at the image. Manny had always loved his kids, with a deep piercing love that had never failed to move her. What were they telling him? Were they going through some kind of nasty custody thing? And how the hell had all this come about? Helen remembered Concepcion as a small, sweet feminine woman who seemed utterly absorbed in Manny and her kids.

But the questions didn't matter now, of course. Helen would probably never have the chance to find out, anyway. Manny hated her. He'd be more than willing to consider Helen a suspect in Alice's death.

Helen's mind gratefully left the subject of Manny and went back to Alice. One thing had emerged from this nasty little almost-confrontation—the police were looking at Alice's death as suspicious. If Helen was a suspect, then they didn't believe Alice had killed herself. Helen shook her head. Of course she was relieved to think she didn't have direct responsibility for Alice's death, but was murder any better?

Standing in the wind, staring down Broadway toward the Embarcadero, the fear she'd felt in the café suddenly drained away. People pushed by her, running for buses or trains, glancing at her with irritation. Helen barely noticed them, absorbed in the way her rage had replaced fear. Manny could go fuck himself. This was not about her dead friendship with Manny. This was about her own survival. She looked up at the high-rises lining the street. Tall and cold and lifeless—gray and solid in the wind. Her rage felt solid, too, like a glacier looming up out of the cold sea. She stood and savored it, welcoming its cold weight. She moved forward.

The February wind, buffeting through the tall office buildings, fought her as she made her way across Broadway to the high-rise where she'd be working for the next week. She waited her turn to enter behind a throng of commuters coming up from the BART station and pushing through the huge glass revolving doors. As she fished her agency-issued ID badge out to flash for the security guard she glanced up.

The guy with the Yankees cap who'd been staring at her in the café leaned against the brick wall of the drugstore across the street, looking her way. So much for the uneasy peace she'd made with herself just now. Maybe he was just waiting for the bus, or maybe he was staring into space. No reason to think it had anything to do with her. She turned all the way around, staring directly at him. He pushed himself away from the wall and turned to look at the display in the drugstore window, apparently totally absorbed by the low prices for space heaters. Suddenly nervous, she wedged herself into the last of the crowd. As she waited for an elevator, she looked back through the smoked glass. He was still there, head bent and hunched against the wind. Yes, he was talking into a cell phone. Helen kept watching until he disappeared in the crowd.

All day as she sat at her desk Helen scribbled notes. Alice's name. Then Walt Greeley. The White Horse. Friday night, ten-thirty. Tuesday evening, more than a week later—when she found the body. On and on it went. She fidgeted through the hours. Like so many other temp jobs she'd had for the past six months, since her return to California, this one seemed to require only that her ass be warming a chair for eight hours. The doodles under her pen gradually formed themselves into a face—a rough approximation of the bartender at the White Horse. What had his warning about Alice meant? Surely Manny and Jordan had talked to him by now. Maybe he'd mentioned she'd been asking about Alice. That kind of pursuit on her part could have put her in either a negative or positive light to the police.

That realization put the image of Manny's face in her thoughts. She sighed and felt the familiar sinking feeling in her stomach. Her past would never leave her alone—never. She was still thinking about Manny—and about being pursued by the police—when she went back to the bar after work.

This time a different bartender stood before the rows of gleaming bottles. Bulky and solemn, he polished glasses while talking to a young blonde at the bar. Helen slid onto a barstool, mentally taking a tally of what was in her wallet. Yes, she could afford a beer, but only one. The bartender placed the open bottle and a glass in front of her without a word, then went back to his conversation. Helen sipped slowly, hoping for a chance to ask him when the other bartender would be back. Two guys in suits sat at the other end of the bar, but other than that the place was empty. Typical for a Monday night, she thought. She was halfway through her beer when something the blonde said made her sit up.

"So you never met Alice yourself?" The blonde's voice was deep, quiet but well projected. "I'm just trying to figure out what happened to her. The police won't tell me much."

Helen sipped her beer and watched the bartender shrug and shake his head. The other woman at the bar had her back to Helen. From behind she looked young—at least held herself like someone several years younger than Helen. Thick wavy blonde hair fell in a simple cut along her shoulders, across a pale gold sweater. Helen took in the solid shoulders and sturdy hips, the large strong hands cradling a cup of coffee. The woman sighed as the bartender shook his head. He muttered something Helen couldn't catch, and the blonde pushed herself away from the bar.

"Okay. Thanks anyway. I appreciate your talking to me. You know where to call me if you find out anything?" He nodded, and she started to walk away. Helen saw her face as she walked by. Older than she had first appeared, maybe mid thirties. Worry lines creased her face, more lines gently carved around her eyes and mouth. She was heavy under the sweater, but it was the heaviness of health and strength. Just as she placed a hand on the door Helen stood up, putting the last of her cash on the bar.

"Excuse me—" Helen was taller than her by several inches. Green. Her eyes were green, large and wide and full of light. The lines on her face told of smiles and laughter. She pushed her thick hair from her eyes and looked up at Helen. Shit, Helen cursed herself. Quit staring at her eyes and say something. "You were talking about Alice Harmon? You knew her?"

"Yes." The woman took a step closer, eagerness in her face. "I did. You did, too, then?"

Helen took a deep breath, let it out slowly. This was not going to be simple. Maybe this was the ex-girlfriend. "I just met her a couple of weeks ago. She was—I took her home from here one Friday night."

The blonde smiled and shook her head. "Yeah, I heard Mike cut her off early. She must have gotten an early start that night."

"Not for the first time, then."

"No, I'm afraid not. Once or twice they called me when she'd had a bit much." Those green eyes glanced away, clearly remembering, and filled with sadness. "I thought that last time I got her into a twelve-step program it was going to work. Obviously it didn't." She looked at Helen again. "I'm sorry. I'm Maggie Evans."

Helen took her hand, felt its strong grip, and suddenly felt relaxed and warm for the first time in weeks. Then she realized she was holding Maggie's hand far too long and let it fall. "Helen Black."

"Helen. Good to meet you. I just wish it was under different circumstances."

"Yes." So do I, Helen thought, so do I. Just wish I wasn't scrabbling up from the shit pile, trying to put my life together and watching it come apart at the seams. Wish I wasn't so used up and you weren't so young and strong and real. Wish you didn't have big green eyes.

But Maggie was saying something. "So you hadn't seen her since two weeks ago Friday night?" She moved away from the door and led Helen back to the bar. "Damn, I just wish the police would tell me a little bit more. I can't stand thinking of her in there for four days."

Helen closed her eyes briefly and decided to talk. "I found her. Last Tuesday."

"It was you?" Maggie sat down on a barstool. "I thought—but

what happened? Hang on a minute." Helen tried to ignore the way Maggie's hand rested on her arm as she turned back to the bartender. "Ray, could you bring us a couple more beers? No, Helen, this one is on me."

Helen went through the story, leaving out the parts about Alice weeping for her lost lover and pawing at Helen. Maggie listened intently, staring down at the bar and frowning. "I'm afraid I don't know any more than that," Helen finished. "I don't know how she died or when, exactly. I only know the police are treating this as a murder, not a suicide."

"Lying facedown on the floor."

"Yes." Maybe better not to mention the phone beside her. Maybe Alice had been trying to call Maggie when she died. Maggie didn't need to know that.

Maggie suddenly smiled, looking past Helen, her chin in her hand. "Alice was—well, she was a lot of things. She'd had it pretty tough. Nobody seemed to give a damn about her. I don't think she gave a damn about herself, either. I had just started feeling like I was getting somewhere with her, and now this."

Helen was about to ask how Maggie had known Alice when the door burst open. Three men, laughing and hanging onto one another, tumbled inside. One of them waved at Maggie and called to her.

"Hey, Rick! You still coming over on Sunday?"

"I wouldn't miss it, Maggie." He grinned and looked with interest at Helen. "I might even talk these guys into coming, too," and he punched at the shoulders of his nearest companion. His two friends pulled him farther into the bar toward the pool table.

"Did you meet Alice here, too?" Helen asked.

Maggie shook her head. "No, she started coming to a support group I helped get started. Then I started seeing her on Sundays once in a while. Off and on, you know? Not regularly."

Helen frowned, not understanding. "You're a therapist?"

Maggie'e eyebrows lifted in surprise. "Me? No, no. I'm a minister. I got appointed to this congregation just a year ago. Alice used to come to my church."

"Your church." Terrific. A clergyman. Clergyperson. Or cleric. Whatever.

"Yes. The MCC over on Webster near Broadway. The Metropolitan Community Church," she went on at Helen's blank stare. "Have you ever heard of MCC?"

"Yes, I have. The gay church."

Maggie smiled. "Well, lots of people think of us that way. But actually only about half the congregation is gay. Mostly it's just people." She looked away again. "I thought maybe Alice felt at home there. Well, you don't want to hear about all that, I'm sure." Maggie reached into her pocket and pulled out a business card. "Alice's memorial service is this Saturday. Why don't you come?"

Helen took the card. Magdalen Evans. "Magdalen? Very unusual."

Maggie rolled her eyes and laughed. "Remember, the Mary with the seven demons? I come from very devout Catholic stock."

Helen couldn't help smiling. "Guess your parents are pretty pleased, a priest for a daughter."

"That's a whole different story, Helen." She moved again to the door. "Come by on Saturday." She smiled again. "Ten o'clock."

Helen felt the ice build up inside her. Green eyes and a beautiful smile. And most likely a lovely partner of many years. Cats and dogs, even kids. Shit, what was she thinking? Someone like Maggie would see her only as a charity case, nothing more. Not as a woman. And anything to do with church turned Helen's stomach. But Maggie was still standing at the door, waiting for a response.

"Maybe. Maybe I will," Helen said stiffly.

"If not Saturday, just give me a call at the number there. If I'm not there leave a message."

Helen nodded as Maggie left. The room felt cold and dim, the laughter from the pool table very far away. Helen looked down at the card, traced the rainbow printed over Maggie's name, then tucked it safely into her wallet. This is about Alice, she reassured herself. Nothing more, nothing less. This was about finding out who Alice was and why she was killed. And about getting Manny off her back so she could get on with her life.

She fought to keep the memory of big green eyes out of her thoughts as she drove home in the darkness. Cat was waiting at the door and greeted her with a hoarse yowl.

"Yeah, yeah, I know. I'm hungry too." Helen poured cat food into the plastic bowl and watched the animal eat. She looked better—a little cleaner, a little less frantic. Still pretty skinny. And still mad. Helen crouched down on her heels, making sure there was plenty of room between her and the dish of food. The cat looked up with baleful eyes, then went back to its food. "You're the only one who knows what happened to Alice. And you're not talking, are you?"

Helen kicked off her shoes and sat down on the chair. She found Maggie's card and looked at it for quite a while before going to bed.

Chapter Five

Helen edged her way into the church Saturday morning. She'd driven by the building twice, unsure if she had the right address. Nope, she decided, after referring to Maggie's card—this must be the place. Despite the fresh paint and open door the church still had the look of an abandoned warehouse, surrounded as it was by broken bricks, boarded up windows and "for lease" signs. Then she'd seen the sandwich board on the sidewalk, bright with fresh paint and awkward lettering. Helen let the car idle for a few moments, wondering if she should turn back. But staying in her own apartment, with a cat that continued to yell at her and boxes of her pitiful belongings awaiting unpacking, seemed even less inviting than going through with the service.

Parking was easy in this neighborhood—most of these buildings had clearly been empty for a long time. The building directly across from the church had apartments for rent over the abandoned storefront where two men sat on the stoop and watched her lock her car. She smiled to herself. The car was far too old to warrant any worries about theft.

She'd been hoping to sneak in and out unnoticed but the small gathering would make that impossible. Inside, there weren't more than ten people in attendance to pay their final respects to Alice Harmon. Every head turned to watch as Helen crept up the aisle toward the middle of the room. Small printed notices lay at the end of each pew. Helen took one up and pretended to study it while catching her breath. She hadn't set foot in a church in a couple of years. The last time had been a disastrous Sunday visit with her Aunt Edna, back in Mississippi. Lots of stares, lots of gossip, lots of smiling faces matched with cold eyes assessing the wayward niece from California. Lots of shouting about hell and judgment, too. Worn hymnals full of lugubrious sentiments referring to blood and punishment. Helen hadn't bothered to pay attention to any religious services in prison after a brief talk with the chaplain assigned to her wing. He'd licked his lips a lot and muttered on about perverse sexuality behind bars while staring at her tits.

Helen looked around the room and noticed with relief that it didn't resemble any church she'd been in before. It was quite small, for one thing. The pews didn't match—some were lighter wood than others, and the carvings on the ends varied, witnessing former lives in a large number of different religious establishments. Brightly colored banners took the place of stained glass windows. Helen couldn't see a cross or crucifix anywhere. Instead rainbow symbols and interwoven circles were draped behind the simple pine altar.

She turned her attention from the building to the mourners. Most of them had graying hair and a good assortment of wrinkles. One or two, surrounded by big black plastic bags that apparently contained their earthly possessions, looked like they'd just come in off the street to get warm. Through a door behind the altar Helen glimpsed a big coffee urn and several boxes of tea bags. That, at least, bore some resemblance to the evangelical church meetings of her youth.

The similarity ended with Maggie Evans sitting in an ordinary folding chair to the side of the altar. Today she had her thick blonde hair pulled back into a plait. A length of cloth in rainbow colors draped her shoulders and hung down smoothly across the front of her plain white robe. She sat silent and erect, eyes downcast, palms flat on her thighs. Helen could see her breathing slowly in and out, her face calm and still as if in meditation. Traffic noise filtered in but the stillness of the church made it seem very far away. Helen looked back down at the program. Thank goodness, no hymns or singing on the menu. Just a few comments by Reverend Evans and silent prayer.

Idly she read the lines on the first page of the program. Familiar words, from the third chapter of Ecclesiastes. This was clearly a modern translation, not the good old King James Helen had grown up with. But the words still caught at the mind and heart, like always.

There is an appointed time for everything, and a time for every affair under the heavens.

A time to be born and a time to die; a time to plant, and a time to uproot the plant . . .

She scanned down to the end of the passage, the words surfacing up easily in her memory after years of Sunday School.

A time to keep, and a time to cast away.

A time to rend, and a time to sew; a time to be silent, and a time to speak.

A time to love, and a time to hate; a time of war and a time of peace.

Well, someone had cut Alice's time short. She had no time to speak any longer.

Helen turned the program over and her eyebrows lifted in surprise at the remarks printed there. Work with Cesar Chavez and the migrant workers in the early Seventies—protests and demonstrations against the U.S. involvement in Central America in the Eighties—most recently an activist opposed to the Persian Gulf War—the Alice Harmon Helen read about here was a far cry from the woman weeping on the sofa a few weeks ago. Helen studied the lines about her life and tried to reconcile the two images but failed. What had happened to Alice? Why?

She heard movement beside her and watched out of the corner of her eye as a heavy woman settled herself next to Helen on the uncomfortable pew. The woman turned a blank face to Helen, staring impassively. Her tattered coat and grimy hands spoke of a night, or perhaps many nights, spent out on the streets. Maybe she'd just come in to get away from the cold, have a cup of coffee or whatever was on hand. In fact, many of the people scattered around the small chapel had that same hunted look in their faces. Maybe it was the empty look in their eyes, their evident poverty, that propelled her thoughts back to the past. Back to five years ago, in Mississippi.

Helen was suddenly back in the prison chapel, enervated by the stifling heat and the stifling, suppressed fury of hundreds of women. Not to mention the stifling evangelical fervor of the little balding minister preaching hell and damnation to them, week after week. Knowing that her attendance might help her get out early Helen had managed it, week after week, sermon after sermon. Sex was the big topic, she remembered. And the evils of being a woman. Helen could still see the sweat shining on the chaplain's little round face, his buck teeth spitting out saliva as he had ranted about physical desire to a captive female audience. Helen swallowed hard, reminding herself she was safe in Oakland now, far away from the chaplain and his hot little hands fiddling with his Bible while he looked them over with hard glittering eyes.

Suddenly Maggie Evans was standing in front of the altar. When everyone else stood up Helen did, too. She bowed her head as Maggie invited everyone to pray with her in whatever way they wished. Helen couldn't think of God at this point—only of Alice. Did her past hold the key to how she died? Once again the bartender's face loomed in her mind, his warning sounded in her thoughts. She had to talk to him.

Wait a minute. There was no way Helen could be poking around in this. Alice was dead. Nothing Helen did could change that. Any interference on her part in the police investigation would only result in her getting into deep shit. She'd learned her lesson before.

Helen suddenly realized that everyone else was sitting down. Abruptly she took her seat and watched Maggie. Too distracted by the sight of Maggie standing poised and composed in front of the simple altar, Helen allowed herself to be lulled by her deep, resonant voice. Maggie spoke of Alice's years of service to the community, her strength and generosity behind the scenes. She portrayed someone gentle and caring who worked tirelessly for social justice and human rights for all people. Maggie's soothing voice spread calm across the nearly empty room, infusing thoughtful reflection into what would otherwise have been a depressing testimonial to a wasted life. Helen realized with a shock that the last time she'd been to a funeral had been after her Uncle Loy died. That last visit with Aunt Edna marked a huge chasm in her life, resulting in prison and the destruction of everything. She couldn't help worrying if this would end the same way. Once again—maybe for the last time—Helen thought of Alice sitting on the sofa, weeping over her loss. Already the memory was fading, and she couldn't see Alice's face clearly in her mind's eye.

She looked up with a start. The service was over. Helen watched as the others moved awkwardly out of the pews. Three women stood near the altar, waiting their turn to speak with Maggie. Helen hung back a little, not wishing to intrude but wanting to talk to her again. Maggie shook hands with and hugged each of them, and at last they moved off. They glanced curiously at Helen but didn't speak. Maggie came down off the dais and sat down with Helen in her pew.

"I wasn't sure you'd make it, Helen." Helen noted with surprise Maggie's eyes were red. From crying, presumably. "Thanks for being here."

Helen looked down at the program folded in her hand. She felt embarrassed. Embarrassed that she couldn't drum up any tears for the dead woman, embarrassed at the visible emotion on Maggie's face. It had been so long since Helen had allowed herself to be that vulnerable in front of anyone. "I had no idea Alice had been involved in all this," she said, gesturing with the flyer. "Pretty impressive."

Maggie sighed and leaned back in the pew. She rolled her head luxuriously in a slow circle around on her shoulders. Helen wondered how stiff Maggie's neck was—wondered what her skin felt like under the collar of her robe.

Enough of that, she ordered herself. "Those women—they were friends of Alice's?" she asked, more to distract herself than to get any information.

Her eyes still closed, Maggie shrugged. "They were in the support group with her. Alice hadn't been going all that long, and she wasn't a regular. I don't think any of them knew her well." She opened her eyes and turned to look at Helen. "But you say you didn't know her well, either."

Helen cleared her throat. How much should she confide in Maggie? "Well, having found her, I just wanted to be here." Shit, that was lame. Maggie wasn't stupid, she knew there was something else going on. Helen inwardly cringed under her steady gaze. "Oh, and I was thinking—what I could do about her cat."

"Her cat."

"Yes." Helen stumbled on in spite of Maggie's blank stare. "I mean, I'm not even sure I can keep a cat in my place. I don't know its name. And I don't think it likes me very much." She showed her arm to Maggie.

Maggie touched the skin around the most recent scratch. "Good lord, you should put something on that."

Helen pulled back abruptly, aware of Maggie's startled response. It had just been unexpected, that gentle probing touch.

"Seriously," Maggie went on, "it might get infected. I think I have something in the bathroom, up in my office."

"Well—I don't want to keep you from anything."

"It's no trouble at all. Why don't we go up to my office?"

Maggie must have sensed Helen's hesitation. "Unless you'd rather wait here. I need to get changed anyhow."

"I'll just wait here, if that's okay."

"No problem. Why don't you fix yourself a cup of coffee? The kitchen is right through there," Maggie called over her shoulder. A few people were standing around with teacups. Helen stood alone in the middle of the church, unwilling to go mingle with the congregants, and was suddenly aware of the sounds of the street. In the distance she heard police sirens. A truck rumbled nearby. Someone drove past the church with stereo thumping, the low dull thud receding as the car moved down the street. She ventured out from the pew and looked at the banner hung over the altar. Suddenly the fabric moved in a draft. Helen turned around and faced strong sunlight. The door closed as quickly as it had opened, and the room fell back into shadow. Helen blinked at the sudden change in light. Then one of the shadows moved.

"Excuse me—I thought there was a service here today."

"There was." Helen went up the central aisle toward the door. The shadow moved again as the woman stepped closer to the door. "I'm afraid it's over now. I'm sorry."

She wore a thin black raincoat over jeans so worn that the fabric had faded from blue to almost white in patches near the hem. A few long wisps of white hair escaped from the hood of the raincoat. Startling to see white hair framing such a young face, Helen thought. Or was she so young? It was just that her eyes were so large and clear—a translucent blue, her skin pale and somehow untouched. Like someone who'd been shut away from the sun for a long time.

"Maggie—I mean, Reverend Evans—will be here in a moment, if you'd like to talk to her, Ms.—"

The woman didn't speak. She looked over Helen's shoulder, then back at Helen. She glanced down at the sheet of paper still folded in Helen's hand, then reached down to take one for herself from the nearest pew.

Just then Helen heard Maggie's voice coming from the kitchen behind the altar. "Found it. I thought I had some in my first aid kit."

"Wait, you'll want to see Maggie. She saw a lot of Alice recently."

"No. No, I'd rather not."

Maggie had joined them by now. She'd shed her robe and held a thin tube of ointment in her hands. Today she wore a green sweater that matched her eyes. Her braid had started coming apart. She tossed hair out of her eyes and smiled at them both.

"Maggie, this woman was just asking about Alice's memorial service."

"No, actually I wasn't." There was no mistaking the ice in her voice. She pulled her raincoat closer around her. "I was just leaving." She wadded the flyer up into a ball and shoved it in her coat pocket as she hurried out of the church.

Helen and Maggie watched her go. "You want to tell me what that was all about?"

Helen shook her head. "I don't know myself." Maybe the ex-girlfriend. Someone from her past, another political activist. "You didn't recognize her?"

"Nope." Maggie handed over the tube of ointment. "As a matter of fact, Helen, I don't really know who you are, either." A smile took away the sting of her words. "Why don't you stay for a bit? I could use a cup of coffee. And I think we have some cookies left in the kitchen."

Helen rolled the tube in her palms, suddenly irritated with Maggie—her smiles, her friendly gestures, her prayers and platitudes, her happy little church meetings. Who the hell was she to prod and poke like that? It was none of her fucking business what Helen knew, who Helen was, or what connection Helen had with Alice. "Thanks for the ointment, but I'd better be going."

Maggie's face fell but she covered quickly. "You're welcome. You know where to find me if you want to talk."

But Helen had already darted out the door after the woman in the black raincoat. Damn Maggie for making me lose her, she thought. And of course Helen knew, the farther she got from the church, that it was all a bluff. It had been the offer of kindness and compassion, the willingness to extend not just first aid but possible friendship. Helen caught a glimpse of herself in a broken window as she crossed the street. Yes, she looked as haggard and worn out as Alice Harmon. No wonder Maggie acted interested. Helen could easily be her next charity case. Friendship wasn't possible between the two of them. Maggie was so—so fucking normal. And Helen had too many invisible scars to play that game again.

She stared down Webster. Of course there was no sign of the woman. She'd had more than enough time to get away from the church. "Shit." She got to her car and had her hand on the door handle when she heard it. Someone crying.

Helen stood silently on the sidewalk. Where the hell was it coming from? To her right. Yes, there was a recessed doorway over there, fronting the neighboring building. Something shifted in the shadows and Helen moved farther back, standing against a parked mover's truck. She went around the back of the truck and peered cautiously toward the doorway.

The woman was wiping her face, her shoulders still shuddering from sobs. She turned her face to the sky. Helen caught a glimpse of the delicate-boned face twisted in grief. Then the woman folded her arms across her chest and started walking, her head bowed, her footsteps slow and heavy.

"Fuck, this is stupid," Helen muttered. She took a few steps away from the truck—the woman didn't turn around. Hopefully too caught up in grief to notice Helen behind her. Helen followed her, feeling more and more foolish. She'd just go to the end of the block, she decided. Anyway, the woman would probably get into a car and drive off.

But Helen followed the black raincoat all the way down Webster until it merged with Broadway. They weren't far from where Helen had had her last office job, in fact. Before she knew it, they were on Broadway heading toward the BART station. Here at least there was the cover of a large crowd, swarming up and down the escalators from the underground rail system to bus stations and parking lots. For a moment Helen lost her, then she spotted her long white hair just at the entrance to the station. She descended toward the trains amid a large group of people.

Helen darted across the street and forced her way through a group of preteen giggling girls and elbowed her way onto the escalator. She saw the woman with white hair insert a ticket into the entrance barrier and disappear down another set of stairs. "Damn it!" Helen hissed, ignoring the stares from people hurrying to their trains. She looked at the lines formed in front of the ticket dispensers and realized she'd lose ten minutes waiting to get a ticket. Besides, she had no idea where the woman would have ended up. The stairs she'd taken led to trains headed for anywhere in the system, from Fremont to San Francisco to Contra Costa County.

Okay. Helen took a breath and headed for the escalators. Just inside the Broadway exit she saw a Yankees cap off to the side. The man from the café, who'd followed her earlier that week, looked right at her for a moment. Then he turned back toward the escalators and disappeared.

Chapter Six

"I see you're a coffee drinker."

Maggie smiled and nodded. "I have to have a couple of vices. Coffee is relatively cheap and it's legal, so it's a pretty good one to maintain."

Helen watched Maggie stir sugar into her drink. Once again Helen was distracted by those long, strong fingers, the broad flat hands. For the past couple of days Helen had tried not to imagine those hands clasped in her own, those hands running over her own body. She'd tried to forget Maggie's green eyes, but that was going to be impossible today. Today Maggie wore a tight-fitting forest green pullover. Deeper green than her eyes, but somehow that just made her eyes glow even more. The shirt also etched Maggie's broad solid body, her firm shoulders and arms. She'd pulled her thick dark blonde hair back in a loose ponytail that showed off the broad flat cheekbones, the quick easy smile.

She was beaming that smile full strength at Helen now. "Lucky you got Monday off. And very nice of you to give up your day off to help me with Alice's things. What kind of work do you do, Helen?"

Here we go. "I'm temping right now. My new job starts tomorrow at the insurance agency." Better that than to describe Brenda's irritation at her this morning for asking for Monday before she got started on the new job. "I'm hoping to get something permanent soon, though."

"I know things have been bad in the corporate world for a while. I hear a lot of that at the church these days." Maggie's smile turned sympathetic. "How long have you been temping?"

Helen looked up from her coffee at Maggie's innocent face and clear-eyed smile. How could she tell her the truth? That she'd been doing odd jobs since getting out of prison, literally living hand to mouth if it wasn't for grudging help from relatives and a dwindling supply of friends? "Quite a while now."

Silent for a few minutes, Maggie was obviously waiting for her to take up the thread of conversation.

Helen cleared her throat and decided it was time for small talk. "So, where are you from, Maggie? You a native Californian?"

Maggie shook her head and licked foam off her lips. "No, a transplant. From Wisconson, actually. I went to school at Cal for a while before I realized what I needed to be doing." She smiled and looked out the window at the pedestrians on Telegraph Avenue. "I stayed just a couple of blocks from here, actually, shared a tiny apartment with three other women going to Cal."

Helen made a mental map in her mind. The café, Mother Hubbard's, a lesbian hangout for as long as Helen could remember, was about half-filled with customers perched at the bars or reading textbooks at the tiny rickety tables. Most of them were much younger than herself or Maggie, Helen realized, although a few gray heads popped up in the murky light. The rain had stopped for the moment, and she noticed that most of the customers kept looking up from their books or newspapers out onto the street, their faces relaxing at the sight of bright sunshine filtering through the wet dark branches. Beneath the increased traffic noise Helen heard birds greeting the day. The promise of warmth, welcome in the chilly drizzled mist of February, brushed against the picture windows at the front of the café. Helen felt her spirits lighten as the door opened, letting in another pair of young women and the sudden surprising warmth and light.

Outside, up and down Telegraph Avenue, Helen could see the usual mix of students wearing backpacks, moms pushing strollers, the street vendors. And the usual smattering of street people. Many of them were kids—kids, by Helen's definition these days, being anyone under twenty-five. Wearing the Goth uniform—lots of black, lots of leather, multiple piercings and tattoos—they presented a common front to the other people crowding the street as they asked for money. They didn't have the lean, pinched look of the older street people, the ones who clutched tattered blankets around them and glanced dispiritedly at passersby. "I don't remember so many kids hanging out a few years ago."

"I think there are a lot more of them since I lived over here," Maggie said. "It's hard to tell if they're really runaways or kids from the suburbs thinking it's a great joke to hang out on the street. Probably a good number of both." A sad smile crossed her face.

"So going to Cal was just the start for you, then?" Helen asked. Better keep the questions going on her side, so as not to give Maggie any room to ask her anything. "What were you studying?"

"English lit, of all things. Like the world needs another dreamy-eyed English major talking about Virginia Woolf and Jane Austen. Yeah, that first year was a year of discovery in more ways than one." She chuckled. "Not only did I fall in love with one of my roommates, I fell in love with God."

"What happened?" Helen asked, genuinely curious. For just a moment she could see Maggie ten years ago, young and bright and untouched, dealing with the shock of realizing who she was.

"It was pretty bad at first," Maggie admitted. "She was working on a degree in child psychology. We'd been to high school together, best friends all that time—you know, joined clubs together, went to the same church, double-dated. The works. Got this apartment together with a couple of other girls. Then the shit hit the fan when I found out she was sleeping with some fraternity guy. It wasn't serious, I know it wasn't, but I just exploded." She laughed shakily, as if the emotions and turbulence were still very real and very present. "I told myself I was angry because Toni was going against God's will, having sex outside the sanctity of marriage—but of course it was just a cover for the real issue."

"So you weren't ever a couple?"

"God, no. Toni would have been disgusted with me. No, one of our other roommates sat down and had a long talk with me—brought me to places like Mother Hubbard's, some of the bookstores that were open then, to a few meetings with other young women. Young women like us." Maggie's hands curled around her empty glass and a small smile curved her lips. "We slept together a few times, but it didn't develop into anything serious. I think she saw it as her duty, to sort of encourage my coming out."

"And God? How did that happen?"

Here Maggie's face seemed to close in. She studied the table as her smile faded. "That was even harder. Lots of priests and nuns in my family, lots of good conservative Catholics. They—they didn't give me any support. Still don't, actually." She forced a laugh. "Don't know what I'd do if it weren't for student loans. The Graduate Theological Union isn't exactly a free lunch." She looked up again, her expression defiant and her eyes alight. "But it doesn't matter, as long as I'm doing what I was meant to do."

A waitress appeared. "Anything else?"

Helen insisted on paying the bill, grateful for the interruption. She had no doubt that Maggie was about to start asking Helen about her own life. "Thanks for meeting me here, Maggie," she said as she held the door open for them.

"Thanks for the call. I was hoping to hear from you, even though I roped you into helping me go through Alice's things." Their progress through the crowds gathering on Telegraph—it was nearly ten o'clock, prime time for the street vendors to set up their wares—prevented further small talk. Helen felt a twinge of guilt. What would Maggie think if she told her why she volunteered to help? The chance of finding something to clear her own name, of getting some hint as to why Alice was dead, weighed very heavily against any benevolent impulse she might have felt. Or any desire to see Maggie again.

"I was afraid I'd have to do this all by myself," Maggie went on as they turned off Telegraph onto a quieter side street. "But I didn't want to put it off any longer, not after I got the letter."

"What letter?"

Maggie stopped suddenly, shamefaced. "I guess it doesn't matter if I tell you. Not now."

"Tell me what?" Helen stood on the sidewalk and watched Maggie make up her mind. "You got a letter?" she prompted. They'd reached Helen's car, and Maggie's was parked a few feet away.

Maggie sighed and leaned against Helen's car. "It got to the church office right before the memorial service. I mean, I was going to go ahead and do the memorial service regardless, right? I had it all planned and set up. Then this letter and check arrives—"

"A check?" Helen interrupted. "From who?"

Maggie shrugged, pushed her sunglasses down against the brilliant mid-morning light. Clearly, Helen thought, she was deciding what she could and could not say to Helen about this benefactor. After all, who was Helen? A total stranger who'd carefully revealed nothing to Maggie about herself or her motives.

"Okay, Helen," Maggie said slowly, keeping her gaze on the trees overhead. "I don't know who you are—and you've been really cautious around me. No, don't say anything"—her hand went up—"I know when I'm getting a bit of a run-around. But you showed up for Alice's memorial, and you're taking care of her cat. You cared something about her. And I'll be damned if I just let her fade away into oblivion. You seem to feel the same way."

Helen knew better than to speak. Maggie sighed and went around the car to the passenger side. "I'll tell you on the way."

Helen lit a cigarette, careful to roll the windows down first, as they drove down Telegraph toward Alice's apartment. The heavy-duty garbage bags and folded boxes she'd picked up the night before slithered across the back seat of the car as she turned off Telegraph.

"It was a cashier's check," Maggie said, breaking the silence. "For a whole lot more than I needed to take care of things. By the time it got there I'd already made arrangements to have her remains cremated, already set up the memorial. I mean, there wasn't really anyone else to do it, as far as I knew."

"And the letter?"

Maggie sighed, let down her hair and rubbed at her scalp as if suddenly tired. "Just printed out on a sheet of plain white paper. Asking me to take care of things with the money and if there was any left over to use it for something Alice would like." She smiled and shook her head. "A lot of money, actually."

Helen gripped the steering wheel tight, hoping Maggie would tell her how much. But the other woman was silent, and she didn't dare ask. "No idea where it came from, then?"

"Nope. The envelope had a San Francisco postmark, though. So it's somebody local. I thought I'd use the extra money for the support group. Maybe see if we could get a rehab program going. Well, seed money for it, anyhow."

Helen suppressed a whistle. Must have been a substantial amount of cash, then. Rehab programs required professionals and cost a lot. She started to ask more questions—did Maggie know anything about Alice's family, for example, or what kind of work she did—then stopped herself. This will get you nowhere, she lectured herself. You're lucky Maggie has told you this much. Don't push it.

"There's something I don't understand, though," Helen began carefully. "I know why the police wanted to talk to me—I mean, I was right there on the spot, I found the body. But how did you find out so quickly about her death?"

Maggie shrugged. "They wouldn't tell me much, but I think they found my name and phone number there. My guess is that they didn't find too much else to indicate she had other friends. But I got the call late at night. They didn't tell me why, at first." Her voice had started to shake, and she took a deep breath. "Maybe they called me from right there in her apartment, over her body. That's the image I keep getting. And the police officer—well, it doesn't matter now." Maggie stared fixedly out the window, her chin set and determined.

Helen could guess how she'd gotten the news—an impersonal call, the flat uninterested voice telling her of Alice's death. The interest on the other end of the line only in who Maggie was and what her connection to the corpse was, with no real concern about the shock of such news. She'd done enough of that herself. How much longer before Maggie pushed Helen for some answers about her own interest in Alice? Better make the most of this while she could.

Helen flashed on the memory of Alice's body sprawled across the narrow entrance to her apartment. The phone resting on the floor by her hand, the book splayed across the dirty carpet—could it have been some kind of address book? Maybe the police had simply noted the names and phone numbers on the open page of the address book, then redialed to see if whoever answered matched one of the names.

As they waited at a stop light, Helen chewed her lip and chewed her thoughts. She hadn't noticed the man from the coffee shop since Saturday. Shit, both she and Maggie were in a lot deeper than they should be.

"So what's going on in there, Helen?"

Helen jumped. Irritated drivers were tapping their car horns behind her. "Just wondering who sent you the check. How they knew who you were and where to find you." And I wish like hell I could get my hands on that letter, see what it actually said, she thought. What would it take to stay in Maggie's good graces long enough for that?

"I'd like to know myself. I guess Alice said some good things about the MCC, or about the support group."

They drove in silence to Alice's street. The surroundings were less grim, less ugly in the soft morning sunshine. The series of storms had seemingly washed away some of the sense of depression hanging over the aging rows of apartment buildings, as well as swept a good bit of trash down the gutters. Even the fading, peeling paint of Alice's building looked less scabrous in the gleam of light. They took the roll of garbage bags and several boxes out of the car. Helen debated going back to the super's door, then decided against it. First they'd see if they could get in without him, going to ask his help only as a last resort.

They were in luck. The door was closed but not locked. Bright yellow crime scene tape criss-crossed the doorframe. It fluttered slightly in the cool breeze coming up from the stairwell. One end of the tape had loosened. It drifted back and forth across the door, the ragged end of plastic making a faint *scritch* of sound on the wood. Helen paused, her hand in midair as she reached for the doorknob.

"It's okay, Helen. I talked to the police—to that Lieutenant Hernandez—and he said they were finished and we could go in today."

But Maggie had misunderstood Helen's hesitance. Maybe it was the image of Alice's body on the floor. Or the yellow tape warning off intruders. Or the memory of Manny Hernandez. Most likely a combination of all those things. But suddenly she was there again, at another crime scene, with another dead woman lying before her. That had been a much younger woman, her pale blank face turned up to the moonlight, a deadly black blossom spreading across her chest. Helen could still feel the grip on the gun that had killed her, still feel the drip of sweat from the hot Mississippi night crawling over her skin and see the lights from police cars pulled up around the ditched car where Victoria's body lay across the front seat. Helen had stood and watched as the Mississippi state troopers had strung similar yellow tape around the site of the car. She'd felt their eyes on her, those troopers in their big beige hats, sweat staining their shirts under the arms and down the back. Felt their curiosity and disgust. Helen didn't know which was worse—that she'd killed a woman, or that she was a lesbian. She'd known what they were thinking. What all of them had thought, from the troopers to the judge and jury to her own lawyer. What horrible things had she done to corrupt this young lady before killing her? What obscenities had Helen perpetrated on Victoria before that final obscenity of death?

The yellow tape had snapped and fluttered in the breeze that night, the welcome breeze that fended off the soggy heat and cooled sweat on the skin. Just the way it moved in the cold air of Berkeley, miles and miles away from Mississippi.

"Helen?" Maggie's hand on her arm made Helen start. She edged away from the door until her back hit the iron railing of the walkway. "Are you sure you want to go in there?"

Helen turned, a surge of anger wiping the past from her thoughts. Who the fuck was this woman, to be so patronizing? To turn those bright green eyes full of pity and kindness on her, to imagine that her self-made God and religion had anything to offer? She welcomed the fury. It built a safe wall between the two of them. Right now Helen needed every barrier she could find to use between herself and Alice's death—between herself and Maggie. And the anger swept away the sudden fear roused by being here. Not to mention how it felt to have Maggie touch her and look at her that way.

"God, I'm sorry, Helen. I'm such an idiot. I didn't think what it would be like for you to see this again." Maggie sighed. "Not after you found her like that." She reached out to Helen, stroked her arm. "Please forgive me."

Helen jerked away from her. "I'm fine," she said through gritted teeth. "Just let it go, okay?" Then she saw the look in Maggie's eyes. It just enraged her further. A softness, a tenderness—something caring and compassionate. She stared into the darkened apartment. "I'm fine," she repeated. She didn't want to look at Maggie, didn't want to mistake her pity for something more meaningful.

Besides, the feeling couldn't be anything but pity. Helen had no doubts about what she must look like to Maggie. Old, graying, haggard. Isolated. In fact, she probably looked a lot like Alice had looked. She just knew that Maggie's concern came from nothing more than pity, no matter how much she wished it could be something else. That knowledge fed her rage, fueled it even more as she realized how much more she wanted from Maggie. And how impossible that desire was. There's nothing but a dead body bringing us together, she told herself. Fuck it all, anyway.

Helen watched Maggie drop her hand, watched her back off as she took in Helen's expression. Helen felt ice come over her, the way it used to when she was working. Really working, as a private investigator. She'd always used the ice, and it felt so fucking good to feel that again. Like the day she'd had her encounter with Manny, the day she'd felt like a big white glacier, clean and cold and solid, floating in an endless black sea. Maggie's face went blank with surprise. Helen almost laughed out loud at the puzzlement she read in those green eyes. For a moment Helen felt the sting of panic that she'd somehow deeply offended her. Ridiculous. Maggie was just glad to have another pair of hands helping her sort out Alice's things. Maybe looking for recruits to her church. Wasn't that what they all did? Convert people? Drag in the lonely, the frightened and the stupid? Give them a place to go once in a while, the pretense of belonging in the world.

"Helen? What is it?" Maggie's voice was quiet and careful. She stood on the landing outside the door, shivering in a sudden burst of wind that howled up the stairs. Over Maggie's shoulder Helen could see the sky darkening, clouds building over the sunlight. The scraggly tree by the railing shivered too, spattering them both with raindrops from the previous night. Maggie reached up to wipe her cheek and Helen thought she saw the other woman's hand tremble.

Helen shook herself and turned away from Maggie's shocked face. Without a word she reached up to the yellow tape and began to rip it down, tearing it into shreds. The scraps of bright yellow plastic flew from her hands into the breeze, scattering themselves up toward Telegraph Avenue. The rain started as they went inside.

Chapter Seven

"What a mess."

"I agree." Helen leaned back on her hands and stretched her feet out in front of her. They'd only just done a first run-through of the bedroom. Already the living room was piled with boxes and bags of Alice's belongings. Helen eyed the stacks of clothes and shoes and books wearily, wondering how many years Alice had been in this apartment to have gathered so much stuff around her. Or maybe Helen had no real point of comparison. For a good part of the past few years, Helen had been living without much in the way of possessions. Being in prison kept material possessions down to a minimum. You didn't want to give anyone else the chance to take something from you. "This is a huge job."

"Yeah." Maggie sighed and slumped down on the sofa. "I'm thinking of asking for volunteers from church to help. Maybe people from the support group."

"Would they do it?"

Maggie gave that little grin Helen was beginning to recognize and associate with her. Maggie's grin. "You never know. People have a way of surprising you."

"That's certainly the truth." Helen surveyed the past three hours' work sitting in piles around her. Shoes were stuck into the paper grocery bags Alice had tucked in the closet. There were still two or three pair sitting on the floor, old cracked leather and broken ties that couldn't have been worn in many years. The clothing, some of it already packed in the set of luggage Helen had pulled from the closet, sat in piles around the room and folded on the armchair in the corner. Three boxes of paperbacks, all generic bestsellers with a slight leaning toward the mystery genre, were stacked against the wall by the door. She continued to gaze at the pathetic piles, the gatherings of an entire lifetime. It said very little about Alice, other than that she had very plain taste in clothes and liked to read bestsellers. Helen had hopefully paged through some of the books, scoffing at herself as she did so. What did she expect, that the family will or a dusty birth certificate would leap out at her from the pages of a bodice-buster romance? But if only there'd been something. Anything. A letter, or a postcard. Besides, she couldn't just rifle through all the books and all the pants pockets—not in front of Maggie. The minister was no doubt already suspicious of her, maybe wondering if she'd done the right thing to have Helen come in and help her.

Helen rolled over on her back. The rain had just stopped and sunlight persisted, despite weather warnings last night of more storms on the way. Shadows dappled the stained ceiling as light made its way into the room, creating an almost pretty lace effect that hid the worst of the marks. Helen glanced over at Maggie, who was loosening her hair.

"I'm really beat. This is harder work than you'd think. I remember when my Aunt Betty died, a couple of years ago. She'd been in the same house for over forty years, I think. You'd not believe what she had piled up in the attic, covered in dust."

"How long do you think Alice was living here?" Helen sat up

and waited as Maggie chose her words. "She had been coming to your support group for a year or so, right?"

Maggie shrugged. "I have no idea. In the group people share what they're ready to share about their personal lives. I hate to say it, but I just didn't know Alice as well as I should have." She stretched, knocking over a stack of papers as she did so. "Oh, no."

"Here, I'll get that." Helen reached out to straighten the awkward pile, sneezing in the dust. It was one of three stacks they'd pulled out from under the bed. None of them looked recent, and Helen had wondered why Alice would have kept them. And kept them hidden.

"Look at this, Helen." Maggie bent over a newspaper. "It's about Alice." Sure enough, there she was, smiling at the camera and standing with a group of people. They held a banner that bore the slogan *Si, se puede* painted in ragged letters. Alice's free hand was raised defiantly in a fist. In the background were rows of trees or shrubs, and line after line of other protesters carrying signs and banners. "This is all from her activist days." Maggie leafed through the pile, clearly impressed at each story. Helen looked over her shoulder, steeling herself against responding to the line of Maggie's neck, her warm breath, the smell of her hair as it spilled down in the dusty golden light. "Here's another one about Alice. Wow. The *Chronicle*." This time she was seated at a table, holding a clipboard and looking seriously into the camera. A man, short and stocky and dark, sat across the table and held a telephone receiver to his ear.

Helen marveled at the difference between the Alice of these stories and the Alice she'd met not long ago. Here Alice was young, willowy and strong, with long straight dark hair flowing over her shoulders. The eyes that gazed fearlessly into the camera were alive with energy and purpose.

Echoing her thoughts, Maggie said quietly, "She looks happy. Happy and alive."

"So what happened?"

Maggie sighed and restacked the papers. "Who knows? I only

knew she was active in political struggles because she talked about it in the group, mentioned it a few times. I just thought it meant she did a few marches back in the Sixties. Like I said, we try not to pry too much. I never got the chance to know her as well as I'd have liked."

Maggie pulled her feet up, hugged her knees to her chest and looked down, brooding.

Maybe it was just booze and the ex-girlfriend, Helen mused, and not necessarily in that order. "Wonder why she kept all this under the bed, why she didn't have it out so people could see it. In a scrapbook. It's something to be proud of, don't you think?"

Maggie snorted, a short sharp noise that could have passed for a laugh. "What people? For all we know no one but you had ever visited her here, Helen. Besides, maybe she couldn't face it."

"Couldn't face what?"

"What she'd been, and what she'd become. Looking at the past directly, really facing it, can be painful." Maggie spoke in low tones but Helen heard the anger in her voice. She looked away, back to the evidence of Alice's past glories. What private ghosts haunted Maggie? she wondered. What did Maggie have hidden away from herself, under the bed?

"She couldn't let go of it, either. Just tucked it out of sight," Helen ventured.

"Yeah." Suddenly Maggie stood up. "I need to get something—coffee or tea or something. It must be, what, one o'clock now?"

"Yeah, we've been here since ten. Food sounds good." Neither one of them acknowledged the presence of coffee and tea in the kitchen. It felt all wrong to use Alice's food for their lunch. "There's some kind of coffee shop on the corner, near Telegraph."

"Coffee and sandwiches okay with you?" Maggie had shrugged into her jacket and was out the door before Helen could answer. The door banged shut behind her, then moved open a few inches, letting in the air and sunlight. Helen went to close it, then froze in the doorway. Here was where she'd stood that day, looking down at Alice. Okay, now was her chance.

She turned and looked down at the floor. Alice's head had been up there—a faint smudge of chalk marked where the police had outlined the body. And the phone was over here, between the body and the door. Then that thing that might have been an address book was on the other side, not far from the lunch meat package. Helen took two steps and came up against the little table where the phone sat. Gingerly she lifted the receiver, noticing the dark smears where it had been tested for fingerprints. No dial tone, so Walt had gotten that shut down already. There was nothing else on the table, no address book. If there had been one, of course Manny and his cohorts would have taken it.

Helen stepped back into the doorway and studied the floor. At least the lights still worked. She flipped the switch and crouched down close to the wood. Plenty of stains on the floor, but nothing that clearly looked like blood. And no marks from the crime scene officers to indicate that any of Alice's blood had been spilled here.

She moved into the living room. The problem was, the place was so dirty, so covered in old tired stains and grime, it was hard to know what might have mattered, if anything. Same thing was true of the carpet. Given the cat's behavior, some of this might have come from the animal venting its spleen and a few hairballs on the worn carpet. If only she could remember more details about the night she'd been here! But she'd had a few drinks herself that night, had only wanted to get away from the weeping woman.

Helen stood in the center of the room and made herself pay attention to the furniture. Okay, sofa over here. That armchair shoved in the corner. And the ugly glass-topped coffee table, right in front of the sofa—

She stopped and stared at the indentations in the carpet, here and here, right next to the coffee table. Like something had been sitting for a long, long time and recently moved. Helen carefully moved the coffee table so its feet fit perfectly in the indentations. What about the rest of the furniture? She prowled the room, first looking at the carpet, then at the surrounding furniture, keeping herself alert and ready for Maggie's return. Yes, the dark patch and long indented line in the carpet were hidden when she pulled the sofa over to the left a few inches. And the shadow-like stain on the wall behind the armchair disappeared when she adjusted the chair to hide it. The tall etagiere holding knickknacks was too heavy for Helen to move by herself, but a similar mark on the carpet told the same story. Someone had moved everything around and not bothered to move it back.

Still no sign of Maggie. It was one-thirty already. Helen stood in the center of the living room and chewed her lip, thinking hard. Ordinarily, scene of crime officers wouldn't disturb anything at all, leaving things exactly as they found them. And she could still remember Manny's lectures about what happened to careless detectives who stumbled through a crime scene and fucked up the evidence. She had no doubt that he still drilled the lesson into the heads of everyone who ever worked with him. Besides, it had taken a certain amount of effort to move some of the furniture around—the sofa, for example. And there was no way she was going to try to shove that huge bookcase over. So—what did it all mean? She couldn't bring herself to believe it had been missed. She glanced at the odds and ends filling the bookcase. Sure enough, the dust showed clear outlines of where some of the assorted cups and vases and ashtrays and ceramic poodles had lain for weeks, if not months, then been recently displaced. And that greasy black smear was likely more tests for fingerprints.

Helen folded her arms and stared down at the newspapers and magazines strewn around the living room. What the hell were they supposed to be looking for? The only thing of interest so far was the decaying stash of clippings and papers Alice had stowed away under the bed. And that stash told only of past glories that no one but Alice herself had cared about. Or had someone else found something of interest there? If so, why hadn't they just taken the pile with them? They wouldn't have been missed.

Just as she was kneeling down to go through the papers Helen heard approaching footsteps. The door opened just as Helen sat down cross-legged a couple of feet from the sofa. Okay, look busy. With her back to the door Helen started putting shoes into a box.

"Thanks for going out for lunch, Maggie," she called over her shoulder. "How much do I owe you?"

"Depends how far back you're counting."

Helen hid her surprise by keeping her face turned away as Manny Hernandez and Jordan entered the room. She kept putting shoes in the box. "Are you here to help us get things cleared up?" she asked, standing up to face them.

Jordan stayed in the doorway, his face hidden in the shadows. He seemed to be fascinated by the trees outside, keeping his gaze turned toward the street. Watching him stand there, clearly trying not to pay attention to what was going on in Alice's apartment, Helen was virtually certain this was Manny's idea, not his.

Manny shrugged, his eyes scanning the room, lighting anywhere but on Helen. "Looks like you've got it under control. Who's 'us,' by the way?"

"Maggie—Magdalen and me. I'm just pitching in, it was her idea." Shit, quit making excuses. Better yet, turn the tables a bit. "What are you doing here?"

Manny finally looked at her. She wished he hadn't when she got the full impact of his cold contemptuous stare. "We got a call from Walt Greeley, the superintendent downstairs. You remember him?"

"Of course. I guess we should have let him know we were going to be in here today." She went back to sorting through shoes, realizing that she was picking up and putting down the same pair over and over. Fuck, get ahold of yourself.

"Magdalen. The minister."

"Yeah, that's right." Helen stood up again and dusted her hands.

"How'd you get so tight with her all of a sudden?" Jordan made a noise and moved away from the door. He took a couple of steps inside the room and waited behind Manny. There was no mistaking the worry on his face. "She your new girlfriend now?"

Helen was so stunned she couldn't respond. Just then a shadow appeared in the doorway behind Jordan and Maggie came in, balancing two tall paper cups and carrying a brown bag.

"Is there some problem, officer?" she asked in her official

church voice, the one Helen had heard at the memorial service. Maggie set the cups and bag down on the little table next to the phone and came to stand beside Helen. "Can we help you with something?"

Helen barely registered the rest of the exchange between Jordan and Maggie. She was too focused on staying calm under Manny's glare. Fortunately he took to pacing restlessly around the room, avoiding Helen as if she had leprosy. "I think Mr. Greeley just got nervous, hearing voices and footsteps over his head."

"Perfectly understandable, Lieutenant. I'll make sure I let him know next time we're here sorting through her things." Maggie smiled and made a sweeping gesture around the room. "As you can see, there's a lot to be done. I asked Helen to give me a hand. I don't think the two of us will be enough."

Helen moved across the room and took up her coffee, aware that her hands were shaking. Hot, sweet and loaded with caffeine—the first sip calmed her and she felt able to pay attention. Manny was now fixing that glare on Maggie, although she deliberately ignored him and paid attention to Jordan.

"Manny, why don't you go back down and call this in—let's get that out of the way." He raised his eyebrows when the other man made no move to leave. "I'll go talk to Greeley. You go on to the car."

Manny shrugged and headed for the door, brushing hard against Helen. "Good idea. It's starting to stink in here anyway."

Helen gasped at the burning sensation on her arm—then she realized his rude gesture had sloshed hot coffee out of the cup. Damn that was hot. She winced in pain, mumbled an excuse and hurried to the kitchen. She had cold water running over her arm when Jordan came to stand beside her.

He spoke just above a whisper. "Look, I don't know what happened between the two of you years ago, and I don't give a shit. Just stay out of the way and don't step into the middle of this one."

Helen laughed ruefully as she turned off the tap. "Jordan, I didn't ask for this. It just shit all over me, all right? I'm in it whether I like it or not." She turned to see real worry lines etching his youthful face. "Besides, it looks like Manny's the one that needs a lecture, not me."

"Come on, he's going through hell right now about his kids—"

"Do not make excuses for him, Jordan. He's on the verge of doing something he won't be able to talk his way out of. You work with him every day, you've seen what he's like. Tell him to take some time off before he loses everything."

"You think I haven't done that?" He ran a hand over his face, his expression fading into exhaustion. "He's already been talking to a shrink, got written up by the suits in administration a couple times. One more and he's down for the count."

"Then get him to back off of me. Not for my sake, but for his." Jordan's face was gray and drawn in the weak winter light. She knew how close partners could get, how much like a marriage it could be. All this was taking a toll on Manny's partner, too.

Jordan looked down and leaned on the counter. "Like I said—just stay the hell out of this one. You two have some kind of history and you don't need to dig it up, not right now, with what he's going through."

Okay. The boys' club all over again. She held her dripping arm over the sink. "Why did you put a tail on me? Whose idea was that, yours or Manny's? Your Yankees fan is not very good at his job. I spotted him right away with that damn hat. Besides, aren't you supposed to work in teams? Someone is screwing up bad on this one."

Jordan pushed himself away from the counter and stared in genuine surprise. "I don't know what the fuck you're talking about." He snorted in disgust and walked out of the kitchen muttering, "I don't know who's more paranoid, you or him. Just stay away from this."

You mean, stay away from Manny, Helen thought as she heard the front door slam behind him.

She was looking for something to dry her arm with when Maggie came in. "You want to tell me what that was all about?" she asked in a calm, careful voice.

"I wish I knew." No paper towels, no dishcloth hanging up.

Maybe there was something in one of the drawers. Her arm felt better, despite the red blotch going from elbow to wrist. "Sounds like Walt thought he heard a ghost."

"Looks to me more like you and that Hernandez guy have a few ghosts to deal with."

Helen closed her eyes and felt sick. "Not now, Maggie. I—I just can't go there right now." She heard a rustle and knew that Maggie had left the kitchen. The coffee sloshed in Helen's stomach, threatening to come back up. She needed to eat something. Jesus fucking Christ, why couldn't anything in her life ever just go smoothly? Just once in her life, just once. "Please," Helen breathed.

And now she couldn't even find a napkin to dry her arm. She slammed a drawer shut, cursing aloud when it didn't close. Something was jammed in there. She yanked on the drawer until it spilled onto the floor. Finally—a spindly roll of paper towels. Relieved, she tore one off and gingerly patted her arm. Still hurt, but it wasn't serious.

Maggie poked her head in. "Everything okay?"

"Yeah, just got a little too eager in here."

"Okay." The smile was back on Maggie's face. At least for the moment, at least to get the job done today. "Let's eat, then I'm going to pack some more of this stuff."

"Be there in a minute." Helen picked up the drawer and tried to fit it back in. It wasn't jamming—no, there was something stuck back there. Remembering the way Alice hid her things under the bed, Helen reached in and felt a lump of—what? Papers, wadded up. She got a grasp and pulled it out.

Yellow-edged stubs lay on her palm. Computer printing. Dates, times, rows of numbers. Pay stubs. Helen fanned through the tight wad of folded papers. These were recent. She looked over the mess from the drawer she'd scattered across the linoleum. Yes, it was an odds-and-ends drawer, filled with receipts and bank statements.

Helen heard Maggie say something. "Coming." After a moment's hesitation she tucked the wad into her pocket, then went to have some lunch and help Maggie.

Chapter Eight

The phone kept ringing as Helen struggled with the door to her apartment Friday evening. Cat—she still hadn't come up with a good name for it—yowled along with the persistent ringing. "Okay, okay, give me a minute!" she grumbled as she finally got inside. She heard the answering machine click on as her grocery bag split open. Cans of tuna rolled across the living room, crunching over the instant soup mixes. "Shit." Cat looked with great interest at the small cans, batting the closest can under the sofa. "Why don't you get a job?" she said as she rounded up the tins.

Then she heard Maggie's voice. "So I'll have to cancel our plans to go back to Alice's place tomorrow," she was saying.

Helen's heart sank and the grocery bag landed in a heap on the table. So telling her about being a private investigator back in the good old days had been a mistake. She shouldn't have opened her mouth. She should have found something else to talk about over lunch and all that afternoon as they'd worked together in Alice's apartment. Thank God she hadn't said anything about prison—just that she was hoping to get in on another line of work. Of course Maggie hadn't bought that lame excuse. Now that she'd had four days think it over she'd decided to wash her hands of Helen once and for all. Of course she was canceling their Saturday plans.

Then Helen registered a quavery tone in her voice. Making an ungainly dive over Cat and Cat's new toys, she managed to grab the phone, switching off the answering machine.

"Maggie? Hi, I just got in. What's up?"

Maggie drew a shaky breath, then let it out in a big sigh. "I can't come over tomorrow. Something—something came up."

"I got that part." Helen heard Maggie's voice crack, tears threatening to break through. "What came up? Are you all right?" She fought down panic at the idea of Maggie's being hurt or in trouble. Not a good sign, to be this worried just because Maggie sounded out of breath. Immediately she conjured up a couple of scenarios worthy of eye-rolling contempt. Someone stole the collection plate. The organ had a crossed wire. Or the covered-dish social bombed because everyone brought Jell-O Salad. But her thoughts came to a halt with Maggie's continued silence. "Hey, what happened?"

"They broke in again."

Jesus. Maybe it was whoever had gotten into Alice's place. Now they were after Maggie. Helen felt that icy calm come over her. "Maggie, are you all right? They didn't hurt you, did they?" She was surprised at how calm she sounded, how easily the professional tone came back to her. No time to think about that now, though.

"What? No, no, it's not me. I'm fine. They broke into the church offices." Now Helen could hear the tears in her voice. "I thought we'd gotten past that. I thought we were part of the community now."

Helen twisted the phone cord around her fingers and watched Cat rolling on its back, stretching luxuriously among the tea bags and coffee filters. One paw stretched up toward a bunch of bananas. Helen bent over to move them out of reach. "You said 'again.' Who did this?"

"I'm not sure. It must be the same ones as before."

"What happened before?"

Maggie told the story in bits and pieces, speaking more easily as she went on. The last time was three months ago, but the church had been vandalized twice during the past year. Whoever had broken into the church in November had painted obscenities about "fags" and "lezzies" all across the sanctuary. They'd also smeared what had proven to be feces across the altar. That time, the offices had been relatively unharmed, just a few scratches on the door. "But that's only because we learned the first time," she said. The first episode, which had taken place right after the church opened its doors in April last year, had included a couple of smashed computer terminals and shredded files. "Fortunately one of our members has his own alarm business, and he installed a system for the offices for practically nothing. And we got donations of computer terminals. We were lucky they didn't set fire to the place, I guess."

"The alarms are just for the offices?"

"That's right. We were hoping to raise funds to extend the system to the chapel, but there's nothing really that expensive in there. You saw it, Helen. Just pews and chairs."

Maggie was close to tears again—Helen could hear her voice cracking. Just keep talking, Helen told herself, keep asking questions. She didn't think she could stay strong and distant if she heard Maggie cry. "So when did this happen?"

"It must have been last night. Thursday night. I was in the office yesterday afternoon, and I locked up around six and went home. Then I got here this evening, hoping to find some extra boxes for Alice's place, and—well, the place is pretty messed up. I don't know how they got around the alarms this time, but they trashed the office." She sighed. "Furniture overturned, filing cabinets broken into, stuff broken and thrown all over the room."

"Anything else written on the walls?"

"No, just a mess." She cleared her throat. "Look, I'm sorry to dump on you like this. I—I thought I'd be okay tonight, but I think I need to stay here and take care of the office. Maybe we can try for Sunday afternoon?"

Helen chewed her lip and prodded her foot at the box of crackers on the floor. Cat rolled over and sat up, alert, watching intently. A paw swiped at her shoelaces as Cat sprang into attack. "Are you planning on staying there for a while, Maggie?"

"I guess so. I mean, there's just me right now. We only have a part-time volunteer secretary, and he's gone for the weekend."

"I'm coming over. No, don't say anything. I'll be there in about half an hour."

Maggie sighed. Helen thought her breathing sounded easier now. "Are you sure, Helen? I hate to take up your Friday night like this—"

Helen almost laughed out loud at the thought of her exciting evening. Better not to tell Maggie that she'd planned to read a paperback mystery from the secondhand bookstore downtown. Well, that and trying not to think about Maggie. "See you at the church in half an hour."

It actually took her twenty minutes to get the groceries away from Cat and get to the church. The building was closed and locked but Helen saw lights from the back of the chapel. She tiptoed down a narrow alley, all her nerves alert for the least noise or movement, but all she heard was the sound of her own feet scraping across old debris. It was too dark to see anything beyond vague shapes outlining a dumpster and a pile of flattened boxes ready for recycling. A narrow band of light reached into the alley from a porch lamp that switched on just as Helen rounded the corner. A motion sensor, probably. Above the porch light Helen could make out the words CHURCH OFFICE in clear black lettering. She stood for a moment, looking around. Office buildings, dark and silent, rose on either side of the alley. Maybe the buildings were abandoned. Behind the office Helen saw a parking lot half filled with cars. Beyond that, an apartment building with windows faced out toward the parking lot and church.

No reason for anyone to pay attention to what happened in the alley at night. The church office might reasonably have people working late from time to time, and unless someone screamed bloody murder no one would pay attention. Helen shuddered at the thought of Maggie caught in the crossfire of a break-in.

"Helen?"

Helen stepped across a large oily puddle that gleamed in the light as Maggie opened the door. She'd have to warn Maggie about opening the door at night without checking to see who was there. "Hope I didn't scare you."

"No, I'm glad you're here." Helen had to resist the urge to take Maggie in her arms. Maggie wiped at her cheeks and Helen took in the reddened eyes and swollen nose and lips. Maggie's hair tumbled loose and soft over her shoulders, and there were dirt smudges on her faded shirt and jeans. "It's good to see you." She forced a smile, forced a level of brightness into her voice. Helen guessed Maggie had kept her grief private, however, and decided it was better not to comment. "Come on up. Just be prepared, okay?"

It wasn't quite as bad as Helen had feared. She looked first at the intact computer terminals—two of them, one on a big desk against the far wall, the other on a long table. Two chairs, both straight-backed with worn plastic cushions—one brown, one black—had been overturned beside the table. They must have come from someone's kitchen or from a secondhand furniture store. The table looked like a hand-me-down as well. Brightly colored posters, proclaiming tolerance and peace, lined the walls. Helen saw a few tacks remaining on the wall where an additional two posters or prints had been displayed. Shreds of paper dangled from the tacks, as if the prints had been ripped down.

A white metal desk, similar to the kind found in hospitals and medical offices, sat in the corner beneath a picture window that showed a stunning view of the parking lot and apartment building she had noticed earlier. An uneven stack of papers were piled high next to the computer monitor. A potted plant—she was bad with plants, could barely tell a cactus from a bromeliad—rested on the corner of the desk, surrounded by black smudges of potting soil where she guessed it had been knocked over by the intruder. In the opposite corner stood an oil-filled radiator, switched off for the moment.

Something small and square lay on the floor under the desk. Without thinking Helen reached down to pick it up. She looked down at the picture frame in her hands. Maggie, a few years younger and wearing a cap and gown, smiled up at her. The woman whose arm rested around Maggie's shoulder had a big grin only for Maggie. Helen looked away from the happy faces and put the picture back on the desk.

The room was otherwise barren. Helen stood in the center of the small office, staring down. A tall filing cabinet lay on its side, the drawers bent against the cheap linoleum, files and papers splayed out in a messy fan in front of the long work table. She crouched down, peering at the front of the cabinet. The lock at the top had been scratched at, then wrenched open. Not a neat job. Not very professional.

"I managed to clean up a lot of the mess," Maggie said. Helen got up and looked at her leaning against the wall. Her face suddenly looked gray and drawn. She rubbed a hand wearily over her forehead, wincing as she spoke. "You know, chairs overturned, the stuff on my desk all tossed around—I can't get the filing cabinet back up, though. Too heavy."

"Did you call the police?"

"Yeah, they left right before I called you. Poked around, took some notes, same old thing to them. They're not going to be able to do anything, Helen. This is minor compared to what Oakland cops usually have to deal with." She knelt down and shoved the filing cabinet. It didn't budge an inch.

"I can help you with that, if you want." Helen took a couple of steps closer. "Are you sure you don't need to get home and get some rest? This can wait till tomorrow."

"No." Maggie pushed herself away from the wall. "I have to get it done now, before I collapse." Helen sighed and joined her on the floor. Together they emptied all the files from the drawers, stacking them on the work table. "We can sort that out later. Let's just see if we can save the cabinet."

Between the two of them they got the cabinet up and standing against the wall ten minutes later.

Maggie fussed at the bent drawers, the twisted lock. "I don't know if we can still use this or not," she muttered to herself.

"Maggie, let's get dinner or something. You need a break."

"Damn, it won't shut!" Maggie suddenly started weeping, her face turned to the wall and her shoulders shaking. Helen hesitated, then reached out to gingerly hold her shoulders. Maggie leaned back in Helen's arms, her face still turned away. Helen tightened her hold, trying not to think, trying to pay attention only to Maggie and not to her own surge of desire. Maggie's breathing finally eased into something less ragged. Gently she disengaged from Helen's arms with a sigh. "Sorry, Helen. Guess this seems pretty small stuff to a private investigator. I don't know why I'm shaking like this. It's not like I was hurt or anything. It's just files."

It was shock talking, of course. Helen kept her hands on Maggie's arms.

Maggie burst out, "Where's the damn Kleenex?" She found the box and grabbed a wadded-up handful.

"Don't be sorry. You've been through an awful experience." Helen watched her as she wiped her face and sat down at the desk, leaning her head in her hands. "Come on, let's go get some food. Do they have any cookies left in that kitchen? I think I saw some kind of chocolate chip things in there."

It was the right thing to say. Maggie smiled and pushed herself away from the desk. A few minutes later they were sitting in the tiny kitchen next to the chapel sipping mint tea. Helen had skipped dinner to get to the church, but she found some muffins that weren't too stale. Crackers and cheese slices from the most recent social rounded out supper. "Why do you think the police wouldn't take this seriously?" she asked as she finished the last sugar cookie.

Maggie snorted, staring down into her empty teacup. "What

could they do? Last time they dusted the whole place for fingerprints, found way too many, nothing they could use. I told them not to bother." She snorted. "They weren't all that eager to do it anyway. Guess they're getting tired of my calls."

Helen watched Maggie's face. Now that she'd had that cathartic bout of crying, Maggie seemed easier talking about it. She chose her questions with caution. "So, they did what, ripped down some stuff from the wall? Turned over furniture?"

"No, I took down the posters." She made a face and glanced up at Helen. "They put—well, they'd written some stuff on them."

"Like what? 'Burn in hell, homo,' what?"

"Just one word. 'Lesbo.' Almost innocent, like stuff from high school. At least from when I was in high school, not like nowadays." Maggie smiled. "And this time they just used a magic marker. Could have been a lot worse, like what they did in the chapel."

"So whoever did this just went into the filing cabinet, basically."

"Yeah, that's about it." Maggie's eyes narrowed. "What are you thinking?"

Helen leaned forward, arms on the table, supper forgotten. "Think about it, Maggie. They had access to the computers, to a radiator that probably would have made a nice little fire if they could get to the oil in it. They had bare walls practically begging for creative artwork. That old table and chairs could have broken up pretty easily. And what did these assholes do? They turned over one filing cabinet and wrote one naughty word on a poster." Helen studied the table, thinking. "What about money? Do you keep any in the filing cabinet?"

"No, not usually. There were a couple bucks' loose change in the desk, they took that. We put the collection in a little safe in the sanctuary. But that wasn't touched." Maggie cocked her head. "What are you getting at? You're asking the same questions the cops asked me earlier."

Helen went on, barely noticing Maggie's sudden wariness. "I'm saying there was surprisingly little damage, given the opportunity. I'm saying these guys, whoever they were, could have busted into the chapel and wrecked it, tried to break open the safe, scrawled all kinds of shit on the walls. Instead they focused on your filing cabinet. The church's records. That's a very odd thing to be interested in if your goal is to destroy the church."

Maggie went still and silent. She looked away from Helen, stared at the sink where a leaky faucet dripped a slow, maddening beat on the aging porcelain. "They're after something else, then."

Helen shrugged, suddenly worried she'd said too much. "Who knows? It's just strange, that's all. Probably the cops have a good answer anyway," she finished lamely.

"Sounds to me like you have some answers, Helen. Or at least the right questions." Maggie faced her again, her green eyes unreadable in the harsh light. "So why do I get the feeling that this kind of scene is all too familiar to you? Just like in Alice's apartment. Just like with those cops. Like you're used to break-ins and strange deaths."

"Well, I just remember from my days as a glamorous private investigator." Helen gave her a crooked smile and tried to laugh while her stomach clenched with—what? Fear? Anger? Maybe just disappointment at how things were going with Maggie. As if they'd be going anywhere in hell, Helen told herself. She cleared her throat. "I'm just commenting on what looks strange to me. Doesn't necessarily mean anything, Maggie." She drank her cold tea and wished the other woman would speak.

"Hey, I'm not mad, Helen." Somehow Maggie's hand touched her own, the fingers resting lightly against hers, not moving or stroking, just lying there. "I just wish I knew something about you. There's more going on than you're telling me."

"I'm just trying to help you, that's all." Helen spoke softly, not trusting her voice to stay calm. She kept her hand poised beneath Maggie's, her gaze on the table.

"Like you tried to help Alice?" Maggie sighed but kept her hand where it was. "Talk to me, Helen. Tell me who you are. Tell me why those cops were talking to you that way at Alice's apartment."

"You tell me something first."

"If I can."

"Who's the woman in the photograph? The one on your desk."

Surprisingly, Maggie laughed. It was the best thing Helen had heard in days. "My ex-girlfriend. Ex-lover, ex-partner, ex-whatever. I met her a couple of years after Toni, the one who preferred a frat boy to me. Grace and I stayed together for six years, but we broke up before I graduated. Can't really blame her. It was hard, being with someone who worked and went to school full time and trying to get some kind of ministry going all at once."

"She doesn't look like an ex-lover in that picture." Helen was proud of how steady her voice was. Maybe in a minute she could look at Maggie, too.

"We've stayed good friends for years, Helen. Grace is a wonderful person, and I value her friendship." Maggie's voice took on a teasing note. "If you come to church on Sunday you might meet her. She sings in the choir. Soprano."

"Does she get to do solos?"

Maggie laughed again. "Only in the shower. Or so her partner tells me."

"One big happy family now, huh?" She risked a look up at Maggie.

"Just a family. Sometimes happy, sometimes not, but there for each other." Now both Maggie's hands were on her own. "Helen, please talk to me about what's going on with you. Tell me what you're thinking."

Helen slowly withdrew her hand, first giving Maggie's fingers a gentle squeeze. Jesus, what should she do? What would Maggie do if she knew she was talking like this to an ex-con, to someone who'd killed another person and been to prison for it? Seeing Maggie like this, her hair down, her face soft and eager, Helen was painfully reminded of the picture on the desk. The smiling, happy, innocent Maggie of that picture would never see Helen as anything but a project to fix up. Like she tried to fix Alice. Another painful reminder—Helen's own tired, gray, aging face in the mirror at Alice's apartment. She might as well have been from another planet, for all the connection there could be between her and Maggie.

Maggie's next words confirmed Helen's suspicion that she was now the minister's new pet project. "At least think about coming to church on Sunday, Helen. Will you do that for me?"

Helen stood up and gazed down at Maggie. The icy calm that had fallen away at Maggie's touch was back in place. Like hell, she thought. "We'll see. I'd better get home. You should go home, too—get some rest."

She left Maggie still sitting at the table and wandered back into the alley, barely seeing where she was going and not really giving a fuck. It had started to rain again, and Helen squinted up at the black sky. A fine mist sprayed onto her face and she cautiously made her way past the dumpster, welcoming the cold and the wet. Maybe it would help her wake up, help her get her head back on right. The hell she'd be a project for some do-gooder with thick golden hair and green eyes—

At first Helen didn't see him in the beige Honda. She picked up her pace as soon as she got to the sidewalk, hurrying to the shelter of her own car. His face loomed in the glow of the streetlight for a moment, then he leaned back into shadow as soon as she recognized the guy in the Yankees cap who'd been following her for days. "What the fuck?" she muttered. Her hand was shaking as she fumbled with the keys. The cold anger that had sustained her as she left Maggie was still there, still strong inside her. She turned, keys in hand, and strode back to his car. Suddenly the engine revved, the headlights flared on, and the car sped off in a blur of rain water and exhaust fumes. It was too dark to make out more than the fact that the Honda had California plates.

Helen stood alone on the sidewalk, shivering under the streetlight. He couldn't have been a cop. He'd been alone in the car and hadn't known enough to stay out of sight. For surveillance, he wasn't worth shit. That didn't make him any less dangerous.

Helen saw no sign of him as she went home to Cat.

Chapter Nine

Helen poked at her salad and looked out the window. Shattuck Avenue shone in the sunlight. Trees lining the street waved branches in the wind over the bicyclists and pedestrians taking advantage of the unexpected break in the weather. Usually Berkeley in February was a dreary round of cold and rain, but once in a while the weather took a turn for spring, warming the air and bringing people outside. The lunch crowd at Chez Panisse this Saturday afternoon seemed to be mostly locals, residents of the quiet tree-lined streets of north Berkeley. Admittedly the lunch menu was a hell of a lot cheaper than the prices Helen had seen years ago for their dinners. Certainly the food was as good as she remembered. She took a sip of water and tried to enjoy the meal. The lentil soup was getting cold beside her, and she reached for the salad. Try to keep something down, she advised herself, wondering why she was so nervous.

"Thanks for taking time out on a Saturday, Katy. Especially since it's Valentine's Day."

“Not to worry, Jan and I have definite plans for the evening.” Katy smiled complacently at Jan. Helen noticed how Jan avoided her lover’s gaze. Trouble in paradise already? She took a piece of herbed bread hoping it would settle her stomach.

That was not as easy as it sounded, given her companions. When they’d first walked in, Katy had stopped talking on her cell phone just long enough to acknowledge the hostess’s greeting and request a table tucked into a corner—“by a window, away from all these people”—and then taken another precious few minutes to look over the wine menu. A brief discussion with the waiter, a handsome young man who deferentially murmured all the right things about the wine, rounded out Katy’s contribution to the wine selection. She’d gone back to her cell phone with a smile of apology to Jan and Helen that indicated the world would end if she didn’t take care of business, despite its being Saturday, then turned her attention to whatever deal of the moment she was setting up. Jan had smiled wryly at Helen as she’d picked up her menu. The young waiter had arrived with a bottle and murmured something in her ear about not using her cell phone inside the restaurant. Katy rolled her eyes and nodded as he filled their glasses.

“God, what a mess. Sorry about that.” Katy had flipped her phone shut only as the food had arrived. “I leave my people alone for one day and they can’t find their way out of a paper bag.”

Helen smiled and sipped the excellent wine. What the hell was this lunch all about? She already knew Katy and Jan had money and friends and power. That they ate at places like Chez Panisse regularly, had nice cars and a house, terrific careers. Helen knew she should have refused the invitation to lunch but it would have seemed ungrateful, given how much Katy had helped her. With a sinking sensation Helen set down her fork. Jan picking her up in the Jag, fancy restaurant, earth-shattering business calls—this could only be about one thing.

Katy’s next words confirmed Helen’s fears. “I thought maybe we could get an update on how you’re doing, Helen,” Katy began. She leaned forward over the table, her expensive silk blouse gleaming in the soft light and showing just the right amount of cleavage.

Helen took in the understated makeup, the hint of perfume wafting across the table, the carefully composed look of concern edged with hardness in her eyes. "Brenda says she's been sending you on a lot of jobs lately."

"Yes, she has. I'm on a new one right now, in an insurance agency. She's really helped me a lot." Helen fiddled with the stem of her wineglass. Wouldn't do to slurp it all down in front of them, not if they were going to ask her to pay up what she owed. "I'm making ends meet, at least. You know how it is," she babbled. "Rents are so high here, and I can't save much. Not with the car and all." Great, that sounded really pathetic.

"Hmm." Katy drummed on the table for a moment. "Well," she went on brightly, "now that you're working fairly regularly, we should probably talk about budgeting for you."

"Budgeting."

Katy's eyebrows went up. "Yes. You know, setting up a payment plan. We could probably get something worked out we'd all agree on, don't you think?" She smiled and cocked her head to one side, as if that made her look more compassionate.

"Sure." What else could she say? Helen gave up on the soup and picked up her wine, drinking most of it down. She glanced around the room, taking in all the prosperous-looking diners and the elegantly rustic setting. How many of these people had scrimped and saved for a meal here—and how many took it for granted as part of their normal routine?

"I have a pretty good idea of what you're earning," Katy was saying, "so I'll get my secretary to put something down and we'll get started on it."

"A contract."

Katy wrinkled her nose and laughed, a tinkling giggle. "It's been my experience it's a lot better that way. Saves time and energy. And then it's a done deal." She actually reached over and patted Helen's hand. "I was thinking we could start next month."

Helen was about to ask what interest rate she'd be charging when Katy's phone rang again.

"Oh, hell," Katy said with a brilliant smile and toss of her head. "Now what?"

Helen took one bite of her soup—yes, it was cold—and went back to the glass of wine. Okay, she had stayed with Katy for what, a couple of weeks? And Katy had loaned her the money to get the apartment. How would that work out in dollars and cents in the paychecks from the agency? She caught Jan looking closely at her as she reached for the bottle. Her clear dark eyes were unreadable as she studied Helen. It reminded her of the way the guards had assessed her on her arrival at the women's prison on Mississippi—being weighed, measured and found wanting. Fuck it, Helen decided. She'd probably never sit in Chez Panisse again, so she might as well take advantage of it. Helen poured the last of the wine into her glass and stared back with a grim smile.

"Great." Katy sighed and rummaged for her jacket and purse. "I have to go to the office. There's a client who—well, never mind. Let's just say that yet again only Katy can do it. Even on a Saturday afternoon." She raised an imperious hand and the waiter scurried over. "Could you just put this on my tab?" she asked as she pulled her jacket on.

" 'Tab'? I'm afraid we don't keep 'tabs,' ma'am," he replied in icy condescension.

Helen looked down at her cold soup to hide her smile.

Katy clucked with irritation. "Is Monty here today? Just talk to Monty, he'll take care of it."

"Go ahead, Katy. I've got this." Jan nodded to the waiter, who lingered just long enough to ask if there was anything else they needed.

In a final flurry of insincere apologies and fond farewells to Jan, Katy left in a wake of importance and clicking heels. Helen and Jan sat in silence, staring down at the table until Helen heard something coming from Jan. It took a moment to realize that Jan was doing her best not to laugh out loud.

"Here's to commerce," Jan said, tossing back the rest of her wine. "That was—interesting."

Helen regarded Jan warily as the waiter took away their nearly untouched plates.

"I'd like some dessert. How about you?" Jan studied the dessert menu and chose bread pudding.

Helen asked for coffee. No more to drink. God knew what Jan would come up with in Katy's absence, and Helen wanted her wits about her. Like it or not, she was tied to Katy for the time being until the loan was paid back. It probably wasn't wise to piss off Katy's girlfriend.

"Don't look so rigid, Helen. The little business arrangement wasn't my idea. Katy came up with that all on her own. God, this is good. You want a bite?" Jan closed her eyes and savored the bread pudding. "You're missing out. They do great desserts here. Come on, Helen, relax! This was all just a big show for our benefit." She sighed and put down her spoon as Helen remained silent. "Look, she wanted us here together so she could toss her weight around. Prove she's the boss and we're just a pair of accessories. Like a handbag, or an SUV."

"Or in your case, a Jaguar, replete with all the trimmings." Fuck, she'd had too much to drink. Helen felt the blood rush to her face. God only knew what Jan would say to Katy about her lack of subservience now.

To her amazement Jan started laughing so hard that a few other patrons turned to look at the hilarity taking place at the corner table. "You thought she bought me the Jaguar? God, no! I bought it myself. My dream car. It's a classic." Her eyes lit up as she described her search for a used Jaguar, the effort she'd put into fixing it up. "All mine, from the ground up." She finished her bread pudding and licked the spoon, letting it fall with a gentle clatter into the empty bowl. "I'd love to get my hands on an old Bentley one of these days, but it won't be easy."

Helen found herself able to breathe again and noted the amused smile playing on Jan's lips. Helen felt icy calm steal over her again—thank God it was still there inside, ready to be tapped when she needed it. "Okay, Jan. Thanks for the lunch and all, but

I'm fresh out of patience for today. Either you tell me what the hell this was all about or I'll just catch the bus home, thank you very much."

Jan shook her head and leaned forward, still smiling. "Like I said. Katy is just jerking our chains. Mine more than yours, I think."

"What do you mean?"

"She's pissed off that I showed an interest in you. Professional, I might add. The minute I heard you were coming back to town I wanted to do a story on you."

"A story. You're a journalist?" Helen couldn't have been more surprised and she knew her voice showed it.

"Yep. Not just a kept woman or another pretty face." The smile faded and the dark eyes went unreadable again. "I still want to do a story on you. Katy doesn't like it when other people get my attention, for any reason whatsoever."

"You're saying Katy was trying to put both of us in our places."

The smile came back. "You dated her once upon a time. You know how she is. It's all about Katy, and God help you if you decide it's about something else from time to time." Jan shrugged. "I figure she left us alone so you could lick your wounds and I could see the error of my ways."

"In other words, so you could see I'm a pathetic waste of time."

"Something like that."

Helen shoved away from the table. "Thanks for the lunch. I had a great time. I'll just get myself home now."

Jan tossed cash on the table and hurried after her. Once they were outside she took Helen's arm and steered her away from Shattuck and toward the side street where she'd parked. Helen was too frozen with anger to react fast enough and lose herself in the cluster of people surging around the entrance to the restaurant. "I meant what I said, Helen. I am interested and I do want to do a story. I've had a couple of pieces in *The Nation*, and now I'm hoping for a series in *Mother Jones*."

Helen snorted. They'd reached the Jag now and Jan had to let her go to get out her keys. "Okay, I'm curious enough to ask why. What could possibly be so interesting about a loser like me? Unless that's the topic of your little article, dyke has-beens?"

"I could use a cigarette, how about you?" Jan got in and opened the passenger door. "Helen, get in. I'll tell you if you let me take you home." Jan drove along the back streets of North Berkeley, taking her time getting into Oakland. Helen refused the cigarette and let her talk. "Actually your story would be part of a series," she started. "On women getting out of prison, how hard it is to take up where they left off."

"So, what, you need a murderer for your collection?" The images rushed into Helen's mind—Victoria slumped dead on the car seat, eyes dull in death. The judge pronouncing sentence, his face pale and indifferent, ready to turn to the next case. The scratchy orange jumpsuit issued by the prison authorities, the fabric harsh enough to give her a rash. The series of depressing affairs with other inmates, often just a relief from boredom or part of the politics of staying alive. The incessant drone of game shows and infomercials on the television set that never got turned off. The grinding pain of trying to work through it all once they let her out. The closed doors and closed faces of trying to get a job. And now it was all going to be a fluffy story in some heart-warming article with an oh-so-politically-correct audience that would have the comfort of feeling pity for the likes of Helen and the satisfaction of knowing they'd never be in her shoes. Ever.

Jan broke the silence as they pulled up in front of Helen's building. "I was hoping for a chance to talk to you without Katy around." She reached into the back seat—Helen was suddenly aware of Jan's strong arms and shoulders, of her neck—and handed Helen a manila folder. "This is a copy of the first article in the series. You read it before you make a decision about talking to me."

Helen sat for a moment with the file in her lap. "Katy knows you're doing this?"

Jan laughed again, that same sharp sparkly noise she'd made in the restaurant. Completely unlike Katy's jagged cackle. "Katy doesn't really care what I do as long as I get into her bed on occasion."

Helen slowly traced the edge of the folder with her fingers. "Is that what this is about, Jan? I don't recall Katy being that good in the sack. Okay, but not that great."

"I met her when I was doing a series on lesbians in the corporate world." The wry smile came back as she turned to look at Helen. "One thing led to another, as they say. I was in between lovers, and it was just so—convenient."

"Convenient." Helen couldn't help an answering smile. "Is that another reason Katy tossed us into the deep end together today? Testing a theory about whether or not it would be convenient for you to hit on me?"

"You're not exactly the convenient type, Helen. But, you're the private eye. You figure it out on your own."

"You forget. I'm not anything anymore, Jan. Maybe a pet project for Katy, but that's about it. I can't afford to turn down Katy's help, even if there are strings attached."

Jan snorted.

"Okay, I guess that means there are a couple more strings attached now. What's going on? What do you really want?"

This time Jan laughed out loud. "You make it sound so evil. All I'm looking for is a story. A chance to go free-lance for good, quit stringing for a two-bit weekly that barely puts gas in this car. A really big break." She turned those dark sharp features back to Helen with a self-assured smile. "And you can give it to me."

"Or you go running to Katy and suddenly she wants immediate payment for everything I owe her, is that it? Make my life difficult." Helen felt her lips stretch into a grim smile. "I don't take kindly to being threatened, Jan."

"What are you going to do, run crying to Katy? Like I said, as long as I keep her happy in bed she doesn't really care what else I do. Come on, Helen, this works all around. I get a terrific story, maybe something prize-winning that writes my ticket to independence. You get all the help you need from Katy. I can help you with that one. What's the big damn deal?" She leaned in closer, until Helen could smell whatever cologne she'd splashed on for the outing. Something dark and spicy that went with the Jag and the leather jacket. "It's a win-win situation, in a lot of different ways."

Helen looked long and hard at her, making a decision. This day had actually become sort of fun, in an unsettling way. Maybe it was the flirting, maybe something more risky. She was out of practice, except for that one awful night with Alice. She shook the memory aside. "Okay. I'll read the article and think about this—if you do something for me."

Jan's eyes went dark and careful again. "If I can."

"It should be easy for a hotshot girl reporter like you." It was a snide remark but Helen didn't care. She dug into her bag and brought out the pay stubs she'd found in Alice's apartment. "I need to find out where these came from. There's a phone number on them, but they're pretty old. Some other information, too. I think that's a payroll company address."

Jan held the bundle in her hand. "Does this have something to do with that woman's death?" Suddenly her face went serious. "You have to give me something before I check this out."

Helen stared out the window, avoiding Jan's eyes. How much should she tell her? Maybe a few bits and pieces. "I found them in Alice's apartment after she died."

"You were in her apartment?"

Helen explained that she'd helped sort through some of Alice's things with a couple of Alice's friends. "I just was hoping we could figure out where her family was. Maybe whoever she worked for would be able to tell us." That was all Jan was getting, she decided. The question was whether or not she'd buy it.

And of course she didn't, not completely. "There's a lot more you're not telling me, but I think I can do this much." Jan slipped the pay stubs into a briefcase on the back seat, brushing Helen's shoulder as she did so. "Us hotshot girl reporters have all kinds of information at our fingertips."

A few minutes later Helen was sitting on her sofa, Cat purring at her side, and reading Jan's article. She felt ashamed at her snap judgment—this wasn't a lightweight entry in a superficial weekly. *Mother Jones* was widely read by hundreds of thousands of Americans. Jan's sharp prose, her grasp of details, made for a riveting read. The real problem, Helen thought as she stroked Cat's head, was whether or not she could really open up to Jan. She just didn't know if she was ready to risk plunging the knife into her own heart, not now when she was struggling so hard to make a life for herself.

And to feed myself and Cat, she thought as she looked for the box of Friskies. Nothing. Helen cursed herself for forgetting she needed to get cat food. Of course her wallet and checking account were bare—and of course Cat had quickly demonstrated she only wanted the most expensive cat food on the market. Not to mention the priciest brand of litter.

"Go get a job, Cat," she muttered. Now what? Too bad she hadn't filched some leftovers from Chez Panisse. Might have cemented Katy's view of her as a loser, might have been good copy for Jan's story—ex-con dumpster diving in Berkeley. They could have a woeful portrait of Cat for the article.

Okay, this wasn't getting Cat fed. Helen remembered seeing some cat food in Alice's kitchen. Hopefully it was still there, and hopefully Maggie hadn't decided to stop by this afternoon. And hopefully Walt Greeley hadn't gotten locks changed yet. She could pick up a couple of cans of cat food from Alice's for the night, and Cat could just handle having a cheap dinner for once.

Her luck held. She crept quietly up the stairs to Alice's apartment, not wanting to alert Walt to her presence. Yes, the key was still under the planter, and yes, it still worked. With as little noise as possible she let herself in. The sunlight that had so brightened her spirits earlier that afternoon still shone through the windows. Maybe all the cold and rain really would go away one of these days—maybe spring was still possible.

Helen scanned the living room and noted that some progress had been made. Maggie must have come here with her work party and boxed a bunch of things up. Good, they'd have less to do next time. Still moving noiselessly she went into the kitchen. A brief search revealed half a dozen cans of Cat's favorite entree tucked into a corner of the counter. That would get them through the weekend, at least, and Helen should get another paycheck Monday.

"Helen."

"Shit!" The cans clattered to the floor. "Jesus fucking Christ, you scared the shit out of me."

"Sorry." Maggie stood in the doorway. "You kind of scared me, too." Maggie took a couple of steps into the kitchen. Helen saw the dark circles under her eyes, the lines of strain around her mouth. "I was in the bathroom and I heard something."

Helen bent over to retrieve the cat food, glad to hide her face for a moment. "Looks like you guys are getting a lot done here." She stood, holding the cans awkwardly. "I ran out of food for Cat."

"I think there's a bag of litter in the bathroom." Maggie disappeared and Helen stood still, catching her breath. "Yes, it's here," Maggie called out.

"Great. You all alone here today?"

"No, but the others left a little while ago. Here, let me help you with that—I think there's a bag over here."

"Thanks." If only she'd quit helping me, Helen thought, if only she'd stop looking at me like that. She tried not to pay attention to Maggie's gentle smile, the tiredness in her voice and movements. She bet Maggie's shoulders hurt, too, the way she was standing. She had a sudden image of rubbing those shoulders, at first through the gold sweater, then down to bare skin. Okay, that was enough. "Hey, thanks a lot, Maggie. I better get home and feed Cat."

And of course her car wouldn't start. Maggie watched from the front of the apartment building as the engine clicked uselessly.

"Fuck, fuck, fuck." Helen slumped down in the seat and the rain began. Clouds scudded swiftly across the sky and water seeped in through the window. She turned at the sound of footsteps running across the street.

Maggie leaned into the window with a tentative smile. "Need a jump?"

Chapter Ten

"Here, let's try this one." Maggie opened a can of cat food and dumped it into the cracked plastic bowl Helen had been using. Cat eyed the brownish mess offered to her, balefully glared at Helen, turned her gaze to Maggie, then crouched by the bowl. Her expression seemed so long-suffering that Helen couldn't repress a laugh. "Guess she doesn't like it very much." Maggie sighed as she stood up.

Cat leaned over and took a small taste—then another. "Thank God," Helen said. "It's always a toss-up if she'll eat. I don't know if it's the food, the new house or what."

"Maybe she's just getting used to all the changes." Maggie leaned against the counter and watched Cat daintily lap at the food. "Cats need adjustment time, just like people."

"Yeah. Listen, thanks a lot for following me home." Helen sat down in a chair, suddenly tired and hungry. Salad and two bites of lentil soup, plus a healthy dose of wine, had been a long time ago.

Not to mention the diversion provided by Katy and Jan. "Sorry I'm not the best hostess right now. I think I'm kind of beat."

"Why don't I fix you something to eat? Lunch was a long time ago."

Great, now she was the charity project again. The last thing she wanted was to have Maggie looking through her bare cupboards and empty refrigerator. "You don't have to do that, Maggie. I'm fine, I just need to get some sleep."

"Well, I definitely need food myself. There's a taqueria on the corner that makes great carnitas burritos. How about I get us something, bring it back here?"

"No, really. I'll be fine. And I'm sure you want to get home anyway."

Maggie went silent, looked down at Cat again. Her bowl was bare, and she was busily licking a paw and running the paw across her face and whiskers. With a twitch of her tail Cat left the kitchen and wandered off. "Sorry, Helen. I guess I was just hoping to spend some time with you this evening."

"Maggie—"

"No biggie. Hey, I have a sermon to finish anyhow." With a forced smile Maggie pushed herself away from the counter. Helen closed her eyes and took a deep breath before following her into the darkened living room.

Christ on a crutch, she really did not need this right now. She didn't need to feel guilty for not being the willing victim for Maggie to heal her conscience with, she didn't need to feel guilty for wanting Maggie.

Helen switched on a lamp and watched Maggie gather up purse and keys. "So, any more news on your break-in?" she asked, hoping to deflect the awkwardness onto another topic.

Maggie shook her head. "I don't think the police give a damn. No serious damage was done, no one hurt. Guess we'll just have to beef up security somehow."

"Were any files missing?"

Maggie looked at her curiously. "No, everything was where it was supposed to be. I mean, if they were looking for money they didn't find it. What else could it be?"

"You're right. Sorry, it's none of my business anyway." Please, Maggie, just get out of here, Helen thought.

"Well—" Maggie opened the door and something small and gray streaked by her feet.

"Shit," Helen muttered, pushing her way past Maggie into the hallway. Cat perched at the head of the stairwell, head turned to see Helen running toward her, then with a flick of her tail darted out of sight down the stairs.

"Helen, I'm sorry," Maggie called. Helen scrambled downstairs and saw Cat huddled behind a straggling potted palm in the foyer of the building. She could hear Maggie running behind her. "She moved so fast, I didn't see her."

"Serves me right. I'm not supposed to have pets here, anyhow." Helen walked slowly toward the palm. Cat glared at her and growled low in her throat. "Come on, you little bastard, come on home now," she said in wheedling tones. She saw the muscles in Cat's shoulders bunch, ready to spring away, and with an exasperated curse Helen grabbed her. "Ouch, shit," she hissed. Cat was struggling in Helen's arms and had managed to swipe a very sharp set of claws over her hand. Blood welled up from the scrape. "Damn critter. That hurts."

"Let me see. God, that's a deep scratch." They made their way back to Helen's apartment, where Maggie insisted on cleaning the scratch. Cat leapt from Helen's arms and hid under the sofa, keeping up a growl the whole time.

Helen lay down on the sofa and closed her eyes. "Yeah, right, little crazy animal. You keep on growling at me and I'll put you out in the rain. You heard me."

"What?" Maggie came into the living room with wet cloths in hand. "Did you say something?"

"No, Cat and I were just having a tender bonding moment." She winced as Maggie wiped at the scratch. "I was just letting her know she's on borrowed time in this house, so she'd better behave."

"Here, let's put this on." Maggie put on the bandage and sat back with a concerned look in her eyes. "Helen, are you sure you're okay? You don't look too well."

"I'm all right, really." She didn't mean to touch Maggie, she really didn't. It was just that Maggie was so close, and her eyes were so big and green and her hair was soft and golden over her shoulders. Helen stared back up at the ceiling and tried to take her hand away but Maggie closed her own hand over Helen's. "Sorry, Maggie, it's been a bitch of a day."

"So tell me about it." Damn it, Maggie still wouldn't let go of her hand. And now Maggie was moving in closer. Helen could feel the warmth from her leg, her side. "I'm a good listener."

"Don't you have a sermon to write?"

"I've ad-libbed it before. Come on, what's going on?"

"Nothing. Everything. Look, Maggie—" Helen looked away, down at her feet, at the floor, anywhere but Maggie's eyes. "I'm not who you think I am. I mean, I don't want you to get the wrong idea about me."

"Then talk to me. Tell me. Who is Helen Black? What's her life about? What does she do, what does she think?"

"I wouldn't know where to start." Helen sighed, finally getting her hand away from Maggie's. She actually felt a bit dizzy—maybe she should eat something. "And I don't want to drag you into this, anyway."

"No one's dragging me, Helen. I think I'm walking in under my own steam here." Suddenly Maggie's mouth was on hers. Helen froze, eyes wide open, hands clutching the cushion. Maggie leaned back and let go of her, watching her closely. Helen barely dared to breathe. "I feel like I should say I'm sorry, Helen, but I'm not sorry. I wanted to touch you, to kiss you. I've been wanting to do this since I first met you."

Helen heard the words, understood them at some deep faraway level of her mind. All she could think about, all she could see, was Maggie's eyes and hair and mouth. All she was aware of was the way Maggie's strong hands had closed around her shoulders and the sensation of Maggie's lips on her own, soft and warm and seeking. Even the smell of her, that warm spicy scent coming from her neck when she'd leaned in close made her heart pound. Helen struggled to remain calm. God, why the hell was she so damn shaky? It was a kiss, that was all. She just hadn't been kissed in a long time, not by a woman like Maggie.

"Okay. Big mistake, I guess." Maggie's face reddened, glowing in the lamplight. She huddled in the corner of the sofa for a moment, then pushed herself up, keeping her gaze turned away. "Sorry. I shouldn't have done that. I'll let myself out."

Still unable to speak, Helen grabbed her wrist. Maggie stood very still, staring down at the carpet. Helen's fingers traced Maggie's wrist, feeling the pulse beating below the skin, feeling the supple muscles and soft warmth. She slid her hand up under the sleeve of Maggie's sweater and found more tender skin. Maggie let out a sigh and Helen felt her tremble. "Why are you shaking?"

"Look, Helen, this isn't me at all. I don't act like this without getting to know someone better. I guess I'm still kind of shook up about the break-in the other night." She moved away, disengaging from Helen and walking out of the room. Helen followed her to where she stood uncertainly in the hallway, rubbing her hand over her forehead. "I believe in commitment and loyalty and all those old-fashioned things. God knows I preach about them enough. I honestly don't know where that came from."

"Well, are you committed to someone right now? Is there anyone besides yourself you have to answer to?"

"No, but—"

Helen traced a teasing finger across the back of Maggie's neck. "Then where's the sin, Maggie? What are you doing wrong?"

Again Maggie escaped from her, this time back into the living room. She sank onto the sofa. Helen knelt on the floor beside her. Maggie refused to look her in the eyes.

For a moment Helen felt like a crouching predator, eager to take all she could get. The moment passed almost as soon as she recognized it. She took a deep breath and laid her hands gently on

Maggie's thigh. "Maybe it's because you just don't really want me. Or because—"

Maggie laughed nervously. "Maybe because I'm scared to death right now?" she said, jumping up and going to the window. "Maybe because I don't know what to do, I'm out of practice, or I can't quite believe I just behaved toward you like that."

"Like what?" Helen said as she approached her from behind.

With one part of her consciousness watching and judging, knowing this was foolish even though it felt wonderful, she leaned up against Maggie's back. She let her breasts press into Maggie, let their soft weight reshape into the hollows there. She let go of Maggie's wrist and quickly brushed back the golden hair. She lowered her mouth to her neck, letting her lips and then her teeth graze the nape. Lightly flicking her tongue across Maggie's lower neck, seeking out the gentle curve of her collarbone, she could feel Maggie's breath quicken, feel the shiver moving up her spine.

"Like this? Or like this?" And Helen reached around her waist, moving her hands around and up just below Maggie's breasts, ignoring the heavy sweater. Her hands increased the pressure as her mouth moved toward the delicate skin near Maggie's ears. Maggie tipped her head back as Helen teased her earlobes. Helen savored Maggie's moan as she nibbled her throat. "You like a little bit of bite, then." Helen smiled as she cupped Maggie's breasts, feeling for her nipples. Maggie gasped as Helen pinched them lightly. Her own nipples tightened as Maggie's grew hard beneath her touch. "No, don't turn around." Helen kept one hand on Maggie's breast and moved the other toward her waist, slipping her fingers into Maggie's jeans. Pressed against her Helen could feel Maggie's breath quicken. Slowly, drawing out the moment, Helen moved her fingers closer and closer to the thick curly hair between Maggie's legs. "Just stay still."

"Helen—"

"Shhh." Helen managed to back them down onto the sofa, her hands still stroking Maggie as they lowered themselves onto the cushions. Now, finally, she reached down and inserted fingertips inside, swirling in slow, small circles across the wet swollen flesh. "Just be still and let me. Let me do this."

Each time Maggie moaned Helen felt a responding pull in her own crotch. It was so thick and wet, so heavy—Helen could smell it, longed to taste it. Not yet, not yet, she told herself. Make it last, make her laugh and cry and scream. At the back of Helen's mind the worry that she'd never have another chance surged up for a moment, but she shoved the thought back down and concentrated on the way Maggie's nipples got hard and heavy, the way Maggie's cunt slid and sucked at her hand. Maggie's hips started to rotate in rhythm with Helen's hand. She felt Maggie's thighs tighten and tremble as she neared climax.

"That's it, that's the way. Come on, come for me, come for me hard," she murmured into Maggie's ear.

Maggie cried out, her body rocking down hard on Helen's hand with her climax as a rush of wet warmth melted between her legs. Helen felt something shift inside herself, some icy core she'd been carrying around for weeks and weeks—something she hadn't even been aware of until the first time she'd seen Maggie. Helen lay back on the sofa, as relaxed and lazed as if she'd had the orgasm. Maggie's breath steadied and Helen pulled her into a tight embrace.

Then, before Maggie could move or protest, Helen slipped out from under her. "We're not done yet." She sat up on the edge of the sofa, pulling at Maggie's jeans. "I think you can keep going."

Maggie lay flat, eyes closed, while Helen dropped jeans and underwear onto the floor. For a few moments she just looked at Maggie's belly and crotch, taking in the smooth curve over her pubic hair and the tightly curled wet hairs covering her cunt. Maggie's thighs glistened in the faint light. Helen traced her fingers along the insides of Maggie's legs, listening to her breathing change into near gasps with each stroke. Then with agonizing slowness Helen parted Maggie's labia and found her clit, swollen and hard and ready. She wet her fingers and began to rub her, using the same swirling circles that had brought her to climax before.

This time Maggie bucked up and down on the sofa, crying out just once with a short sharp jerk as the final wave of pleasure washed over her. Helen lowered her tongue to Maggie's clit just as her orgasm started to wane, pressing in and around her labia as if pulling every last bit of sensation from her cunt. Maggie's legs finally stopped trembling and Helen lifted her head, making sure Maggie watched while she wiped the moisture from her face and lips.

"Was that the behavior you were referring to, Maggie?"

"No. I was thinking more about this, actually," and suddenly Maggie had her pinned down on the sofa. Helen was already hot and wet and more than ready when Maggie's hands found her crotch. She used both hands, fingering Helen's clit while her other hand explored inside. She was soft and gentle, using her hands together in rhythm. Helen kept her eyes open and watched Maggie smile down at her as the pressure increased, just enough to make Helen want it even more.

"Go deeper."

"No." Maggie shook her head. "I want you to work for it. I want you to really reach for it."

"Bitch."

Maggie just chuckled. "So I've been told. I always take that as a compliment." And she moved another finger inside Helen.

With a groan Helen gave herself up to the fullness, the heaviness of Maggie's hands moving inside her. She found herself pushing up to meet Maggie's hands, her whole body straining for that elusive point of release centered in her cunt. Her orgasm came hard and fast, and she burst out with a surprised shout and closed her thighs around Maggie's hands.

"Yes, yes, yes," Maggie breathed. As soon as Helen had quieted, Maggie pulled her up from the sofa. They found their way onto Helen's bed, tossing clothes on the floor along the way. Helen had a moment's qualm at the rumpled sheets, then forgot everything but Maggie's tongue as it teased her nipples. Then Maggie slid across her chest and belly until that tongue rested on her clit and began flicking lightly. Helen heard herself cry out with each stroke. Just when she didn't think she could take another second Maggie opened her mouth and sucked until Helen came again with a long wail of pleasure.

Everything was blank after that. Helen didn't remember falling asleep—she vaguely recalled nestling into Maggie in a heap of pillows and sheets, relaxing into the warmth of the other woman curled around her back. When she opened her eyes again the room was completely dark and Maggie was gone.

"Hey," Helen muttered, wiping sleep from her eyes. The winter chill had worked its way through her apartment. She sat up and wrapped herself in a blanket. Something crackled in the bed and she saw a pale outline on one of the pillows. Switching on the lamp, she squinted at the note Maggie had left.

"Had to go finish some work," Maggie had written. "I'll call you tomorrow afternoon." There was a phone number, too. Helen sat and stared down at the note for a long time, barely aware of the cold creeping down her shoulders and back. Maybe Maggie the preacher was already regretting their encounter. She'd certainly enjoyed herself, Helen was sure, but how did that fit in with her religious convictions? Or maybe Maggie just wasn't sure of what she should do at this point. Or something.

"Quit analyzing," Helen told herself as she clambered out of the bed. It was just after ten. God, it was cold. She found sweats and pulled them on, shivering and trying not to think. She had no clue how she was supposed to think about any of this. As a one-time event? A beginning of something, or an end?

She shivered her way into the kitchen, suddenly ravenous. Thank God for canned soup and crackers, she thought, reaching into the cupboard. The phone rang like a shriek in the darkness. Maybe it was Maggie, Helen thought. She edged toward the living room, waiting for her answering machine to click on.

"Helen, it's Jan. Sorry I missed you. I have some information for you."

Chapter Eleven

Once again the sun had come out. Helen sat in the café Monday morning, wondering if it had been wise to call in sick, sipping her mocha. Outside, the residents of Napa strolled back and forth in front of the quaint boutiques that lined the main street of town. It hadn't changed much in the years Helen had been away—still a cute touristy town full of strip malls with fake Mission-style façades. All kinds of lures led tourists to wine-tastings and headliner shows that would rival the worst Velcro-studded entertainment in Vegas. It was a few miles outside of town, out among the rows of the vineyards, where the real Napa Valley began. The valley of back-breaking labor and thwarted immigrant dreams had resulted in the well-dressed and the well-fed being able to sip at a prize vintage and make pronouncements on bouquet and texture.

She turned her gaze away from the streets of Napa and looked at Maggie, sitting on the other side of the booth. "Maybe I shouldn't have asked you to drive me up here. My car would have made it."

"Yeah, right. Your car couldn't go around the block without a jump." Maggie shrugged and fiddled with her napkin. "Besides, I feel I have as much responsibility for her death as anyone."

"Well, I don't know if this will turn into anything, Maggie," Helen cautioned. "Jan was certain that this private hospital is where those pay stubs were from, but all it means is that Alice worked there. It was a long time ago, and since the hospital changed hands a couple of times since then we may be on a wild goose chase here."

"Still, it's a chance. Someone might know about Alice's family, or where she came from. At least we can try to find that out."

Helen looked long and hard at Maggie. "You didn't have to come with me, you know," Helen said quietly.

"But I wanted to, Helen." Maggie played nervously with her coffee cup, looked out the window, at a menu, everywhere but at Helen.

"Why?"

"Well—" Maggie finally looked at her. "I just needed to see you again, but not at Alice's place. That's why I canceled yesterday. I'm really sorry about how I handled things Saturday night." Her face was bright red now, and she ducked over her cup, trying to hide. "I acted badly. I think I surprised myself."

"Is that bad?" Helen kept her voice careful and quiet. If Maggie was in the mood to talk she didn't want to scare her off. What she really wanted was to touch her again, to smooth her hair from her face, to hold her hand, to see her smile and hear her laugh. To hear her breath catch in her throat again, like it did Saturday night when she climaxed.

"We got off to a kind of strange start and I want to try to make this all a little more normal. Quit staring at me," she said with an awkward laugh.

"If you hang around long enough you'll figure out I'm not normal."

"Thank goodness, neither am I." This time it was a genuine smile. "Besides, a chance to see you and make sure everything was okay with—with us and the other night, it's a chance to make sure

I've done everything I can for Alice. For me, too. The *Chronicle* says the police are not seeing her death as murder, but I still want to get to the bottom of this."

Helen leaned back in the booth and watched Maggie as she talked. So it was all about making Maggie feel better about herself—by coming with Helen today she could tie up Saturday night into a nice neat little package, tuck it away into a drawer and probably forget about it. Same thing with Alice. Helen didn't even try to fight down her disappointment. Served her right for letting herself go the other night. She felt the glacier inside resurfacing like some giant sea creature, cold and silent. Fine. Might as well use this opportunity. It would certainly look better for Helen to arrive at Valley View Hospital with a card-carrying minister than to try questioning people on her own. Anyway, Maggie was right—her car probably wouldn't have made the long drive from Oakland to Napa.

Well, for this Monday morning, at least, she needed to set aside those thoughts and focus on the task at hand. She looked across the table at Maggie, who was taking a bite of toast and studying her placemat. "You okay with doing this?" she asked.

Maggie nodded, pushed her plate away and looked up with a determined smile. "I appreciate doing this. I'm glad we're here together."

Glad. Helen doubted that. Especially since the ride up to Napa had been taken up with telling Maggie about her past. Another big mistake, thinking that by opening up to her Helen could create a real bond between them. Maggie had taken in the news silently, watching the road as Helen regaled her with tales of prison, of her now-dead career as a private investigator, of her tenuous grip on a new life. "Look, Maggie, I'm sorry I didn't call you back yesterday, after I got your message you wanted to cancel, or come to the church, or—or anything. I just wasn't sure what I should do. About Saturday night, I mean." Helen shook her head as she heard her own hesitance. She didn't want to talk about that evening, but she had to get it out of the way so they could both concentrate on the deception ahead. Glancing at Maggie's face, so soft and concerned and full of feeling, she knew there was no way to avoid it. Already Helen felt raw from having unzipped her life and laid it out for Maggie to see. Given the situation—having roped in Maggie to help her on this escapade—she realized she'd have to keep those wounds open for a little while longer. She pushed aside her panic and tried to pay attention to what Maggie was saying.

"I wasn't sure, either." Maggie blushed and folded her hands, prayer-like, on the table, her head bent. Helen had to listen hard to catch her words. "You may not believe this but my—my behavior Saturday was not like me at all. I don't do things that impulsively, as a rule." She managed a shaky laugh. "I'm sorry I took off that way, with just a note. God, how insensitive can you get?"

Helen sighed. Okay, they'd both established that Saturday evening was probably a big mistake, a moment of passion fueled by loneliness and fear. Passion, certainly—she felt a rush of heat creep over her own face as she remembered Maggie's hands, Maggie's mouth. Time to change the subject. "Okay. We start over today. Okay?"

"Okay." Maggie looked up, her small smile fading into concern.

Helen knew instantly, watching sunlight flow like liquid gold over Maggie's shoulders, that the only way she'd really get rid of her was to savagely hurt her. With a fascinated horror she noted how her mind began to churn out ways to dump her. Did Maggie think she was some kind of do-good project? Well, Helen could kick her in the ass with that one, and kick her so hard she'd never get over it. If Maggie was going to use Helen to assuage her nice white middle-class guilt, if Maggie was all about "fixing" Helen's broken state, then Helen could certainly use Maggie for her own ends, too—to find out what the fuck was going on with Alice's death. With a grim satisfaction Helen felt the plan snap into place in her head. She'd fuck this up all by herself, before Maggie could do it.

"Helen? You all right in there?"

"Yeah. Yeah, let's do it."

A few minutes later they were driving along a winding tree-lined road toward the address Jan had produced. Helen looked down at the notes she'd jotted down Saturday night. Jesus, she was owing a lot of people favors these days—Katy, Jan, Maggie. God knew where it would end. Maybe with her in prison again?

"There it is." Maggie's voice broke into her worries. Helen raised her eyebrows at the castle ahead. It looked more like a resort hotel than like the nursing homes Helen had seen before. White pillars and a curving drive graced the perfectly manicured green lawns, and its three stories gleamed pristine white in the sunlight. "Looks like Scartlett O'Hara is going to come out the door any minute."

"In a hoop skirt," Helen agreed. "This can't be a nursing home. I mean, when I was a kid my church made the youth group visit nursing homes. They're supposed to be squat ugly brick buildings that smell bad."

Maggie pulled into an empty space in the vast parking lot, squeezing between a Mercedes and a super-accessorized Hummer. "Well, your friend at the paper—Jan, right?—she said it was a privately owned nursing facility. Private means money."

"Damn. Hope we're dressed okay." Helen glanced down at her simple dark slacks and blouse, her plain black shoes, as she got out of the car. Thank God they'd come in Maggie's sedate Toyota and not her own junked-up clunker. Of course Maggie had dressed for the part—she'd probably had lots of experience in hospitals, Helen thought, maybe while training to be a chaplain or whatever charitable work she'd had to do for training. Helen realized with a jolt that she'd spilled her guts in the car but didn't know much about Maggie's life. Besides the fact that she was amazing in bed, but Helen thought she'd better not go there right now. "Too bad we couldn't get my cousin Bobby into a place like this," she murmured.

"Your cousin?"

"Yeah. I bet a place like this would have been great for him."

"What's wrong with him?"

Helen considered briefly how to answer. "He's developmentally disabled," she finally said. That was better than saying he had the mental ability of a six-year-old, frozen into permanent childhood by spinal meningitis. His forty-year-old body, balding and pot-bellied, had become a prison for an innocent little boy who never had understood why Helen had to go to prison.

"I'm sorry, Helen. Do you get to see him often?"

"Not since I left Mississippi." She was determined not to tell Maggie anything else about her life. Maggie didn't need to know she'd been disowned by her last remaining shreds of family, didn't need to hear about Aunt Edna's contempt or about Bobby's drawings lining the walls of her prison cell or about the way Bobby had wept when Aunt Edna finally told her she had to move out. Put all that under the ice, along with all her ridiculous hopes about Maggie. Concentrate on Alice and how the hell she had gotten a job at a place like this.

Those thoughts carried Helen through the entrance and toward the receptionist. The slender, well-groomed woman, whose fastidious makeup made her seem years younger at a distance, looked as though she belonged behind the counter at a five-star hotel. "Yes, your appointment is for one-thirty. I'll just let Ms. Schubert know you're here," she said with a discreet glance at her watch.

Helen and Maggie sat side by side in a lobby filled with dark heavy furniture. Maggie pretended to flip through a magazine but Helen could sense her nervousness. Maybe conversation would relieve some tension. Helen murmured, "Does this remind you of any hospital you've ever been in?"

Maggie let out a discreet snort and replaced the *Town and Country* magazine on the table. "Are you kidding?" she muttered back disdainfully. "It's like a spa, or one of those places you go to detox with a lot of breathing exercises."

"And I don't see anyone. Not a soul except for our lovely receptionist." Helen wished Jan had given her a little more information, but Jan had been insistent. *Quid pro quo*, she had said. *You scratch my back and I'll scratch yours, Helen.* And an address was better than what she'd had Saturday afternoon. "My guess is the 'residents' here are bored and rich and have lots of time for very expensive ailments."

"Ms. Black? I'm Grace Schubert."

The woman greeting them looked perfect, like a well-preserved Barbie in a navy suit, but her gracious smile got nowhere near her eyes. Briefly Helen introduced Maggie, then stepped back to let Maggie, in her nice dark suit, make a good impression. Helen and Maggie followed Ms. Schubert down a short corridor to her office. The dark and heavy theme was repeated here. Helen took a seat in a comfortable wing chair and scanned the room. Not a bookshelf or a filing cabinet in sight, just chairs and sofa and what must be an antique desk with an empty surface. Apparently Grace Schubert's role was to provide a comforting, almost grandmotherly face to the indelicacies of nervous ailments. Not quite your milk-and-cookies grandma, Helen realized, but perhaps a reassuring older face from the world of money. A revered aunt, maybe. Those had to be real pearls draped over her low-slung bosom, and a matching single pearl in the silver ring. Beautifully coifed silver hair, too—none of that cheap blue stuff. Helen suddenly felt smothered, wished Grace had shown up in a cheap housedress and too much rouge, maybe lipstick on her teeth, but some evidence of real feeling in there. For the first time this morning Helen felt afraid. Up to now it had been all anger, determination and planning. Even her anger at Maggie for being a decent person had been a distraction.

Then Helen realized Maggie had started to speak. "It's been a difficult time for us, Ms. Schubert. We're hoping that you can help us."

"Of course." Those cold eyes—Helen couldn't even tell what color they were, as silver as her hair and jewelry—turned to Helen, assessing her bottom line probably. For a moment Helen had a swift, gut-wrenching memory of one of the guards in prison. Same cold little colorless eyes, same smooth quiet voice that masked an empty heart. This woman was no different, just better dressed. "That's why we're here, Ms. Black. To help you in your time of need."

Like hell. The moment of recognition had jolted Helen out of her scare. She let out a heavy sigh and shook her head, hoping for just the right touch of melodrama. "It's about a former employee of yours, someone who recently died. We're hoping you can help us locate family members."

"Really?" Grace managed to look mildly interested. The staff was surely beneath her consideration, yet she had to feign polite curiosity. "Who was that? Perhaps Doctor Merriweather? He recently retired, I know. Lives in Marin, I believe. But certainly his family would be aware of this."

Maggie smiled back and shook her head. "No. It was Alice Harmon." She kept talking even though Grace's expression had frozen in disbelief, her little pale eyes widening with shock. The only other clue to her inner state Helen noted was a sudden twitch at the corner of her mouth, there one moment and gone the next. "You do know she died recently? Very sad. She was a member of my church."

Helen jumped in, keeping her gaze fixed on Ms. Schubert. It wasn't her imagination—good old Grace had paled a bit at the mention of the name. "Yes, Alice often spoke about Valley View. But I think it was called something else back then—Napa Valley Home, wasn't it, Maggie?"

They looked at Grace. Her composure was nearly complete but Helen saw her hands tighten and twist together. "I'm afraid I don't recall the name," she managed to get out through stiff lips. "Besides, all records of that nature are completely confidential. I'm afraid I can't help you at all."

"Perhaps someone who worked here when it was still Napa Valley Home, another aide or a nurse, would remember Alice. Do you have any staff who are still here from those days? We could talk to them."

"There's no one like that here."

"Are you sure? We won't mind waiting while you check, will we, Maggie?"

Grace's features hardened into a mask of—anger or fear, maybe both. "I assure you, all the staff employed when Alice was here are all gone. There won't be anyone left who remembers her." She stood up with an awkward jerk, accidentally knocking over the gilt pen holder on her desk. "I'm sorry I can't be of help. If there's nothing else—"

Fear, Helen decided. Good. That gave her the edge she needed. Maggie squirmed a bit in her seat but Helen knew she had to push it now. She wouldn't get another chance. "Except you, apparently." Helen ignored Maggie's movement beside her. Now was no time to back down. "According to what you just said you don't know the name, and now you're talking like you know exactly who I mean."

Poor Grace, Helen thought. You sure as hell do know something about all this. The marble mask slipped and Helen saw her mouth quiver. "If you'll excuse me for a moment? I'll be right back." She smoothed her skirt, seeming to take reassurance from the gesture, and clicked out of the room.

Maggie and Helen stared at each other. Maggie's eyes were wide and surprised. Helen knew she hadn't really quite understood what they were getting into. Welcome to my world, she thought.

"Damn," Maggie breathed. "Something is going on here."

"And we're not going to wait around for it. Ten to one she's calling some kind of security. Stupid woman—doesn't realize that will just stir the shit around even more. You saw her, she's completely unprepared for anything to do with Alice." Helen got up, stuffing the pile of paperwork into her bag. "We're out of here."

They hurried past the receptionist, who looked up in vague surprise. Whatever Grace was doing obviously didn't involve the help—another ominous sign if the woman was sneaking around to get security or whatever she was up to.

"Where to?" Maggie asked breathlessly as they pulled out of the parking lot.

"Over here." Helen pointed to a narrow lane between two houses a few blocks up the street from the hospital. "Now we just wait until old Gracie figures out we're gone."

They didn't have long to wait. A few minutes later they saw Grace Schubert behind the wheel of a dark green sedan, driving much too fast for the quiet residential street. Helen got a glimpse of her face, set and white and frightened, as she took off.

Without being told Maggie drove out of the lane and slid a couple of cars behind Grace. To reassure her, Helen said, "Don't worry, she won't figure it out. You saw how shook up she was in her office. She was totally unprepared for this."

"So was I, Helen." Maggie's hands gripped the wheel tightly. "So was I."

Helen sighed. This was not the time for a conscience. She wanted to scream. "You didn't have to say yes, Maggie. I told you we were going to see what we could find out today, and you knew ahead of time what that might involve."

"No, I didn't know." Her face was grim but determined, and her voice held a matching level of coldness and anger. "I didn't know we were going to play cops and robbers."

"This is not cops and robbers, Maggie. Jesus, your church got broken into! You think this is just a good time for me? Is that it?" Helen took a deep breath and concentrated on regaining an edge of calm. "I just want to see where this woman is going. Then you're off the hook, okay?" She slouched down in the seat. Fine. Maggie was like everyone else and Saturday was a big fucking mistake.

The rest of the drive was silent. Neither of them spoke until Grace turned off the main street into a parking lot fifteen minutes later. Just ahead was a tall glass-walled office building.

"Well, here we are," Maggie said. "Any ideas?"

"Yeah. I'm getting out." Helen waited until Grace had gotten out of her car and scurried inside. "Are you going to be here when I get back?"

"Of course. Let's just get this over with and get out of here, okay?"

"Suits me." Helen shut the car door gently, as if something fragile might shatter if she used too much force. No, it was already broken, she thought sadly. Helen rides again. Feeling numb, she went inside.

Chapter Twelve

The Giorgi Building stood out in the quiet street. Helen thought it must be about twenty stories high, towering over the other more modest buildings in Napa. She glanced over her shoulder to see Maggie sitting in the car. The building felt out of place to Helen—too tall, too imposing for its setting. She tagged close behind a trio of women, all dressed dark suits, who were talking over each other as they went inside. Although there wasn't precisely a crowd gathered here, there was enough activity that she felt her own entrance would be unremarked.

It was that doldrum hour, just past two o'clock in the afternoon when office workers were waking up from the after-lunch stupor but not quite ready to wrap up the day and get away from their desks. Helen stood just inside the double glass doors, edging close to the wall display that showed a directory of the different offices there. A long row of black and white photographs lined the walls that stretched up for a couple of stories. Small clusters of people, most of them dressed in what Helen called "corporate drag"—dark expensive suits and dark expensive briefcases—flowed quietly around Helen. Some had cell phones clamped to their ears and carried on conversations with varying degrees of volume and intensity. They moved around Helen, barely registering her existence. With ill-concealed impatience they stared at the elevators and shoved past her to get through the doors.

Helen stepped away from the directory board and spotted a security guard at the main desk. The elderly man, who looked as though he ought to be retired, had a white telephone receiver to his ear. Helen couldn't make out his words but he was nodding vigorously and jotting notes down with furious intensity. Some bigwig in one of the penthouses, maybe, who needed serious butt-kissing. The guard sat behind an enormous semicircular counter that shone black in the soft light. His suit jacket, heavy maroon wool embroidered with the Giorgi name in script, looked too small for his bulk. It stretched awkwardly over his shoulders as he hunched forward. Expensive potted plants almost hid the television screens, four of them, that displayed varying views of the parking lot and the entrances. Helen breathed a sigh of relief that Maggie had accompanied her. She didn't think Grace Schubert had spotted their car but the last thing they needed was to get hassled by some security guard questioning their presence. It was much better for Helen to do this alone.

She went back to the directory and scanned the names. Nothing helpful there—law firms, a couple of investment groups, financial advisors, some kind of public relations company. Topping the list in the single penthouse suite was Giorgi Brothers. Their building, after all—might as well have the penthouse if you were going to own a place like this. It took a moment for Helen to connect the name with the big vineyard just a few miles outside of Napa, the one advertising the wine-tasting tour she'd commented on earlier to Maggie.

She turned around and saw the guard hang up the phone. Before she could approach him two workmen in paint-stained coveralls carrying a stepladder clomped by. "Hey, Joe! How's it shakin'?" one of them called to the guard. The guard smiled and lifted a hand in greeting, then reached below the counter to pull out a clipboard. The workmen, obviously not in a hurry, leaned against the glossy counter and made some joke to the guard, who snickered expressively as he laid the clipboard down. Helen walked the length of the foyer, noting its cavernous depths. Sure enough there was a video camera, mounted high up on the wall over the elevators. She kept going, uncomfortably aware that her image, a tiny stick figure in black and white, was visible on one of the screens next to the guard's counter. Had the Giorgi family merely taken over a building already in place, or had they made it to order?

She spotted another camera tucked discreetly in a corner as she approached the guard station. Distracted by one of the photographs on the high walls, she stopped, risking the guard's attention to her loitering. In the photo a smiling elderly couple was shaking hands with another elderly gentleman. The caption announced the groundbreaking of the Giorgi building a decade ago. So all this display was due to malice aforethought. A glance back to the entrance confirmed that the work crew was still telling jokes to the guard. Helen moved on to the next picture, then the next. All of them showed various and sundry Giorgis doing this or that—smiling with the governor, with the president of Mexico, at local social gatherings with the other glitterati, even a shot with a very recent president of the United States, who looked extremely pleased to be sipping a Giorgi vintage with his host.

The opposite wall showed some of these same people out in the rows of the vineyards, handing out wrapped gifts to migrant workers and standing around a huge Christmas tree that looked like it had been set up in the center of town. The kinder, gentler Giorgis, Helen mused. Then she paused, eyes narrowing, in front of a picture placed on the wall next to the guard station. The pillars of the Valley View Nursing Home loomed in the background of another set of smiling Giorgis. She read the caption: *At the opening of Napa*

Valley Home, in cooperation with mental health officials of Sonoma County. The Giorgi family continues its commitment to service by living up to its motto of caring and concern for the entire community. There was no date on the caption, but the clothes looked like Seventies styles. That would fit with Alice's term of employment, as shown on those old pay stubs. Helen found herself staring at the little family group posed in the shade of those majestic trees where she and Maggie had just been. At one face in particular. The woman was years younger, of course, but Helen recalled the knife-thin features, the pale skin and haunted stare. She'd encountered it recently, at Alice's memorial service. In the photograph the woman appeared to be a teenager. She hung back behind other members of the family, lingering in the shadows. The camera caught her intense stare, full of—what? Hate? Fear? Helen took a step to get closer, study those features more carefully, when someone behind her coughed.

"Can I help you, ma'am?" The workmen were trundling off into the depths of the building and the security guard had turned his attention to her. She made herself stretch her lips in a smile. She was too tense, too eager about this. With a deep breath she forced herself to relax, to try to draw on that ice that always lay just beneath the surface of her consciousness. "Which office are you looking for, ma'am?"

"Actually, I wasn't told which office they'd be meeting in." She leaned casually on the counter, continuing the easy grin. "I was supposed to meet with Grace Schubert today. The meeting is supposed to start in just a few minutes."

The guard was all smiles and obliging help. "No problem, ma'am. They're up in the penthouse today."

"Oh, is everyone here already?"

"Well, don't know who everyone is, ma'am. I just saw Grace Schubert come in, and Mr. Eddy, that's Mr. Giorgi, he's been here all day." He kept watching her and the smile faded a bit as he took in her simple clothes, her lack of cell phone and briefcase. "Why don't I call up there and let them know you're here?" He reached for his phone, his eyes still assessing her low-maintenance look, the lack of corporate savvy that seemed to be a requirement for entering the sacred penthouse.

"No, that's all right—I just wanted to make sure the meeting hadn't taken place yet. They can't do anything without me, anyway." Fuck, that was lame, Helen chided herself as she backed away from the guard. "I'll just go out to the car and get my briefcase." With a final glance at the photograph of Valley View Nursing Home, she managed to keep herself from breaking into a run.

She was almost out the door when the guard barked something into his phone. All caution aside, Helen took off. Maggie saw her coming and had the car started before she slid into the passenger seat.

"Let's go."

"Are you okay?" Maggie asked, backing out in a squeal of gravel and exhaust. Helen kept watch over her shoulder but saw nothing. Maggie weaved through the light traffic of the city—at least they'd avoided rush-hour tangles—with more skill than Helen would have credited her with. "Helen, talk to me. What the hell happened in there?"

"Just keep going. We need to get on the freeway and disappear." Helen kept her gaze fixed on the side mirror. Nothing. It wasn't until they reached the bridge that she began to breathe easier. "I think it's okay. They didn't have time to catch up with us. Thank God that Schubert woman had no idea how to handle the situation."

"Okay, Helen, I've played Keystone Kops long enough for one day. I offered to help you but I didn't think that would involve being in some crappy action flick." Maggie spoke through gritted teeth, her rage barely concealed. Her voice was low and strained, and one look told Helen she was ready to dump her on the side of the freeway and let her make her own way back to town. "I've put up with the mystery long enough. Start talking."

Finally, Helen felt the ice come edging back to the surface. So

Maggie would be like all the rest. A good fuck, but not much else. And who could blame her? Helen relaxed into the chill growing inside her, preparing her for the severing she knew would come.

"Grace Schubert went straight from the hospital to the Giorgi family penthouse. That building belongs to them." Quickly and quietly, as if giving a news report, she relayed what she'd seen and heard, leaving out what she'd seen in the photograph. That was not to be shared—especially if Maggie was about to bail. First Helen had to get her hands on Alice's scrapbook.

"So there's some connection between the wine family and this hospital. Fine. People like the Giorgis own half the state, so what?" It was fear that made Maggie snap at her, Helen knew that, but it still hurt. "Tell me how that has anything to do with Alice Harmon."

"Okay, Maggie. Fine. I appreciate your help today but I'm not going to drag you through any more of this." Helen folded her arms and stared out the window. The sun had faded behind thick steel-gray clouds. No rain yet, but she could see the wind whipping through the trees lining the freeway. They were off the bridge now, and soon Maggie would be dropping her off. Leaving her alone with Cat, with her little dark sordid apartment, with the vain hope that Brenda would have a job waiting for her tomorrow at some other office. Helen hugged herself tightly, shocked at how much it hurt. Why should this one hurt more than the others in the past few years? Hadn't she fucked up enough times before to learn her lesson once and for all? To her amazement she found she was fighting off tears. Shit.

Suddenly she realized the car had stopped moving. Maggie was parked in front of her apartment building. "Helen. I'm sorry I yelled. I—well, I'm just not cut out for this kind of thing. Car chases aren't what we studied at G.T.U.," she tried to joke.

Damn it, where had that icy layer gone? "It's okay, Maggie. I should never have dragged you into this." Not on the strength of one good fuck, anyway. No, that wasn't fair. This wasn't what Maggie had counted on. "I meant what I said, though. I do appreciate this. And I won't bother you with it again." Helen opened the car door. "You'd better go home." Back to your nice safe church and all your nice safe friends, where it's warm and light and people don't get killed.

"No, Helen—" Maggie took her hand and stopped her from leaving the car. "Not like this. Please." She lifted Helen's hand to her lips. "Please," she whispered.

But Helen pulled away, determined to get out before Maggie saw she was close to tears. "I'll call you sometime, okay?" She hurried up toward her building, trembling with unshed tears. She leaned against the outside door, listening until she heard Maggie drive off and out of her life.

Numb and exhausted Helen couldn't rustle up the energy to move for several minutes. Whatever she had felt Saturday night, it was dead now. Dead and starting to rot. Time to bury all of that forever. She might have stood there for a couple of hours if she hadn't heard Cat howling from upstairs.

"Oh, Jesus, not again." Cat had taken to darting out of the apartment at every opportunity. Its brief taste of freedom Saturday afternoon had apparently inspired it to seek repeat escapes. Maybe it wanted Alice, or maybe it just wanted to get out of the crummy little apartment. "Yeah, me too." She sighed in agreement.

She halted on the landing when she that saw her door was open. Cat was crouched, a gray-and-white puddle with green eyes, in a corner of the stairwell. Helen froze, listening hard. The cat kept crying until she reached down to pick it up, then it darted between her legs and down the stairs. She backed down the hallway, hoping the intruder hadn't heard her, hoping she could gather Cat up and get the hell out to call the cops. She turned around long enough to grasp the handrail firmly, and that was when he grabbed her and dragged her back toward her apartment.

The hand around her mouth smelled like tobacco and sweat—bitter and acrid and nauseating. Helen tried biting and kicking but his hold tightened around her neck until she could barely breathe. Still, she gathered enough air in her lungs to try for a scream.

"One sound and you get this," he hissed.

She couldn't move her head but she made out the glimmer of something long and steel and sharp near her chin. Helen let herself be tossed like a sack onto the sofa. Gasping for air, she peered through the murky light of the apartment to get a look at her attacker.

Same Yankees baseball cap, same round doughy face—how many guys could be following her, after all? He stood near the door, knife in hand, not even breathing hard. "What do you want?" she croaked through a sore throat.

"You know what I want, bitch." Still a hissing whisper. Hard to identify. She strained into the sofa, edging away from him as he stepped closer. He kicked her legs apart and leaned in over her, giving her another whiff of stale cigarettes and unwashed clothes. "You want to get sliced up? Then give me that fucking scrapbook."

The photo album. That must be what he meant. "I don't know who you are, why you're following me or what the hell you want. But if you don't get the fuck out of my apartment you will pay the consequences. Do you understand me?"

Of course he knew she was bluffing. He was the one with the knife, after all. And maybe some other weapon she hadn't seen yet. He stood up with a snigger, wiping his nose with his free hand. God, he stank. Forget seeing him in a lineup, she'd smell him from a mile off. She realized she was thinking like this to take her mind off her terror. Her mind blanked, though, when the knife came close to her again, this time at her throat. Then, inexplicably, he took a step back from the sofa. She was so surprised by the way he backed off that she didn't see his fist coming.

Helen found herself knocked onto the floor, staring up at the ceiling, her face numb. She couldn't feel her lips or her chin, but that must be her own blood dribbling down her neck. With an effort not to grunt she pushed herself up.

"That's for you from me, bitch. Don't worry, I'll be back. If you don't have that book for me next time I show up you'll get more than a fist in your face."

Helen shook her head, willing her vision to clear. Yes, he was in fact heading toward the door. He sneered at her over his shoulder.

"Let's just hope that preacher friend of yours has said her prayers, okay?"

His parting words sank in after Helen had sat staring for a few minutes. Her preacher friend. Maggie. Jesus, he was going after Maggie. Shoving aside the pain in her head Helen pulled herself off the floor to reach for the phone.

"Shit, where's her card?" With trembling fingers she found the number and shakily punched in the numbers. She cursed at the recorded message and started talking as soon as the beep sounded in her ear.

"Maggie, it's Helen. Maggie, please pick up. Maggie—"

Hell. This was stupid. Better to get her keys and get over there. She found the purse she'd taken this morning as part of her official outfit to go to the nursing home and heard her keys rattle inside. She paused only long enough to take in the splintered wood of the doorjamb. He hadn't had to work too hard to break in, given the dilapidated state of the building. She wondered fleetingly how long it would take to get someone to repair it.

As she stumbled down the stairs, still in a daze, she found Cat in her favorite hiding place behind the plant near the front door. This time Cat submitted to being caught up in her arms. She spared a moment to look the cat over—no signs of cuts or scrapes. She must have darted out before the guy saw her. Again, very bad work. This was no cop, but Helen couldn't figure out what the hell he was. One of the Giorgi family? Hired help? If he was hired, someone was definitely not getting their money's worth.

Cat whined in her arms as Helen dumped her unceremoniously into the passenger seat. Probably very stupid to bring the cat along, but she didn't want to leave it alone when knife-wielding smelly thugs lurked in the neighborhood. "Start praying, Cat," she said as she revved the motor and tore off toward the church.

Chapter Thirteen

Helen noted the coming and going of doctors and nurses in the quiet hallways of the hospital on Ashby in Berkeley. It was after ten according to the clock on the wall. She'd been there for four hours, since she'd found Maggie at six. No one paid her any attention, which was just the way she liked it. One sympathetic nurse had guided her through the emergency room, making a quick assessment of Maggie's inability to stand, and left Helen in the hallway with a promise a doctor would talk to her as soon as he'd had a chance to look over the results of the beating Maggie had received. So far the only people to talk to Helen, aside from the admitting nurse, had been Lieutenant Jordan. That had been an hour ago.

And here he was again, perched on the uncomfortable plastic chair beside her. She steeled herself for another inevitable barrage of questions, wishing desperately some doctor or nurse would talk to her. "Have you had a chance to talk to Ms. Evans yet?" Jordan asked.

"Not yet." Helen looked at the Styrofoam cup of coffee in his small freckled hands, at the linoleum floor, at the clock on the wall showing that Monday was nearly over—at anything but Jordan's taut expression.

"So, let's go over this again. You met Maggie at the church, found her unconscious on the floor—"

"No, not unconscious." God, how many times did she have to tell them? At least it was Jordan, and not Manny. Helen glanced down the hall, saw Manny leaning against the wall outside an examining room. No doubt he was saving his ire for Helen, maybe building up a head of steam. Certainly his stiff pose and bunched fists didn't bode well for Helen. "Like I said—she wasn't unconscious but she was in shock. I called you guys, then brought her here. And before you ask me again, no, she didn't say anything or identify her attacker."

"So you said." Jordan finished his coffee, made a face—it must have been bitter or cold or both—and tossed the empty cup into the trash. "And you said you have no idea who did this to her."

Helen looked at him squarely, knowing she had to convince at least Jordan that she was being honest. "Look, Maggie and I had an argument earlier today. I stopped by the church to see if we could patch things up and found her like this. You guys know all about the break-ins, the way someone trashed their offices last week. Hell, they've had a bunch of attacks like this. Probably it was those guys, coming back for another round." Hopefully she'd put just the right note of exasperation in her voice, even lobbed the pressure back on the police. She leaned her head back against the wall and pretended exhaustion, forcing her hands to relax on the arms of the chair so Jordan wouldn't see how tense she was.

"Interesting, though, isn't it? You show up, with a record of violence, and suddenly a nice upstanding minister gets beat up. And you say you'd had a fight earlier in the day." Jordan's voice was more musing than accusatory. He shrugged and smiled at her. She knew he was taking in her own appearance, her split lip, the bruises on her face and arms. "That's the kind of coincidence I'm just not comfortable with."

Shit. She shouldn't have said anything about the argument. Better to clam up right now. She didn't want Jordan or Manny poking around in what she was trying to do, but she couldn't allow Maggie to get any deeper into this. She let out her breath slowly. "Are you charging me, Lieutenant? We both know how it works. Either you charge me with assault or leave me alone."

Jordan stood up and stretched. His face was gray, the freckles standing out in ugly patches on pale skin. "Yeah, we know how it works. We also both know you didn't get that shiner from a little tiff with a minister." He glanced down the hall at Manny, then back at Helen, his eyes dark and serious. "Don't give Hernandez any excuses to go after you."

"Is that a threat, Lieutenant?" Helen stood up to face him. Their eyes were level. Looking closely she read anger and fear mixed there. "Because if Manny does anything to me, he'll lose his badge. I'll make sure of it, and I think you will, too."

There was a stir behind Jordan. Over his shoulder Helen could see someone in a white lab coat emerging from the examining room, chatting with Manny while he consulted a clipboard. Jordan sighed and rubbed a hand over his face in weariness.

"You're really worried about him, aren't you, Jordan?" Helen said. "That he's going to go off the deep end because of me. Or what he thinks is all about me and his ex-wife."

Jordan's face was blank when he turned to her. "If I find out you've been keeping anything from me I'm not going to be very happy about it. In fact, I'll be fucking pissed. You don't want that to happen, believe me."

"I hear you." She watched him walk away. The doctor listened to both Manny and Jordan for a moment, grimaced and nodded before coming down the hall to Helen. He was very young, very rumpled, but his eyes were alert and clear. Helen smiled wryly to herself, momentarily distracted by the realization that she was old enough to be his mother, yet Maggie's well-being was in his youthful hands. With a start she had a second realization—that she thought of Maggie as hers, in some way. Not just as being responsible, but as part of her life. Made no sense at all. She shoved the idea aside and waited for the doctor to speak.

"Looks worse than it is," he was saying. "No broken bones but an awful lot of bruising and tearing." He spoke matter-of-factly, glancing up briefly from his notes. "You're her—partner?"

"I'm a friend, that's all." Well, maybe not a friend after today, but the fact she'd brought Maggie in would at least convince them to give her information. "What about the blood? Was she cut up, or stabbed or something?"

"A cut on her forehead," he answered, lifting his own hand to demonstrate. "Head wounds always bleed like the devil, so of course that must have looked really scary. She remembers falling down in the office, and maybe the cut came from hitting something on the way down. I don't think there's a concussion but we'll want to keep her overnight just to be sure."

Helen almost swayed from relief, barely listening to his comments about getting Maggie checked in for observation. She felt the young doctor's eyes on her and forced herself to stand upright. It wasn't until he mentioned the police that her attention focused on him again. "Maybe after the cops finish with her you can go in for a few minutes while we get her room ready upstairs."

"She—she wants to talk to me?"

Again the doctor studied her, his clear gray eyes meditative as he took in her appearance. Helen didn't have a clue how she looked—disheveled, certainly, with a few bruises of her own. "She asked for you. Why don't you sit here a minute, wait for them to come out? Then you can go in." He guided her back to her chair and, with a wisdom beyond his years, left her alone with a single backward glance. Helen closed her eyes tight against the tears welling up. She didn't know if this meant Maggie would tell her to go to hell or maybe thank her for coming by the church. Whatever it meant at least she'd have a chance to see her once more. Maybe just once, maybe not.

She opened her eyes at the sound of footsteps, two people, walking the hall toward her. Jordan trailed behind Manny, still looking drained but determination in his eyes. Manny was a different story. His face was dark and furious, his jaw working as though he'd bitten into something that tasted like shit. Helen stood up again, bracing herself.

Manny stared for a few seconds, apparently getting himself under control. "Well, Helen, she's not talking. Whatever crap you've gotten yourself into, you've got a pal in there. Might as well make the most of it before you get her killed."

"Manny, you're tired and angry, so I'm not going to remember you said that," Helen said, relieved at how calm she sounded. She looked past him at Jordan, who was studying some spots on the floor with great interest. "I will, however, remember our conversation, Jordan."

"What conversation was that, Helen? Don't tell me you're hitting the switch now, kissing Jordan's ass?" Manny leered at her, his fists coming out from his pockets. Jordan saw it, and he moved quickly between Manny and Helen. "Won't work, Jordan. She's a muff-diver, she doesn't mean it. Anyway, she's getting a little old for that, don't you think?" His face went red in the ugly fluorescent light. Beyond the waiting area Helen saw a couple of nurses look worriedly at each other, and one reached for a phone. Calling security, Helen guessed.

Time to break this up. "Keep him on a leash, Jordan, or I swear I will own you both," and she brushed past them toward Maggie's room. The nurse replaced the receiver and watched her as she went slowly toward the examining room. Helen knew she'd have a couple of minutes, no more. Hopefully that would be all she needed.

"Don't you just walk away from me, bitch." Suddenly a hand circled her arm, squeezing hard enough to leave bruises.

Helen stopped, turned around and stared at Manny, her face only inches from his. "Get your hands off, now," she said quietly. She could feel him shaking. "Manny, you are very close to a dangerous line. You don't want to cross that line."

His breath hissed in and out. Helen doubted he'd heard anything she said. "You crossed that line yourself a long time ago, Helen," he said, tightening his hold. "How does it feel, to be one of them? One of the fucking losers you and me used to put away for life?"

Later Helen could never be sure what happened next. She remembered getting out of Manny's grasp. She didn't remember punching him in the face, although the next thing she recalled was watching Manny hold a hand to his bloody nose. Then Jordan was there, scuffling between them and saying something to Manny. He turned to Helen. "He had it coming, I know he did. But you better back the fuck off or you'll be way in over your head."

She took in Jordan's tired pale face, the nurses scurrying up the hall to see what had happened, Manny slumped against the wall with a handkerchief clutched to his face.

"It's all right, he just got a nosebleed," Jordan was saying to the hospital staff. They backed off slowly, clearly not quite believing him. Jordan turned back to Helen. "I mean it. Stay away from this case or you're both going to pay."

That cold clear rage iced up through her body, freezing out the pain in her arm and the fear she'd felt on first seeing Manny tonight. "I don't have much to lose, Jordan. Manny is the one you need to be lecturing, not me." She allowed herself one last look at Manny before going toward Maggie's room. She paused when she got to the door, getting a glimpse of her own face in the dark glass panel. One of them, Manny had said. One of who? Murderers, like the ones she'd shared cells with in prison? Or like Alice Harmon, descending into her own private hell of deprivation and loneliness, trapped in a longing that could never be fulfilled? She looked away and opened the door.

Helen stood just inside the door, letting her eyes adjust to the dim light and to the sight of Maggie's face. With the blood cleared away Helen could see clearly the ugly bruises on her cheeks, the swollen split lip and the bandage that covered one eye. Maggie's other eye was closed and Helen could see her chest rise and fall rhythmically under the flimsy paper gown. They must have given her something for the pain, she realized, something to get her to sleep once they got her upstairs.

Then Maggie's eye opened and she tried to sit up. "No, just lie still," Helen said, moving toward the bed. She pulled a stool over to the side of the examining table and made sure her face was all smiles, as if to say the damage was under control. "The doctor said you'll be okay, they just want to keep you overnight."

"Make sure I don't have concussion." Maggie's mumble came out just above a whisper and Helen leaned in to hear her. "Wanted to say thanks."

"Thanks? For what?"

"Finding me. Bastard heard you in the alley, ran out of there." She scrabbled with a hand and reached out to Helen. Near tears again, Helen clasped it gently. "Never saw him coming, Helen. I think—I think he might have killed me if you hadn't shown up."

Helen swallowed past the threatening tears and took a deep breath. God, she hated to push it but she had to know. "Did you see enough to tell the cops anything? Or did he talk to you?"

Maggie tried to shake her head, grimaced and gave it up. "No. I heard noises in the church, went in there to see what was happening." Something like a smile moved across her swollen face. "Guess I never did show you where I lived, did I? A studio up above the church. Cheap, though. Came with the job."

"You should have called me. Or someone. Especially after the office got vandalized."

"Stupid, right? Go in there alone. But it was dark in there, didn't see a thing. He came at me from behind and pulled me to the kitchen area." She broke off, shaking suddenly with fear or pain or both.

"Okay, Maggie. Don't say anything else, don't try to talk." Maggie's shivers subsided and her breathing steadied. The door swung open and two orderlies made their way in with a gurney. Helen went outside while they got Maggie loaded safely, then watched them as they trundled to the elevators. "I'll pick you up tomorrow, Maggie," she said as they rolled by.

But Maggie was quiet, eyes closed. Maybe already half unconscious—better that way, Helen reassured herself as she went out into the parking lot. It wasn't until she was heading out onto Ashby, quiet now after eleven, that the tears came. Hard and hot and painful, they blurred her vision and racked her chest. Unable to see or breathe she pulled over. Cat, who'd been crouched inside the car for a long time, squeaked out a cry and climbed onto Helen's lap.

"So we finally get to be friends," Helen said as she clutched the creature on her lap. Unbelievably, that was a purr coming up through the scraggly fur. "Mangy little thing," she muttered as the tears eased. "Why couldn't you scratch that asshole's eyes out? Or at least wrestle him for his wallet, or something."

Cat kept purring, rubbing its head on Helen's thighs. It was the first time she'd been able to get a look at the animal's anatomy and be certain it was a female. Helen absently stroked her belly, one part of her mind marveling at the way Cat had decided she was acceptable—another part of her mind spinning around the events of the night. Okay. She didn't have any solid information on who this guy was, didn't have any proof he'd gone after Maggie. So what did she have?

She had the fact that all this had come down right after her visit to Valley View Nursing Home. It was the only connection to Alice's past, to whatever or whoever killed her. Maybe this smelly goon who'd done the dirty work had decided that going after Maggie would keep Helen quiet. He'd been careful, making sure Maggie couldn't identify him, making sure the scene was set to blame the vandals for the attack on Maggie. Brutal and ugly though it was, Maggie's beating had come in the form of a warning.

Helen sat up straight behind the wheel, her hands suddenly still on Cat's tummy. A warning. She'd had another warning recently—right before she'd discovered Alice's body, in fact. She glanced down at her watch. It wasn't yet midnight, there was still time. She eased Cat off her lap, and Cat gave her an irritated look.

"Sorry, I have one more place to go," Helen said as she turned on the engine and pulled out onto Ashby. "I promise you'll get something really special when we get home. Maybe the rest of the tuna salad. How about that?" Cat blinked green eyes and settled down onto the floor under the passenger seat. Helen turned the car around and headed back toward the White Horse.

After grabbing some fast food at a drive-through, she got there after one o'clock. Being a Monday night there weren't too many people coming and going. She found a parking spot on the side street and waited another hour until the neon sign outside was switched off and a few final customers staggered out onto Telegraph Avenue. She didn't have too long to wait until the bartender came out, calling a farewell over his shoulder at whoever was staying behind to clean up.

Helen got out of the car and followed him. He held out his hand, pointing toward a small sports car. Lights blinked and the alarm chirped as he approached. Helen caught up with him while he was opening the door. She was careful to call out from a few feet away—not a good idea to spring on someone at this hour, in this neighborhood, without first expressing friendly intentions.

"Excuse me—"

He turned swiftly, alert to the potential for danger. His leather coat gleamed richly in the streetlight and she could hear it rustling as he brought his hands up, prepared for a confrontation. He relaxed slightly when he saw it was a woman, alone, walking across the street toward him.

"I need to talk to you for a minute."

He recognized Helen when she got close, and she saw his face freeze into irritation. "Hey, we're closed. I'm off the clock, sweetheart." His lighthearted tone was belied by his face, though, and she watched it tense in the light as he turned again to his car. "Better go home now. We open up again at noon." He looked around the street, making sure they were alone.

"Do you remember me?" she asked as soon as she got close.

"Maybe." His face was thin and tight. She heard his car keys jingle as he fidgeted nervously. Of course he recognized her. His eyes went dark and blank and he looked her up and down. She had no doubt she looked like shit—no sleep, an awful night, and her face must have told the tale. He had every reason to be scared if her face showed how angry she was. And it wasn't a hot rage anymore. The shakes and the tears had worked their way out to be replaced by that inner ice. "I see a lot of people in my line of work."

"Yeah, I know." Helen stood in front of him. His height put her at a bit of a disadvantage. "Like me, like Maggie from the MCC in Oakland. And like Alice Harmon."

"She's dead."

"And I'm the one who found her. What's your name again? Mike, isn't it?"

"Who wants to know? Get out of my way, you crazy bitch, or I'll call the cops."

"Actually, I just got done talking to the cops." Helen leaned against his car and spoke conversationally, relaxed and friendly. "We were at the hospital. Maggie was there, too. But she wasn't talking much."

Mike's face froze in horror, his hand clutching his keys with a jerk. "Is she—is she dead?"

"What an interesting question, Mike. No, she's not dead. A bit bruised from the beating, but very much alive. For now." Helen inwardly groaned at sounding like something out of a B-movie from the Forties. But it seemed to be working with Mike, whose weak attempt at bravado melted. He stared down at the street, folding his arms across his chest. Helen was sure she had his attention now. "They don't think she has a concussion but they'll be keeping her overnight."

"Jesus." He let out a long sigh and covered his face with his hands, keys falling to the wet pavement. Helen picked them up and held them as he let his hands fall. "I didn't know—I mean, I never thought these guys would go after anyone. I swear it."

"Okay, Mike." Helen put his keys in her pocket. "Let's go someplace and talk."

"What?" He gaped at her in amazement. "I'm not going anywhere with you! You're fucking crazy, you can't do anything about this!"

"Actually, if you want your keys back you will. I bet you're getting hungry, Mike. Let's find some food and talk for a while."

Chapter Fourteen

The café on Woolsey, just up the street from the bar, was the only place Helen could think of that was open twenty four-hours. She walked back to her car to check on the cat before heading away from the White Horse. Mike stood silently beside the car, noting Cat's presence without comment. Cat had moved to the back seat with only one growl of protest before slinking over the seat and settling down without further comment to the floor.

"Don't suppose you know someone who wants a cat, do you? This belonged to Alice." Mike glared at her, then turned away to stare down the street. Helen decided small talk was not going to help so they walked in silence across Telegraph. Once again rain started to fall in a thin cold mist as they entered the restaurant. There was one other couple there, sitting side by side in a booth and giggling over their burgers and fries—college students, out late on a date. Helen and Mike didn't rate a glance from the kids. Helen guided them to a booth on the other side of the dining room.

For all his height, Mike looked shrunken against the red vinyl seat. He had to be hot in that leather jacket, but he pulled it closer as the waitress brought their food—Helen, still hungry, had soup, Mike had refused anything. Good thing, too, since her wallet was yet again almost empty.

"Sure you don't want anything?" she asked.

"Yeah. I want to get my keys back and go home."

Helen laid down her spoon. "You looked pretty freaked out a few minutes ago, Mike. You could have taken those keys from me if you really wanted to. I think you were just too shook up to make a move. What do you think?"

He shrugged, glanced around the room. The teenagers were smiling at each other and ignoring their food, and the waitress leaned lazily against the cash register, talking on her cell phone to someone. Helen caught the words "bitch" and "crazy" on her end of the conversation.

"No one gives a damn what we're talking about, Mike. You might as well tell me." She raised her eyebrows, realization sinking in. "I think you want to talk to me, don't you? Kind of like a confession. You want to tell someone and it might as well be me." She tasted her soup—not too bad, and she really was still hungry—but kept her eyes on her dinner companion. "What did you do about Alice?"

"Nothing. I didn't do a goddamn thing." He leaned forward suddenly, a sheen of sweat on his face. "I think I'm going to be sick." It didn't come out exactly a whine, but close enough. Helen watched his face grow paler, his hands shaking as they held his head. "Let me think a minute, all right?"

She finished her soup, started on the crackers. She pushed Mike's glass of water toward his hand and he took a sip, his hands still shaking. "Come on, talk. People are getting hurt, Mike. I need to know what happened."

"But you're not a private eye anymore, are you?" The water seemed to help. He took a long swig and leaned back in the booth, his color a little better, his hands still. "What the hell could you do to take care of me?"

Take care of him. Jesus, what the fuck had he done? "I know some cops," she said, cringing inside at the claim. Well, it was true. Granted, the cops she knew didn't like her very much right now, but that was better left unsaid at the moment. "Just tell me about Alice."

"Alice." He waited while the waitress refilled their glasses. "It's nothing, really—just something strange happened. It was the day before you talked to me, asking me about her and her car. Her car she left at the White Horse." He looked up, his hands twisted on the table in front of him. He found his napkin and began to shred it, leaving a trail of white paper pills littering the space between them. Helen wanted to grab his hands and stop his nervous gesture but she kept still, willing him to keep talking, feeling his wide-eyed gaze on her face. "I noticed the car, too. I didn't know what to do. I mean, I almost called Maggie—"

His face crumpled and Helen glanced around the room. The teenagers had left, the waitress was nowhere in sight.

"Jesus, poor Maggie," he whispered shakily. "Okay. The day before you came around, before Maggie came around, this guy came in. He was asking about Alice, too. I mean, it's not like I know Alice. Knew her, I mean. But she was a regular. Too regular."

"So what did this guy want?"

"This is the weird part. He comes up in this big black car, smoked windows, way too expensive for the neighborhood. Way too much for the people that come into the bar, too." By talking Mike calmed down. He'd quit fiddling with the silver and the napkins, and his tension eased as relief came into his voice. "Ugly guy, too. Smelled bad, like he hadn't washed in a while."

"What did he want to know?"

Mike shrugged, looking positively relaxed now. "Just when I'd seen Alice last, where she lived, that kind of shit." He looked down, his face suddenly flushed. "I—I was getting mad at Alice, about the way she cried and carried on when she came into the bar. I was tired of how she came in and wailed almost every night, tired of calling a cab to take her home. We were about to eighty-six her, anyhow." He looked up again, his face defiant. "I just thought maybe she owed them money or something. I never imagined they'd—they'd—oh. God . . . ." His voice trailed off, all defiance gone.

"What did you do?" Helen asked gently. "You told them where she lived?"

"Not exactly," he said in a trembling whisper. "I mean, yes. I told them the building—I mean, Jesus, I had to take her home myself one night when the taxi never showed up." He looked back down at the table, avoiding Helen's gaze. "I swear, I thought they just wanted to talk to her. That's what the guy said, the one who smelled like shit." He took another napkin from the metal holder, started to rip in into tiny pieces. "It's not my fault, what happened. You can't say it is." Then his jaw dropped. "Oh, my God, this guy went to Maggie? He hurt her? Fuck, fuck, fuck."

Helen reached over and grabbed Mike's hands. "Calm down a minute, Mike. You said 'they.' Was someone else with this guy?"

"Maggie's going to be all right, right? You said that, that she's okay."

"Calm down, Mike. There were a couple of guys? Not just the one who needed a bath."

He fidgeted some more on the seat, took another long drink of water. "Christ, if they killed Maggie, too—yeah, yeah, the guy wasn't driving. I watched him when he went back to the car and he got in the passenger seat when they drove away."

"Tell me what the guy looked like. The one who came in and talked to you."

"Jesus, I gotta remember faces. Okay, he was maybe in his thirties. Not tall. Kind of—not fat, but kind of round. Big round face, a Yankees baseball cap so I couldn't see his hair. Smelled horrible, like he hadn't taken a bath in days. Kind of like Alice smelled, actually." He was sweating in big drops now. One fell from his nose, plinked on the table. "Christ, I don't know. Why are you asking me this?"

Helen gave up. The description was close enough to the guy

who'd been following her around, she guessed. There wouldn't be two round-faced men wearing Yankees baseball caps be in the middle of this. Besides, Mike was in no shape to continue, certainly not in such a public place. And anything further might push him to call the cops himself. Who the fuck were these guys?

"So, Maggie's okay? Come on, you said so—"

"She'll make it. By the way, I got a little visit myself. Maybe you didn't see this," she said, pointing at her face.

He looked down at the table. "Yeah. I noticed."

Helen fought down the impulse to slap him across his sweaty little face. His actions had not only helped Alice get killed and Helen into deep shit with Manny and company, but had gotten both Maggie and Helen beat up. Put those bruises on her face, caused that slice in her forehead, wrecked her church, given Helen bruises of her own. "Why didn't you say anything to the cops, Mike?"

"Are you fucking nuts? They would have come after me next." All the pretty youth he was able to keep up in the dim light of the bar had faded into lines and weariness. He leaned forward, resting his head in his hands. "I'd be dead, too. Besides, there wasn't anything I could tell them. It was just two guys. I don't know who they were or where they came from. How was that going to do anything for the cops?"

She pulled his keys out of her pocket and tossed them with a loud clatter on the table. "Go home, Mike." She gripped her hands together in her lap, wanting him out of her sight before she hit him.

"So the cops—you won't—"

"Get the fuck out of here," she said through gritted teeth. She kept her gaze fixed on the opposite wall and waited until she felt the cold wind from outside move through the café and heard the door shut behind him as he went out into the rain. She waited some more, until she was sure Mike had taken off, then paid up the bill. The waitress was still on her cell phone, and she took Helen's money without once looking at her. Good thing, too, or she might not have liked the look in Helen's eyes.

Cat greeted her with a yowl and kept it up until they got back into Helen's apartment. The door was shut, the lock barely hanging onto the splintered wood. Cat prowled around the furniture for a few minutes, then curled up on the sofa and went to sleep. Helen stood in the living room, listening hard, but all she could hear was the rain. For the first time in a long, long time she wished she had a gun. Helen heaved the sofa up to the door with the last bit of energy she had.

Trembling from exhaustion she listened to her phone messages. One was from Jan, who wanted to know when they could do an interview for her article. The other one was from Brenda. She gushed—as always—about the office they were sending her to next. "It starts Wednesday, Helen, and it should run through the end of February. Maybe it will turn into a permanent job, who knows?"

Helen went to the bedroom and lay down, all her clothes on, lights shining. Thank God she had a day to get some rest before going back to work. "I'll never get to sleep," she muttered, but the next thing she knew daylight shone through the tattered curtains and rain pounded on the window. Cat sat solidly on her belly, pressing against her kidneys. "Okay, okay, I'm up." A shower and a cup of coffee later Helen felt much better. She got one good look at her face in the mirror and turned away quickly from the purple bruises. A couple of phone calls later she felt even better—the job was hers starting Wednesday, according to Brenda, and the hospital said Maggie could go home today.

On her way out Helen studied the lock on her door. Damn, this wasn't going to hold. She would invest in something a lot tougher than the flimsy excuse for safety provided by the building, but there wasn't much in her bank account right now. Could she wait until her next paycheck?

Seeing Maggie's battered face a couple of hours later made her decide to raid her rapidly shrinking funds for a new lock that very afternoon, after she took Maggie home. "Are you sure you should go home now? Maybe they could keep you for another day," Helen said as she watched Maggie move slowly into the passenger seat.

"I'm fine. I just need to go home. The insurance won't pay for another night anyway. I'm dreading the bills already." They drove in silence, Maggie holding herself stiff, her face set with pain.

Helen felt a growing sense of uneasiness. What the hell was she doing here? Maggie couldn't possibly want anything else to do with her, not now. Helen would get her safely into her bed, then go home—get out of Maggie's life, leave her alone from here on out. It was the best way. Again the inner field of ice, stretching long and wide and deep, an arctic calm, spread across her heart and stilled her emotions. This was all she could hope for, all she could manage in life. Some kind of work, trying to stay out of trouble, and no more attempts at connection. That was over. Despite the ache that surged up under the calm Helen knew she could face that. What she couldn't face was causing Maggie, or anyone else she cared about, more pain and danger.

"Will you stay here a few minutes, Helen?" Maggie asked just as Helen was about to make an excuse and leave.

Helen looked down at her, lying in the bed. Small and vulnerable and very alone, with her gold hair lank and stringy on the pillow, one eye still covered by a bandage, bruises turning yellow and purple on her face—she was the most beautiful thing Helen had ever seen. "Are you sure you want to stay here?" she asked. "Those offices aren't far away. They may know you live up here." She stopped short of inviting Maggie to stay with her, remembering just in time that her own home wasn't much safer.

But Maggie misread Helen's sudden silence. "I guess it's too much to ask you to hang around. You've taken care of me enough for one day." She managed a lopsided smile. "Thanks."

"Thanks?" Helen repeated, disbelief making her voice crack. "Thanks for getting you beat up, for making you run all over town, for getting your church trashed?" She sat down on the floor next to the bed so Maggie wouldn't have to strain to look at her. "Are you sure you don't have a concussion? I think you need your head examined."

"Just stay with me for a while, Helen. I don't want to be alone."

"Okay."

"I need to tell you something." Maggie slid around in the bed until she faced Helen, wincing with the effort. "I need to tell you why I was in the office last night when I heard noises coming from downstairs. I got a message from the church secretary on my phone yesterday. She called in the afternoon, while we were coming back from Napa."

"What happened?"

"Apparently the FBI had called. They had some questions about our involvement in terrorist groups."

Helen felt her mouth open and she blinked hard. Was Maggie hallucinating? "Maybe I'm the one with a head injury. It sounded like you just said the FBI was questioning you about terrorist activities."

That looked like a smile on Maggie's face but Helen couldn't be sure. "Well, you know, the Patriot Act covers a lot of ground. Apparently the fact that we've sent groups to take part in protests and spoken out against what's happening in Iraq had ruffled a few feathers. So the secretary called our lawyer and was trying to get hold of me all day yesterday. Guess I should break down and get a cell phone."

"I can't believe it. Just because you've taken part in some demonstrations?"

"Welcome to the brave new world, Helen. Interesting timing, don't you think?" Maggie struggled to sit up, and Helen got to her knees to help adjust pillows until Maggie sighed and leaned back in more comfort. "You poke around in Alice's death, and suddenly my office gets torn apart and the FBI comes calling."

Helen got up and began to pace the room. She thought about the pictures on the walls of the Giorgi building—the conservative politicians shaking hands with various family members, the rigid conservatism of their record with migrant workers, the commendations from local police. She stopped pacing and sat by the bed again. "I need to get away from you. Now. I need to walk away from this and make sure I'm nowhere near you again." She swallowed past the soreness gathering in her throat and chest, ignored the ache growing inside. "This isn't your fight. I'll leave you alone."

"But it is my fight, Helen." Maggie reached out, her hand falling on the bed. "I knew Alice a long time before you came into the picture. Someone killed her, Helen. The police are investigating this as a murder. Someone is getting away with murder. And now they're coming after my church. We both know how people like this operate. There's no telling who they'll come after next." The crooked smile appeared again. "If they think we're troublemakers now, they have no idea what they're up against once I really get going."

Helen stayed for a long time, letting Maggie talk herself into conviction, watching her fall asleep. Maggie couldn't know what she was getting into. After years as a cop, more years as a private investigator, and a few years in prison, Helen had a good idea of the obstacle course in front of them. She watched Maggie sleep, studying the bruises and bandages, trying to match them up with her brave words. Words didn't back down people like Manny, or the Giorgi family, or even the bastard who'd done this to Maggie. Words didn't bring Alice back.

Helen felt her eyes drifting shut. Maggie's apartment was warm and quiet. Central heating hummed comfortingly against the cold and wind outside. Carefully she edged a pillow out from Maggie's bed and curled up with it on the floor. She'd stay for a few hours, at least, make sure Maggie was okay before she went back home. Her last thoughts before dozing off were of Saturday afternoon, of the way Maggie's hands and mouth had felt on her body. Maggie hadn't said anything about that, Helen realized. Maybe she didn't want a repeat. Helen listened to Maggie's breathing, tried to empty her thoughts of everything but that—even matched her own breathing to the gentle sounds coming from the bed.

Then Helen slept. When she woke it was evening. Maggie woke up as Helen stumbled in the darkened room.

"It's just me, Maggie. I should get home." With a whispered

reassurance that she'd call tomorrow Helen let herself out. Time to get out of there, she lectured herself as she drove through the wet streets. Time to get someplace where she could think. She'd make a decision about all this after a good night's rest.

After a stop at a hardware store Helen drove home. The paper bag on the seat beside her held additional locks and a chain for the door. Fuck the building owners, she thought, I'll take care of it myself. Helen finally got inside the apartment, feeling inexplicably better. A short nap? Maggie's pep talk? Or maybe it was the sense of things coming together.

"Honey, I'm home!" she called out to Cat. No growls, no snarls, nothing to greet her. Usually the animal yelled at her first thing, insisting on dinner or attention. Not this afternoon. "Hey, Cat! Where'd you go, you little bitch?"

Helen wandered through to the kitchen and noticed the trail of blood on the floor. With a sick sense of horror she followed it to where Cat's body lay, stabbed and still bleeding, on the bathroom floor.

Chapter Fifteen

The following Saturday, Maggie moved stiffly around her kitchen—putting water in the kettle, laying out cookies, setting sugar and milk on the table. Helen had already made the mistake once of offering to do it for her. One frown, creasing Maggie's bandaged brow, was enough to discourage that impulse. Helen sat quietly, holding a purring Cat in her arms, watching Maggie move about.

She tried not to stare too directly and earn another angry look. Maggie's moves were slow and careful, like she was trying not to drop things. The bruises, Helen knew, would last for at least a week. She was lucky she hadn't gotten any broken bones, and Helen hid her own mingled fear and fury by looking down at Cat, stroking her pale fur.

Cat hadn't stopped purring from the moment Helen had picked her up from the vet after work Wednesday. The overnight stay at the vet's kennel had seemed to work a change in the contrary creature. Instead of hissing and growling, she had been affectionate, loving, reaching out with little gray paws every time Helen moved away from her. She rubbed her head constantly on Helen's hands, mouth open and slack with pleasure at Helen's touch. Dr. Morrisey, a recommendation from Maggie, had turned clear gray eyes to Helen, with raised eyebrows, at the sight of Cat's injuries.

"Who did this?" she had wanted to know. Something like cold hard anger flared beneath her steady gaze.

Anger, Helen hoped, not toward her but toward whatever sick fuck had taken a hunting knife to Cat's belly and left her to bleed to death. Helen didn't answer her question, merely looked down at the unconscious animal on the vet's examining table.

After an uncomfortable silence, Dr. Morrisey sighed and gently moved Cat to a different position. "This'll keep her unconscious while I stitch her up."

"She'll—she'll be okay, then?" Helen was shocked at the catch in her voice, the way her throat seemed to close up painfully. Relief washed over her in waves, and she fought down the feelings with a swallow. "She's going to make it?"

"Yes. Good thing I could come in after hours, though. If much more time had passed, even a few minutes—"

Again the cool gray eyes, the heavy sigh. Dr. Morrisey turned to her cabinets, pulling down needles, vials, other tools of her trade. Helen looked at the tray of equipment she'd arranged on the table. This was going to cost her as much as next month's rent, no doubt. Hopefully the surgery would get done first, and they could talk about money later.

As if she'd read her mind, Dr. Morrisey looked up with a wry smile. "Normally I'd charge quite a bit for an emergency procedure like this. But since it was Maggie who called—well, we'll work it out later."

It had been worth it, Helen decided, watching Cat's eyes narrow with pleasure when Helen rubbed her head. Even if she ended up paying Dr. Morrisey for years. Hell, why not owe her, too? Then Helen would be in debt to just about every single human being she'd come in contact with in the past six months.

"So Cat's going to be okay?" Maggie poured hot water, wincing a moment as she leaned over the table, then sat down with a sigh of relief at being off her feet. "Dr. Morrisey is terrific."

"Is she a member of your church?"

Maggie nodded, sipped tea. "One of the first, along with her partner. They're great. Maybe you'll meet them both there sometime."

"Maybe. She was really great with Cat." Helen managed a smile, hoping to change the subject fast. She wasn't about to get started on church membership, not just now. "Guess I should name this little stinker one of these days." Cat's eyes closed and the purring faded as she fell into a doze. "Thanks for letting me bring her over here. I just didn't want to leave her alone if I didn't have to."

"It was the same guy, wasn't it? The guy who found me in the church."

Helen shrugged, careful not to disturb Cat in her lap. "I think so, Maggie, but I have no proof. This little one isn't talking, and you didn't get a good look at whoever it was." She raised her eyes to meet Maggie's gaze. "I think the attacks on me and you, and on poor Cat, were warnings. To me."

"So we were just convenient targets, then." Maggie tried to smile, stopped at the pain it evidently caused her sore mouth. "Why? What warning?"

Helen shrugged. "I can only speculate, but it all happened right after our visit to the nursing home. And with going after us, and Cat, he was hoping I'd get scared off."

Maggie stared evenly at Helen. "He really thought that? To scare us?"

"Why not? Someone is dead, Cat should have been dead, you could have been in a coma, or worse." Again the tight throat, again the threat of tears. Helen took a swallow of hot tea, grateful for the scalding to distract her.

"Who knows—if he hadn't heard you coming he would have probably done a lot worse." Maggie sounded matter of fact. She reached for a cookie as Helen eyed the bruises on her wrists. They did look a little better. "So maybe he calls in the FBI, to finish me off?"

"How did that go, by the way? Did you call them back?"

Maggie tried a smile again. "Not exactly. I have a good friend who's an attorney, I had her contact their office. Nothing more yet, but Terry—the lawyer—she thinks they're not done yet. But, Helen, I don't understand." She leaned forward on her elbows. "How exactly does that all tie in? I mean, this is some guy who's not much better than a street thug. How the hell does he pull in the local FBI office on some trumped-up anti-patriotism charge? It doesn't add up."

"That's what I wanted to show you today. Hang on a second." Helen put Cat back in the carrying box she'd made from a cardboard box and a heap of soft old towels. Cat stirred briefly, yawned, subsided back into sleep. Helen picked up the thick file she'd brought in with her and slapped it down on the table. "Thank goodness for Brenda."

"Who's Brenda?"

Was Helen imagining the jealousy in Maggie's voice? Probably. "She's with the temp agency. Brenda got me this job in a big office where I don't have much to do all day. It started Wednesday and should go through the end of the month. I sit on my butt and play on the Internet between phone calls." She flipped open the folder and sat down as she pulled some of the papers out for Maggie to see. "It's amazing what you can find when you Google something these days."

"Like what?"

"Like the name 'Giorgi.' I found tons of shit about the Giorgi family." Helen paused. "They don't just own a winery and a few big buildings in Napa. They have a pretty long history, and it isn't very nice."

Helen sat back while Maggie leafed through the printouts, studying Maggie's face. Maybe she shouldn't stay much longer—Maggie looked white and strained under the bruises. Helen had a fleeting image of tucking Maggie into bed, of smoothing the sheets over her body, then fought the picture away.

By the time Maggie looked up she had herself under control again. "Okay, so the Giorgi family is rich and powerful and has conservative ties. So they've not exactly been the friend of the migrant worker, or of environmentalists. So what? Connect some dots for me here, Helen." She let the pages fall from her hands and sat back. "I'm not seeing the picture."

"What was it Alice did, all those years as an activist? What did we find in those old papers? The workers at the Giorgi vineyards were a big part of that movement. Alice was right there, with them. And—not only Alice. The dot that connects it all is something you didn't see that day we were in Napa." Helen described the woman at the memorial service, the one whose face showed up in the portraits at the Giorgi building. "There's some kind of connection here, Maggie. There's no other reason."

Great, Helen thought, sinking into silence. Maggie was shaking her head, moving away from the table toward the sink. She doesn't believe me.

"Okay, it's a working theory, you're right. But it does make sense." Now she was coming off as a hard sell, as if she were trying to convince herself as well as Maggie. Said out loud, Helen's theory did in fact sound ridiculously far-fetched.

"Maybe there is a connection. But this will never fly with the cops, Helen. Will it?"

"No. It's just some ideas. I have to make sense of this somehow, and this is the only thing that adds up so far." I should never have said anything, Helen told herself furiously. She should have waited until she was sure, not just tossed out a bunch of stupid theories. But theories were all she had—that and a deep-seated burning rage every time she saw the stitches on Cat's delicate belly, every time she saw the ugly marks on her own and Maggie's faces. Abruptly she moved to round up the loose sheets and stuff them back into the file.

"Helen—don't be mad."

"I'm not angry. Really." Helen stopped, looked across the table at Maggie. Her green eyes were hidden in shadow and she looked small and frail sitting alone at the table. Helen sat down again. "You're right. It's ideas right now, nothing more."

"You should—you should let it drop. I mean, don't do anything else on my account."

Helen raised her eyebrows at the flat, unfeeling tone of Maggie's words. "What is it, Maggie?" Maggie didn't move a muscle, didn't look up from her cold cup of tea. Without thinking Helen reached out and gently encircled Maggie's hands with her own, both of them clasping the cup. "What did the FBI say to your lawyer?"

To her astonishment and dismay Helen saw tears glistening on Maggie's cheeks. She wept soundlessly, shoulders shaking slightly. "They—" She took a deep breath and struggled for control. "They're going to try to get a warrant to search us, to go over all our records and make sure we don't have connections with terrorist organizations."

Helen nearly laughed out loud. "That's fucking ridiculous, Maggie! What the hell do they mean by 'terrorist organizations'? The SPCA? The local Brownie troop? You have nothing to worry about."

Maggie shook her head. "It's not as stupid as it sounds, Helen. Our anti-war protests are a mark against us, and we've formed coalitions with peace groups that are already on hit lists." She withdrew her hands and twisted them, her fingers white and strained. "Even if they don't find anything they can make our lives really, really difficult. I've already had a couple of newspapers calling—I have no idea how they found out about this—and we have a couple of grant proposals on the table. Terry—my lawyer friend—she said they specifically mentioned the grants."

"What are the grants for?"

"A soup kitchen, a daycare place for seniors. Even a playground for the neighborhood." Maggie shook her head, smiled through her tears. "Lots of big dreams. Now they may all go in the shit pile."

Helen abruptly got up from the table, shoving her chair away with a clatter. She paced the kitchen, anger growing inside her and breaking through the inner ice floe. It was all her fault. She herself was the cause of this. "Don't worry, Maggie," she heard herself say. "All of this is going to go away very soon."

"How?" Now Maggie got up and blocked Helen's path, forcing her to stop. "What do you have? A bunch of news articles about the Giorgis, a mysterious woman at a funeral and a bunch of boxes from Alice's apartment that are still sitting in my garage, waiting to go to the dumpster. That's it."

Helen let Maggie cry out her fear and frustration. Cautiously she placed her hands on Maggie's shoulders and pulled her closer. Only when Maggie stopped shaking did she pull back.

"Sorry, Helen," she said in a shaky voice. "I'm not mad, not really. I just got so upset when Terry told me what they—what they're planning to do."

"Well. They haven't done it yet." Helen kissed her eyelids, tasting the salty wetness of Maggie's tears. "And they won't, if I have anything to say about it." She bent forward a little, her lips traveling to Maggie's mouth.

Slowly she pulled Maggie back into her arms and kissed her. Their tongues met, Maggie slow and scared at first, Helen tentative and not wanting to exacerbate recent wounds. Helen grazed her hands over Maggie's back and shoulders, her heart pounding hard as Maggie finally relaxed. A few minutes later they were in Maggie's bed.

"I won't hurt you." Helen unbuttoned Maggie's shirt, trying not to wince at the scrapes on her ribs.

"I know you won't. Just touch me, Helen. Please." Maggie lay down with a sigh and Helen watched her welcoming smile—a smile that was becoming familiar to her.

This time the sex was lazy, a pace demanded by Maggie's delicate condition. Helen turned her strokes and caresses into a teasing game, drawing out pleasure as long as she could. "No, honey, not yet," she whispered as Maggie sighed and shifted under Helen's hands.

With slow fingers Helen circled the soft wet folds of skin, both hands working to bring Maggie to orgasm. It came finally, a long lingering shudder crossing Maggie's thighs and belly, until she lay still, savoring the pleasure.

"No, not now." Helen snuggled next to Maggie, relishing the warmth of the sheets around them as the wind and rain beat against the bedroom windows. "Don't worry about me."

"Doesn't seem fair, Helen." Maggie nestled against Helen. "I want it to be good for you, too."

"It is, Maggie. You'll have your turn when you get those bandages off, I promise you."

"Helen—" Maggie raised herself up to look into Helen's face. "I'm sorry I got so mean in there. About the Giorgis and all that work you did, getting information. You're right, there's something there."

"But, like you said, all I have is Internet articles, some woman I don't know and boxes of Alice's stuff in your garage." Helen suddenly felt cold. She sat up. "Boxes of Alice's stuff. Here, in your garage?"

"Yes. The support group finally got her apartment all cleaned out, and now we're getting rid of it." She lay down again, nestling against Helen. "Boxes and boxes of stuff, dishes and shoes and—well, you saw it that day. The other folks from the support group were thinking of having a garage sale." Maggie shuddered. "Sounded kind of gruesome to me, actually. Besides, someone from her family might still show up and want to go through it."

"Maybe." Helen could hear drowsiness in Maggie's voice. She held her close until her breathing evened out in sleep.

Helen eased out of the bed and found her clothes. On her way out to the garage she tiptoed past Cat, awake from her own nap in the box.

"Just stay quiet for a while, Cat," she whispered. "I've got some work to do."

Downstairs, she grimaced at the creaking from the garage door and let herself into its darkness. The overhead light revealed an imposing number of boxes, lined up and ready to go to whatever doom Maggie decided for them. "I could use a cigarette," she muttered as she set to work.

Chapter Sixteen

The sun shone brightly through the windows of Maggie's living room Sunday morning. Helen awoke on the couch, blinking hard at the unexpected light. She sat up with a start, unfamiliar with her surroundings, and immediately regretted the swift movement. Her arms and shoulders ached with the effort of moving Alice's belongings around the garage last night. She slumped back against the cushions, stretching her legs cautiously. More than once she'd bumped up hard on her shins against the boxes as she'd tried to shift them around the cold cement floor. All she'd gotten for her trouble was stiff muscles. The one thing missing, the one thing Helen had been looking for, was nowhere to be found.

With a groan she rolled off the couch and went to the kitchen. No sound emitted from the bedroom yet. She found Cat sleeping where she'd left her before crashing on the sofa. The bowl of milk beside Cat's box was empty. Helen crouched down beside her and Cat stirred, opened her eyes and started purring. "I need to get us both home," she whispered, stroking Cat's head. Cat pushed up against Helen's hand. "But not before caffeine."

A few minutes later Helen sat nursing a cup of strong black coffee at the kitchen table. She stared morosely at the file folder marked "Giorgi family" and wondered where the hell Alice's scrapbook had gone. She didn't need a rehash of the missing girlfriend story, but maybe there were some pictures of her time with the protesters amongst the other photos. That is, if the killer hadn't gotten to it. Maybe that had been the point. Maybe Alice's death was an accident.

"Yeah, right," Helen muttered. If this guy had had no trouble breaking into a church and Helen's apartment, what was to keep him from just getting into Alice's place and taking what he wanted? Maggie was right—it made no sense. Who gave a rat's ass if Alice had some old pictures? Why kill her? And why would it matter that Alice had been active in the civil rights movement? Nobody cared about that kind of shit anymore.

Helen heard movement behind her. She finished her coffee quickly and braced herself to face Maggie again. Before she could stand up she felt two arms going around her, a face close to hers, lips on her neck.

"Good morning," Maggie murmured into her ear, following the greeting with a kiss. "You're a morning person, I take it?"

"I can be. When required."

"Too bad. I hate getting up early. But it's always the way with couples—one person likes to get up early, the other person thinks noon is too early." Maggie released her and stepped around the table. "Good, you found the coffee."

"Yeah, help yourself." Helen picked up the folder and thought about how to get the hell out of there. It just felt wrong, for some reason. Wrong to be in Maggie's kitchen, wrong to be so cozy with her after fucking her the night before. Wrong to hear her talking about being part of a "couple," most of all.

"Whoa, that's strong." Smiling, Maggie leaned against the counter, cradling her mug with both hands. Helen watched her in surprise. She looked a lot better than she had last night. Not radiant, exactly—that would be too much like a bosom-heaving romance novel—but definitely better. Sex agreed with her. "You want some breakfast?"

Helen paused, a part of her reluctant to go, a part of her internally screaming in panic. "Uh, no, not really. I'd better get going. You must have a lot to do today. Sunday, after all. Big day for preachers, I would imagine." She grabbed the folder and collected Cat, still purring away in her box. "I should take care of some stuff myself."

Maggie watched her gather her things. "I'm taking the morning off from church," she said quietly. "Got a friend to cover for me until I look a little less dramatic." She followed Helen to the door and stopped her only as Helen was almost to the stairs. "I'm not the enemy," she said, taking her arm and pulling her close. "Go ahead—take care of business. But one of these days you have to quit running."

"I'm not running." Stupid comeback, when she was itching to get out the door and away from Maggie. Of course she was running, even though at the moment she was somewhat encumbered with a cat in a box.

Maggie smiled again and leaned on the doorjamb. "If you say so. I'm not going anywhere, Helen. I'll be here when you're ready to talk about this."

Helen took a deep breath. "Things are happening very fast here, Maggie. Maybe it's a little too fast for you."

"No, that's not it. It's—well, it's different for me. That doesn't mean it's a bad thing." She stroked Helen's cheek, the gentle touch fast becoming a caress. "I think it's time, anyway."

"Time for what?" Helen leaned into Maggie's hand. "For getting hooked up with a crazy woman who doesn't know who she is or what she really wants?"

"It's like what we read at Alice's memorial service. A time for everything. Maybe now is a time for me to stop doing things the way I've always done them. Time for changing a lot of things in my life." She smiled and gave her a quick kiss. "And it's time for you to go, I know."

"I'm sorry." And she was, Helen realized. Even if she had no idea what was going on, she was sorry to leave Maggie now. "I will be back, I promise."

"I know." Maggie stayed in the doorway until Helen was downstairs.

Helen breathed a sigh of relief and drove as fast as her old clunker would take her back home.

Home to a messy apartment. Helen gently unloaded Cat into the living room, uncertain if she would balk as she had Wednesday evening at being back in the place where she'd been attacked. But Cat just looked at her, gave out an odd little growl that turned into a purr and walked gingerly toward her food bowl. She looked up piteously at Helen, then twined around her leg before sitting by the food bowl again. Helen couldn't help smiling. She took a can of food from the cupboard. "Here you go."

As soon as the cat was chowing down the very expensive, vet-approved soft food, Helen went back to look at the new lock she'd installed. Not that she trusted that very much—but until she could scrape up the funds for a new apartment she was stuck. She pushed aside the thought that Maggie would let her stay with her for a while and made more coffee. Suddenly hunger took over, and she let Cat eat some of her scrambled eggs while she sat in the morning sun and thought.

She'd talked to Mike from the bar. She'd found out what she could from Maggie—stop thinking about Maggie, damn it! She had found out what she could from the Internet about the Giorgi family and its hold on the Napa Valley, a hold people like Alice were committed to breaking. She'd gone through all of Alice's remaining things and found nothing. What was left? She pushed aside her empty plate, reached down absently to pet Cat's head and went back over everything from day one.

Okay. That night in Alice's place. Not a pleasant memory. Helen gave up—just drunken sobbing and hints of trouble. Then there was the bartender at the White Horse. She didn't think she could get any more out of him. And of course the day she'd found Alice's body. She shook her head, trying to get past the horror of seeing Alice dead on the floor and recapture the details around the body. The phone on the floor. The cat screaming. The furniture all slightly moved around.

Nope, it was no good. That had been it—Helen, then Manny and Jordan. No one else.

She sat up straight. There had been someone else. "Shit." She grabbed her jacket and keys and fled out the door. Traffic wasn't too bad on an early Sunday morning and she got to Alice's neighborhood in less than fifteen minutes, just after nine. She found parking on the next block, just off Telegraph, and walked quickly to the building, barely noticing how warm she was in her coat under the sun. She stood silently for a moment on the sidewalk. Maybe this was foolish, storming here in broad daylight. She kept going, onto Telegraph, heading up toward Berkeley. She went inside a liquor store and pretended to look at newspapers for a few minutes. The cashier glanced her way, perhaps afraid she might steal something, then went back to watching cartoons. Helen went back outside. Nothing. No one.

She took a deep breath, reminded herself better safe than sorry, and headed back to the building. She was reassured to hear Walt Greeley's television set was still going strong. She pounded on the door, making sure she'd be heard over the cacophony inside. To her great relief Walt opened the door almost immediately.

His eyes narrowed. Helen reeled back—apparently bathing wasn't one of his top priorities. Or maybe this was something new since he'd seen Alice's body. "Hi, Walt," she managed to cough out. More smells came wafting out from his apartment. Surely it hadn't been this bad a few weeks ago, when she'd watched *Jeopardy* and *Family Feud* while Manny and Jordan had been upstairs with Alice's body.

Walt stood and stared, saying nothing.

"Strong silent type, I guess."

"Huh?" He squinted, peering down at her. Much of his body was concealed behind the door, but Helen was relieved to see a faded pair of jeans, a stained T-shirt. "What'd you say?"

"Hey there, Walt. Remember me?"

"Fuck, no. You one of them people selling church magazines? I told you to stay away from me."

"No, I'm not selling anything. Let me help you out here, Walt. We met a few weeks ago, when the police came by. For Alice. Upstairs."

He remembered, all right. His face went from puzzled to fearful as she spoke. His jaw clamped tight shut and he made a motion as if to shut the door on her.

"Hold on, Walt. I just want to talk to you." She got a leg inside. "I just want to see it again. That thing you took from her place. You can keep it, I promise. I just want another look."

Walt froze, his hand clenched on the doorknob. "I don't know what you mean."

"Yes, Walt, you do." Come on, come on, just let me in. He finally released the door, his jaw dropping in surprise as she pushed past him. She took a deep breath and regretted it. Walt's seclusion from life had worsened since she'd seen him last—the windows were tight shut, keeping out not only cold but fresh air. Through the door of the kitchen Helen could see trash piled up and overflowing the waste can by the sink. Dishes were piled up on the table and the counters, matched by more dishes in stinking heaps on the floor around the television set.

Sets, rather. Two, no, three additional sets. One looked very familiar. Helen moved closer. Yes, this looked like what she'd nearly knocked over in Alice's apartment that first Friday night. The last time she'd seen Alice alive. She peered around Walt into the dark hallway leading into the kitchen. All those boxes of things—pictures and books and ashtrays and stuffed animals—maybe none of them had started out as Walt's possessions. Maybe he'd been taking things from his tenants for a long time. The kind of things no one would miss, or maybe just imagine they'd lost or thrown away. Nothing important, just the ordinary detritus of ordinary people. A television set, though—that was a fairly big item to steal. Walt had graduated from odds and ends to the big time.

"So it wasn't just her scrapbook. It was her television set, too." Helen turned around to see Walt twisting his hands in front of him, hanging his head. "What else did you take, Walt?"

"Nothing! No one is going to miss that stuff, anyway. She didn't have any friends or family or anything, not till you and the other ones came around." He looked up and Helen winced at the tears in his eyes. "You was just going to give it all away, anyhow."

"Others. You mean Maggie? The people from the church?"

Walt sniffled and drew his hand across his nose. "That's what they said, they was going to give it away. So it didn't hurt a damn thing if I took it, right?"

"That's called stealing, Walt. You know what that means? That means you've broken the law." Helen took a step closer, putting on her best snarl. "You're in trouble with the police."

Walt's gaze darted around the apartment. Helen wondered how much of the clutter had found its way like this into Walt's apartment. How many previous tenants had noticed the odd item missing? And that was fear, not anger, in his eyes now. He fidgeted, getting more and more uncomfortable as she stood there staring in silence.

"Remember the two cops who were here the day we found Alice?"

Walt stared back down at her, breathing hard now. "They already talked to me. They know I didn't do it."

"Is that right?" Helen smiled, not a nice smile at all. "Are you sure about that, Walt? Sometimes they follow people around for days, watching them. How do you know they didn't watch you take those things?" She glanced around the apartment. "They just might show up again and ask you some questions about it. About Alice's death, too."

"Jesus, I didn't kill her! I didn't even know the bitch, okay? Jesus fucking Christ!" He turned and punched his fist into the wall, leaving a gouge in the plaster, a trickle of chips tumbling down to the floor. Helen shuddered, looking for a way to get past him. Bad, bad idea. He leaned against the wall with both hands, his breathing harsh and heavy. "All I did was take a couple things. TV set, some dishes, shit like that."

He seemed to be calming down. Helen took in a shaky breath and turned around, hoping she had her face under control again. "No one else knows about this? You haven't told anyone?"

"Why would I do a stupid thing like that? Lots of people would think it was wrong." He looked over at her, his eyes dark. "Just like you did. No, I didn't tell anyone. Not even those people who came by later."

"Who, Walt?" She felt a sliver of fear run through her. He was fucked up, he smelled bad—but Helen had seen him put a hole in the wall. Surely he could take care of himself if it came to a fight. "A man? Did a man come by to see you?"

"No, it wasn't a guy. It was this old skinny woman, long white hair. I thought she was a ghost, first. You know, coming around for Alice or something." Walt stood still and hugged himself. "She a church lady, too? Or a cop?"

"No, Walt." I don't know who the hell she is, Helen thought. Wish to God I did. "Come on, Walt"—she sighed—"let's have it."

"You'll give it back?"

Jesus. "Yes, I promise. I'll look through it right here, you and me together." If I can keep breathing that long, or if this game show doesn't drive me nuts. While Walt disappeared into the depths of the apartment, Helen turned down the volume on all three television sets to a tolerable level. Walt frowned when he came back in, glancing suspiciously at the sets then at Helen. She ignored his irritation and focused on the leather-bound book he carried.

He sat down next to her on the sofa. Helen bit her lip and did her best not to shy away from the odor that fogged his body. He blew out a sigh. "Okay. You can look at it."

“You have to let go first, Walt.” He handed it over and leaned back, his weight crunching something under the cushions. Probably a long-forgotten bag of chips. Then Helen opened the book and began to turn the pages. She remembered seeing Alice’s face, that house, from the Friday night weeks ago. Helen was nearly overcome by a wave of sadness. Sadness for Alice, dying alone, perhaps not even knowing why. And all that was left of her life, of her memories, was a dilapidated scrapbook. Even if Helen found what she was looking for, it was doubtful anyone would ever know who these people were, what their lives were about. Alice was gone—and so was all she ever knew. Helen looked at her hands on the old black pages, so old they almost crumbled beneath her touch. She remembered standing and looking at herself in Alice’s mirror that night, horrified at the vision of aging loneliness she’d seen reflected there.

“You going to look or just sit there?” Walt shifted nervously on the sofa. Helen pushed down her thoughts and feelings, reached for the inner ice floe and found it. Then she turned the page again.

Chapter Seventeen

Spring was definitely on the way now. The weather was positively warm for a Saturday in March. Had it only been a month since she'd met Alice? Only a week since she'd spent the night at Maggie's apartment? Odd how just the sense of sun and warmth returning could lift her spirits, she thought as she pulled into a parking space a few blocks from the parking lot where the garage sale was taking place. Maggie's phone message telling her about the event at the church had roused mixed feelings in her. It was only after a long debate with herself she'd decided to show up.

Under the car seat lay the scrapbook she'd looked at in Walt's apartment a week ago. Helen wasn't sure why she was taking it to Maggie—maybe just as a way to prove there was something going on? She grimaced as she recalled how she'd talked Walt out of it. He was not working with a full set of wheels, that much was clear, and further threats of police questionings had been more than enough to persuade him to give it up. Besides, Helen wasn't about to leave it lying around. She wanted the scrapbook within easy reach at all times. Especially after she'd seen more pictures of the white-haired woman.

She hadn't always had white hair. Some of the pictures, judging by the clothes, had been taken during the Seventies. Then, her hair was still long and straight and shiny—but it gleamed golden over her thin shoulders. Still the same haunted face, the same too-thin bony body. But the smiling face that looked out at the camera had something besides pain and fear in it. Usually the pictures showed Alice and this woman together, smiling or laughing or looking at each other. In the shadow of Alice's strong muscular body, the thin woman had seemed to gain some of Alice's strength and spirit. Despite the changes wrought by time and trouble, Helen was certain the woman from the memorial service was the same one in these pictures. Maybe she was the ex-lover Alice had talked about.

And now here she was, rattling off to show Maggie her prize. What did it prove? That this woman—girl, then, probably—had some connection to the Giorgi family? So what? What use would it be to Maggie? Face it, Helen lectured herself. You're just trying to find some reason, some reason that will convince yourself, that you need to see Maggie again. Especially after the way you've run out on her, more than once.

Helen had debated with herself for nearly a full week about whether or not to call Maggie. She'd gone to the job Brenda had arranged, this one in another insurance office. Cat was healing and almost back to her old crotchety self. Still it hadn't been enough to distract her. In the end, she cheated. Leaving a message on the church office's answering machine was a cowardly way out, she knew, but it was all she had the courage for. As she waited for the beep to leave her awkward message, she had to listen to a series of announcements about upcoming events. When she heard the words "garage sale this Saturday" Helen knew she had to be there. This was what Maggie had talked about last weekend, a way to finally clear out Alice's belongings. Helen had set the phone down gently without leaving a message. Maggie would probably make an appearance at the garage sale, and maybe it was better to say what she had to say in person.

Despite the effects of the spring sunshine, the way light hit the raindrops on eaves and trees and windows, Helen felt her stomach clench as she walked around the corner to the church parking lot. She'd been rehearsing her speech for a week, but it never sounded good enough. We shouldn't be together, she might start, because you're too good for me. Very lame. Or—there was the excuse that Helen would only get her hurt, just like Maggie got beat up because of her. That one was a little better, and certainly it was the truth.

Helen shook her head. Maggie wasn't likely to care about any of those reasons. Helen had carefully scanned the papers all week, checked on the Internet and listened to local news. There had been one brief story on a local listener-supported radio station relaying the FBI's interest in a local "gay" church, but it was only a headline. Nothing else. Maggie and her lawyer must have faced them down, which wouldn't surprise Helen at all.

She brushed against a lamppost as she moved aside for a cluster of people making their way to the church. Her movement dislodged a flyer from the pole, and she stooped to pick up the announcement for the garage sale. *A fundraiser sponsored by the Beginnings 12-Step Group, in honor of Alice Harmon. All proceeds will be used to repair and restore the church office.*

She looked up at the church. People were approaching the parking lot in twos and threes. Not a bad crowd for a garage sale. And yes, there was Maggie, standing near the church entrance in a black shirt and pants and a white collar. Helen hadn't seen her in "uniform" since Alice's memorial. It was startling. A relief, too, to see that the bruises had faded and her eyes were bright and clear. She was smiling and nodding to a couple, two elderly men, who spoke animatedly with much waving of hands. Helen found a quiet corner beside a table full of ancient crumbling books and watched Maggie in action. Strange to watch her doing her thing, strange to see Maggie as a professional person in her own right.

Helen froze and drew herself up with a gasp at the thought she'd just had. Someone behind her said something, and she turned around swiftly. The woman selling old books drew back—Helen realized her face must convey something of what she was feeling—and Helen smiled and shook her head. The woman backed off and paid attention to her other customers. Helen wandered off through the tables, past small kitchen appliances and dishes, to consider what just went through her mind. So she didn't see Maggie as an adult, mature person, capable of making her own choices and thinking for herself. That Maggie needed—what?—needed Helen to take care of her? Needed Helen to rescue her? Jesus, Maggie had had the guts to break away from her family, her former life, and embrace a life that was filled with uncertainty, few rewards and more than a few challenges. And it wasn't an ego trip for her, Helen was certain of that. Maggie would fight for her life and for the lives of those she ministered to. Hell, she'd beaten back the fucking FBI.

"So, have you seen anything you can't possibly live without?" Maggie picked up an old steam iron and held it out toward Helen. "I'm sure this worked like a charm thirty years ago."

Helen smiled and caught her breath. Maggie's face was almost back to normal—the puffy yellowish-purple marks were almost gone, and her green eyes were sparkling. They shone, like her smile, with a lightness Helen couldn't put down just to the sun or the warm air or the good turnout for the event. She hoped it wasn't because Maggie was happy to see her. Maybe showing up had been a bad idea after all.

"Guess I could use it as a doorstop. Or were you actually thinking I might iron my clothes?" Helen looked down at her jeans and T-shirt. "Surely you've seen enough of my wardrobe by now to know better."

Maggie set the iron down with a smile. "You look fine to me, Helen."

Helen felt her resolve begin to melt under that gaze. She cleared her throat and looked out across the busy parking lot.

"I'm surprised to see you today," she went on quietly as she walked away, leading them both to the church's side entrance. She sat down on the steps and motioned for Helen to join her.

Helen hesitated only for a moment, then sat beside her. The concrete was cold under her back and legs, cold and hard enough to bring back a sense of reality. She hugged her knees and took a deep breath. "I've been thinking a lot about you."

"Me, too. About you, I mean." Her voice was carefully neutral.

Helen risked a glance—her face was neutral, too. No encouragement, no discouragement. Hell, she wasn't making this any easier. Better stick to a safe topic. "The FBI leaving you alone for now?"

Maggie shrugged. "For the moment. I don't think they're finished. We got one story out on Berkeley public radio. I think that scared them off for a little bit. They don't need any more bad publicity." Maggie turned and smiled again. "We're holding our own, Helen. Besides, there's nothing for them to find. We haven't broken any laws, done anything wrong. We've just exercised our rights as stated in the Constitution."

Like that will stop them, Helen thought. But there was no mistaking the set of Maggie's jaw, the way she looked almost eager for this fight. Helen studied her shoes. This was no way to break anything off, not in this public place, not when she herself had just realized how arrogant she'd been about Maggie. "That's good to know, Maggie. I hope—"

"What? What do you hope?" Maggie leaned in closer and Helen could feel Maggie's breast pressing up against her side.

Helen looked up again and prepared to pull away. She froze as she stared out into the crowd, completely taken aback by the familiar figure moving from table to table. She held something in her hand—one of the brightly colored flyers announcing the garage sale. Whoever she was, she had to be living close by.

"Helen? What is it?"

Helen said nothing, just watched the tall thin woman in the cheap black raincoat move quietly through the knots of people laughing and talking in the makeshift aisles. Her long white hair, gleaming in the sunlight, was easy to track through the crowd. "Shhh, hang on a minute," she whispered to Maggie, who drew back and, clearly puzzled, followed Helen's gaze.

So far the woman didn't know she'd been spotted. She looked like some kind of ghost, her head bent as she browsed. She's looking for something, for some one thing, Helen decided. Just then, the woman stopped and took her hands out of her coat pockets. A small pool of quiet seemed to open up around her as she reached a pale hand to the glassware before her on the table. Alice's glasses and dishes, Helen realized. She remembered all too well the long dusty afternoon she and Maggie had spent packing them in newspapers for their journey from Alice's apartment to the church offices. The woman picked up a glass, set it down again, then ran her hands over the other things on the table. Helen got a good look at her face as she bent over the assorted odds and ends, the detritus of Alice's life. The woman ignored the pretty young man behind the table who smiled and tried to get her attention. She backed away from the table and looked up and away. Her eyes, large and pale and luminous, met Helen's. Helen was too far away to determine the color of her eyes but she easily identified the look of anger on the woman's face. Anger—followed by recognition.

"Shit, she spotted me." Helen began to unfold herself and stood up on the steps. She glanced down at Maggie. "I've got to talk to her, Maggie."

"Will you be back?" Maggie's voice held no inflection at all—it was as neutral as her expression. "I'd like to talk to you, too."

"Maybe not today, Maggie, but I will be back. I promise." For whatever her promise was worth these days.

Maggie stood up, stroked Helen's arm and walked away. Helen turned back to watch the white-haired woman dart through the crowd. With a muttered curse Helen took off after her. She reached the street just a few seconds behind her. Helen took a deep breath and broke into a trot. The woman was fast, she had to give her that—she was just a dark blur at the end of the alley. Helen bumped past a box of trash and emerged onto a brightly lit side street. A few yards to her right was Broadway, nearly deserted on a Saturday. And the BART station was a few yards beyond that, to her right.

"Oh, no, you don't. Not this time." Helen pushed her way past a man sitting on the corner, holding a cardboard sign asking for money, ignoring his cry of anger and surprise. Instead of heading down the BART stairs, into the underground station, the woman glanced behind her. As soon as she saw Helen she ran past the station and around the corner. The stretch of office buildings, some abandoned and condemned, was deserted today. Helen caught a glimpse of the black coat flipping in the breeze and disappearing inside one of the empty buildings. "Fuck." She sighed and gazed up at the ten—no, make that twelve—stories of the condemned building. She shook her head and went inside.

At first she couldn't see a damn thing. Dark and dim, with the stench of stagnant water and trash assaulting her, she knew the surroundings were dangerous. God only knew how long the building had stood empty, open to the elements. And God only knew who else was inside besides them. Helen heard scurrying off to her right but made herself stand still. Good decision—a moment later she saw two very large rats that would have given Cat a run for her money scuttle off into the darkness. Somewhere water dripped in large echoing plops. The wind blew through the broken windows, sending down cold air from high above. Helen stood her ground, waiting.

Gradually her eyes made out shapes in the murk. Piles of wood, rotted through and stinking, mingled with twisted metal pipes and loose cables swinging in the breeze. No, she realized, that's not a cable. The woman knew she'd been seen. She backed against the wall, slipped on the wet surface, then picked herself up and started running.

It was just enough for Helen to get a good start on her. She caught up with her just as she was trying to wedge herself through a narrow crevice made by two pieces of sheet metal. Helen grabbed her arm and pulled hard. She heard a high sharp cry—and the woman was on the ground at her feet. Helen paused to take a deep breath and tried to lift her up.

Big mistake. She had picked up a long sharp piece of broken glass. Ignoring the bleeding on her own hands, she swiped it at Helen's face, nearly nicking her eyes. Helen reared back as the woman struck again, this time going for Helen's throat.

"Fuck!" Helen shouted, her angry outburst echoing against the walls covered with mold. Enough. Enough. She pinned her down.

The rage surged up through the glacier of calm she'd been nurturing since—it must have been since she got back to California, having left Mississippi and prison and family behind. Having left herself behind. The Helen who had watched Victoria die at Helen's own hands, the Helen who had survived the years in prison, the Helen who had made the decision to try again in California. Nothing was left of her. She felt the emptiness, felt it flow into her and wash clean everything inside. Everything but rage.

Helen stared down at the woman. She straddled her, leaning in close, but somehow the woman looked very, very far away. Her white hair, thin and brittle, splayed out onto the oily concrete like a shimmering fan. She still clutched the glass, and her hand moved in little twitches. Helen lifted her hand and slapped the woman in the face as hard as she could. Then she slapped her again, then again.

The woman stared up, her mouth bloody and eyes wide with surprise and pain. The sliver of glass clattered on the floor beside them. The woman lay still beneath Helen's legs. Helen caught herself, hand upraised, ready to strike. With only a mild sense of shock at her behavior Helen rolled off of her and sat on the dirty floor. She noticed she was breathing hard. Shaking, too.

"Sit up. Goddammit, sit up!" The woman jerked upright, holding her face in her hands, slender fingers probing her bleeding mouth. Helen twisted around to see her face and felt a wave of nausea pass over her. She fought for control of her rebellious stomach and tried to think. She didn't know who the fuck she'd just been beating up. There were certainly a lot of people on the list now. The asshole who attacked Maggie and sliced up Cat. The Giorgi family and their friends at the FBI. Maybe even Alice. Maybe Maggie.

"Who are you?" The whisper bounced off the walls, sounded shivery and alien. Helen reached inside for the ice. Yes, it was still there, thank God. "What do you want?"

She'd be okay. Helen hadn't broken anything but her lip. "I want to talk to you."

"Did they send you? Are you here to kill me, too?"

"No." How to start? Helen stared down at her face. She knew what this woman's name was. Alice had mentioned it several times that night. What the hell was it? "No, I'm not here to kill you."

"The hell you aren't." It was still a whisper, but stronger this time. "I should have killed you, just like they did to Alice."

Suddenly Helen remembered. "Jenny. You're Jenny. Alice talked about you." Helen stood up and reached her hand down. "Come on with me, Jenny. We have a lot to talk about."

Chapter Eighteen

Jenny accepted the soda from Helen and winced as she held the cold metal can to her swollen lips. "Job will be back soon, you can't stay here long." She pronounced it *jobe*.

"Job?"

"Yeah, like in the Bible." Jenny squinted up at her. "You ever read the Bible?"

"Some." Helen flashed back to her childhood, years of Sunday school, church camps and all-day revivals. "Now and then. Like at the memorial service for Alice we both went to. Remember?"

"He call himself Job. I don't know if that's his real name and I don't give a flying fuck." Jenny popped open the can and took a sip, hissing as the cold Dr. Pepper hit her split lip. "Shit. There wasn't any beer left?"

"No, just what you have in your hand." Helen sat down on one of the overturned crates that served as furniture in Job's living room. They were upstairs in the abandoned warehouse. She glanced around, making mental apologies to her apartment for thinking it was ratty. A couple of fat roaches scuttled along the baseboard next to Jenny's bare feet. "How did you meet him?"

"What, now we get small talk after you beat me up?" Jenny sighed, tossed the empty soda can onto the heap of empties moldering under the window and leaned back on the mildewed cushion propped against the wall. "He picked me up outside a bar a couple of months ago. He'd just got a job, he said, he wanted to celebrate by buying a couple of beers for the best-looking woman he could find. Me, of course."

Helen shrugged. She stood up, too restless to stay still, and wandered over to the window. They were eight stories up. In the distance she could see the Embarcadero circling Jack London Square. Farther still there were boats of all kinds, moving in and out of the Port of Oakland. "It's a good hiding place, Jenny. I doubt your family would think to look for you here."

A snort from Jenny made her turn around. "Oh, they'll figure it out one of these days. Much as I've enjoyed Job's hospitality, I won't be able to stay a whole lot longer. They'll get to him, too." Her face crumpled and her thin fingers trembled over her face. "Jesus, I don't know what to do, where to go," she whispered.

Helen crouched beside her. How the hell was it that she was here trying to comfort a woman she'd nearly killed a few minutes ago? Her hesitance made Jenny look up. "Jenny, look, I'm sorry I—that I lost it down there, when I found you. It's just that when I saw that glass in your hand, I couldn't take it." Her attempt at saying sorry died on her lips when she saw the disgust on Jenny's face. It looked even worse with the cut lip and the bruised cheek, and for a moment Helen thought of Maggie.

"Spare me the guilty conscience. You're only here because I need to know. I guess you need some answers, too, don't you?"

"What do you need to know?"

Jenny closed her eyes and leaned against the wall. "Are the police going to take me back to my family? Make me go back to them? Alice won't be there to take care of me if I go back to the hospital." At the mention of her former lover's name tears squeezed out from Jenny's eyelids. "Fuck, I can hardly believe it. I thought she would live forever." She jerked forward suddenly, and Helen felt a hand grabbing her shirt, pulling her down. She was stronger than she looked. Right now those pale eyes were hot and glaring at Helen. "What did you tell the police about me? Please don't let them take me again. I'll kill myself first!"

"Calm down, Jenny. I haven't told the police anything because I don't know anything to tell." Christ, she meant it, Helen thought. Maybe this Jenny did belong in a hospital. She was practically frothing at the mouth, her little fists grinding into her lap. Instinctively Helen reached out to take her hands in an attempt to relax and calm her down.

Jenny reared back as if Helen had hit her. "Please let go of me."

Helen got away and went back to the crate. She didn't like that light in Jenny's pale eyes. She also didn't like the way Jenny had been so eager to slice her up, self-defense notwithstanding. Jenny sat still, arms folded tight across her chest, while Helen told the whole sorry story. About meeting Alice in the White Horse, and Alice's subsequent crying jag. About finding her body a week later.

"You found her?" Jenny asked, her eyes wide and horrified.

Better do some careful editing, Helen thought. "I don't think she suffered, Jenny. I think it was quick and painless." Fortunately Jenny didn't press her for details about the body. Besides, they had more important things to worry about. Like maybe the Giorgi family had hired someone to follow Helen—and presumably to find Jenny.

At the mention of Napa, Jenny stiffened as if a rod had been pushed up her ass. Her eyes flew open wide and she tucked her feet under her, folding herself up very small.

Jenny sobbed quietly on the sagging cushion, her drink forgotten. She covered her face with her hands and Helen watched tears trickle between her fingers. Helen decided Jenny wasn't ready to hear about Helen and Maggie being followed—she might completely go over the edge if she knew Helen suspected the Giorgi family of hiring someone to do their dirty work. Finally Jenny took in a couple of shivering deep breaths and let her hands fall into her lap.

"I've been going crazy, all this time. Thinking about what my family would do to me if they found me here. What they'd do to Job. What they've already done to Alice." More sobs, but quieter this time. "Just leaving her there to die, trying to call someone for help. All alone at the end, reaching for the phone. For help that wasn't there. Oh, God, why couldn't I have been with her?"

I shouldn't have told her anything, Helen thought, watching Jenny cry. She stood by helplessly until the weeping subsided.

Silence, for quite a stretch. What kind of answer could Helen give to that cry of pain? She listened to traffic for a while, then broke the quiet. "I'm sorry, Jenny. Sorry for you, for Alice."

Jenny barked out a laugh. "Janetta Giorgi. That's my real name. It was Alice that called me Jenny. Yeah, that was me in those pictures. Nice little family album, huh?" She pushed her hair out of her eyes and sighed. "There's this one they let me out of the hospital for, where I'm standing with my father and the governor. You see that one?" She snorted. "Should have seen all those nurses fussing over me, washing me up and getting ready to roll me out like a good little nutcase. They had me pretty drugged up, too. All I really remember is a lot of men talking and laughing. My mom was dead by then, there was just my dad and a whole bunch of aunts and uncles. One big happy fucking family." Suddenly she started to weep, big silent shuddering sobs.

Helen waited for them to subside, chewing over her own thoughts. "The hospital in Napa. Where Alice worked."

"Why the fuck do you think Alice worked there?" Jenny asked in a quavery voice. "She wanted to get me out."

"She helped you escape, you mean."

Jenny smiled, her eyes glazed over in reverie. "Good old Alice. She was in love with me, I know she was. God, those pictures—she'd keep pulling them out, talking about our 'good times.' Jesus, good times." She looked squarely at Helen, as if daring her to pass judgment.

"It was all a cover, then? Alice was your ticket to freedom." All the protests, the demonstrations, the march on Sacramento with Cesar Chavez—a way out of whatever plans the Giorgi family and its millions had for Jenny. "So, they—they, what? Locked you up because you were gay?"

"What? Oh, Jesus, no. You aren't too quick on the uptake, are you? No, they locked me up to get at my money." Jenny squirmed on the cushions and finally gave up on trying to find a comfortable position. "My family doesn't care who I fuck, as long as they could get their hands on what my mother left me." Her face crumpled again. "I don't think Alice ever knew how much I was worth. Still am, actually. If they could get me committed, my loving father could have it all. I couldn't risk Alice being hurt because of me. And if they were willing to put me into a hospital and keep me drugged, God knows what they'd do to Alice for helping me."

Helen looked out the window again. It was cold and dark, with steel-gray clouds building over the bay. More rain, more cold winds coming in. "So as long as they can't find you—"

"There's nothing they can do. My mother left it to me and it's mine." Jenny had control of herself now. She got up and came to sit near Helen. Helen, remembering the strength in those thin arms, the hate in her colorless eyes, moved back instinctively. "He'll never get it, not while I'm alive."

Not the best choice of words, Helen thought. She went over to the window. Nothing down there, just a bunch of trash blowing in the wind.

"You think we were followed here, don't you?" Jenny breathed at her shoulder.

Helen shrugged, hoped her face looked calm. "I doubt it. Whoever this guy is, I haven't seen him in a while. But it's a safe bet he'll keep looking." The two of them looked at each other, both of them understanding exactly what Helen was saying. If this guy hadn't hesitated to kill Alice, there was no telling what he'd do.

Jenny's face went blank again. "I should get out of here, before they get to Job, too." She stood thoughtfully in the middle of the room, staring down at the floor. “He’s been nice to me. God-awful in the sack, but not a bad guy.”

Helen watched her as she stood there lost in thought. Eerie, how the woman could vacillate between violent emotion and stillness in the space of a second. Was that a survival trick from her institutionalized days, or a sign of instability? Helen was certainly no judge of mental stability, but it suddenly occurred to her that she had only Jenny’s word for it that she’d been put away out of spite and greed. The only other thing supporting her story was the fact that Alice was dead and she and Maggie had been attacked—Cat, too. It didn’t necessarily add up to the truth.

“I need to go.” Helen grabbed her jacket and stood awkwardly by the door. She sure didn’t want to hang around and run the risk of meeting Job, or the guy sent by the Giorgis, but she felt she had to say something. “I’m sorry about what I did to you. In that building. I don’t usually come unglued like that.”

But Jenny was standing close to her now, her hand on the door keeping it shut. “Really? I’d say coming unglued was one of the things you did best. I’d say you probably don’t do it as much as you’d like to.”

“Thanks for telling me what you did. I have to go.” Helen’s hand shook on the doorknob. She wasn’t sure what she was feeling—guilt, confusion, anger. Nothing made much sense beyond her need to leave.

“How’s Mickey? Do you know what happened to her?”

Mickey. Another White Horse habitue, perhaps? Someone from the hospital? “I don’t know Mickey.”

“Shit, they probably put her to sleep. Or she just ran away.”

Cat. At least the creature had a name. “Alice’s cat. Mickey is fine. She’s with me now.”

Jenny let her hand fall from the door. “I won’t be here if you come back.”

“I know.” Helen took off, almost at a run, clattering down the stairs and into her car. Rain couldn’t be far behind the cold wind blowing up from the water through the downtown streets. She made herself sit still in her car, watching for a reappearance of her one-man surveillance team. Nothing.

When she got home Mickey was fine, yowling at the rattling Helen made opening the door with its series of new expensive locks. Mickey proceeded to weave around her legs until Helen put cat food in her bowl.

"I don't quite know what to do here, Mickey," Helen said as she stroked the cat's back. Mickey looked up, purring, from her dinner, batted her big green eyes, then finished off the food. "Should I keep after this? Should I just forget about it?" Her hands moved down Mickey's flank as the cat sat on her haunches and began to groom, running a paw over her whiskers.

Helen touched the edge of the stitches that stretched across Mickey's belly. The cat tensed for just a moment, then resumed cleaning herself. Helen sat on the floor and watched her finish her ablutions. Just because she had found Jenny and had a few more pieces to the puzzle didn't mean that the anonymous thug wouldn't be back. Nor did it mean that she wasn't still a suspect, with Manny and Harmon waiting in the wings for just the right moment.

"Wish you'd do something besides purr," Helen said as she reached for Mickey again. The cat rubbed her head up against Helen's hand. Amazing how a brush with death had transformed her from a feral ball of smelly fur to a placid purring creature that couldn't get enough of Helen. "Like get a job, or buy me a house—"

Buy a house. Own property. Jenny had claimed to be sitting on top of millions of dollars' worth of real estate. Said she was worth a lot more dead than alive. Millions coveted by the Giorgi family, despite their ostentatious wealth and power. And how the hell could Helen know if any of it was true?

She sat cross-legged on the floor, her back against the refrigerator. Mickey slunk off into the living room when Helen stopped petting her. "Napa," Helen said out loud. Some of this had to be on public record, surely. At least property ownership, even if she'd never get a look at a bank account.

For the moment, though, she felt finished. Deflated. Empty. Just lying flat on the floor of her apartment, down next to the dust piles, was all she could manage for now. The floor felt good against her back. It felt real. Unlike the last few hours. Somehow finding Jenny had taken all the air out of everything. The sense of urgency had drained away, leaving only a blank hole. Everything fit—so why was she feeling like this? It wasn't as if she could take any of this to Hanson. Helen needed to make sure her own ass was covered, but there really wasn't anything she could do for Jenny. Still, if there was a chance to clear her name with the police she should follow it up. Maybe check some of this out in Napa. But what would that do to Jenny's safety?

Helen realized she was spinning her wheels to keep from thinking about her own behavior this afternoon. The rage that had flared up through what she called her glacier inside. Something about the whole mess was cracking her self-control. She remembered seeing herself in Alice's mirror—what she'd seen then was an aging, lonely dyke. Today she'd seen someone else, someone capable of murderous fury. Which was worse?

She'd just picked herself up off the floor when the phone rang. It was Maggie. After saying hello, Helen asked, "How are you feeling?"

"Much better." She was being deliberately light and cheerful, Helen realized, trying to stay neutral and not offend. "Just wondered how you are tonight."

"Doing all right. How'd the garage sale go?"

"Well, not too bad. We got enough for a decent paint job on the office. I don't know when we'll get another computer, though."

"Maybe I can find one lying around at the insurance company Brenda sent me to." An awkward silence ensued. "You doing okay? Not hurting, or anything?" Helen finally asked.

"Still a bit sore. Nothing serious. I was just thinking—well, I know it's kind of late notice, but—are you busy tonight? Thing is, we have all these leftovers, and people brought stuff by when they heard I was hurt."

"I can imagine." Shit, Helen thought, here I go again. But the pleasure, the warmth easing into her back felt so good she couldn't resist. Especially after the ugly scene she'd enacted earlier today. Somehow she had to banish that Helen, the one ready to kill Jenny, from her thoughts. Somehow she had to convince herself that some level of happiness was possible. Even for her. "From my own churchgoing days. The whole covered-dish thing, right?"

"You guessed it." Maggie's chuckle sounded relieved and excited. "Tater Tots casserole."

"Jell-O Salad, the green kind with sliced carrots in it."

"Canned sweet potatoes with those burnt marshmallows on top."

"Macaroni things with that orange glow-in-the-dark cheese."

"We have just described the regular diet of a pastor. It's amazing I'm still alive."

Yes, amazing. Helen felt herself smiling. What the hell? Who knew where she'd be after tonight? "Why not," she heard herself say aloud.

"Why not?" Maggie murmured.

Helen suddenly wanted—no, needed—to look at those green eyes again, to feel her golden hair, to touch her face. "I can't leave you alone to face all of that. I'll be right over." Napa can wait, she thought as she grabbed her keys and headed out.

Chapter Nineteen

Helen stood up and stretched. She looked outside the window of the Napa café where she and Maggie had shared a cup of coffee before going on to the hospital. She still felt a little dazed from the previous weekend. In one Saturday she'd gone from slapping Jenny around to making love to Maggie, not forgetting the garage sale of course. Then she, Helen Black, had actually sat through a church service the following morning. She'd been amazed to find herself enjoying it—and enjoying even more the sight of how much the church members loved Maggie.

Helen had no idea how long she'd been sitting there, over a cup of coffee grown cold, a half-eaten sandwich. It was fully dark out. Helen noted with amazement the time on the wall clock—past ten. A man had just locked the door and began switching off lights. The noise was what had roused her. Time to head for home.

"Anything else?" The waitress, the same one who'd been there when Maggie sat with her, looked out the window with Helen as she left the check on the table. "Bet we got rain coming again."

"Again. Sorry, I didn't realize how late it had gotten." Helen left money on the table and picked up her notes. She told herself again that it had been worth it, to take off this Monday from her new temp job with the plea of a dentist appointment, to get the information on Janetta Giorgi. She darted to her car as the rain started, sat at the wheel and thought about what she'd found out. Janetta—Jenny—hadn't been lying. At least certain kinds of property records were available to the public. And Jenny, if anything, had underestimated her own value, certainly in monetary terms. It wasn't just land. She was heir to commercial properties, apartment buildings, acres and acres of land. So that much at least was true. The vineyards, too. And that was just what Helen had found out so far by looking through public records in Napa this afternoon.

What about the rest? Helen leaned back against the seat and sighed as wind whipped raindrops across her windshield in fat spatters. It was absolutely up for grabs. No way to really know, since the Giorgi Vineyards were privately held. That limited how much access Helen had to information. And how the hell was Helen supposed to dig anything else up? Maybe Jan?

Whoa. Helen gripped the steering wheel, turned the key in the ignition. She shouldn't even be doing this much. She needed to leave it all alone, go back home, hope Brenda hadn't canned her for taking the day off and stay the hell away from all of this. So Jenny had title to a lot of very valuable property. So what? A runaway from a mental hospital was claiming her family was out to kill her. So what? Helen shuddered at the thought of Manny and Jordan looking over her shoulder, watching what she was doing.

And she turned the key in the ignition again—pumped the gas pedal again. Shit. Once again this rusting bucket of nuts and bolts had decided to go belly up. Helen hated to think of calling Maggie yet again to bail her out especially at this hour of the night. Maybe Jan? If she gave her the interview, Jan would probably come zipping up in her little sports car and get her home safely. But what about the car? She couldn't afford a motel stay in Napa.

With a heavy sigh Helen went back to the café and knocked on the door. The waitress lifted the blind and saw her, shouted something over her shoulder. "Come on in and use the phone," she said. "Just make it fast," she added in a whisper. "Joe wants out of here."

"Thanks so much." She dug through her backpack and came up with the number Jan had left her. But neither Jan nor Maggie were answering the numbers she had. Was Maggie out on some kind of ministerial call tonight? She couldn't remember if Maggie had mentioned it. Helen left messages, aware of the waitress watching her.

"You need a jump?" she called out from behind the cash register.

A few more minutes spent fixing cables, and the car revved into life. "Thanks," Helen shouted over the noise. "What's your name?"

"Barbara. You gonna be okay?" Barbara came around the car and peered in, clearly doubtful about the car's ability to make it down the block. "You got anybody you need to be called?"

Helen smiled. "I should be okay now. Thanks a lot, Barbara." To her immense relief the car kept going, sounding strong. She made the turn out of the parking lot and headed toward the highway. In the cold and rain the streets were deserted. It was already nearly eleven. The frontage road leading up to the highway was the same—a lone car passing her by now and then as she neared the on-ramp toward San Francisco. She got as far as the turn-off to the ramp when it died with a final shuddering clunk. "Fuck!" she screamed, slamming her hands painfully on the steering wheel. With a last spurt of movement the car shifted onto the shoulder. Helen looked up and down the stretch of road. A couple of cars whizzed by, splashing mud and gravel and rain against her car door. She grimaced as she switched on her blinkers. Hopefully the police would come by—highway patrol—or a friendly motorist with a cell phone.

A black car slowed as it approached, pulling off the main road onto the shoulder. Helen sighed with relief. Pulling her jacket up over her head, she opened the door. The wind had picked up and she struggled to slip out and hurry as fast as slippery gravel would allow toward the late-model Ford. She automatically noted its opaque windows, the California plates.

"Thanks for stopping," she called out, shivering against the wind. "Maybe you could just call the highway patrol for me, or do you have—"

The words froze on her lips as the window rolled down and a heavy, pale smiling face looked out at her. She'd recognize that Yankees cap anywhere. The last time she'd seen him he'd been standing in her apartment, pointing a gun at her. The same gun he was pointing at her now, in fact. Helen stood still, barely feeling the rain on her back. Would he be stupid enough to shoot her here in the middle of the highway? Then again, how many cars had Helen seen driving by in the past few minutes. None, except for his. Besides it was pitch black out here, no lights, no moon or stars to show anyone what was going on. She was alone.

"Get in. Now." When Helen didn't move his grin faded into a sneer. "You want to die out here on the road? Get the fuck in the car." Helen heard the dull snick of the safety released from the gun. She walked slowly around the front of the car, slipping in the mud and gravel. The rain began to drive hard, pelting against her back with painful intensity. She wouldn't get five feet from him without him taking a shot, even though it would be stupid for him to try to kill here right here. But brains didn't seem to be in large supply for him. She wouldn't put it past him.

As she reached the passenger side of the car an eighteen-wheeler made the turn onto the ramp. Its horn blatted out a warning as it neared the car. Helen ducked down during the moment of distraction.

"Fuck it!" she heard him cry out from inside the car.

Helen kept crouched down. Her jacket snagged on the shrubbery lining the road and she wiggled out of it to make her way more easily. She forced her way through the tangled foliage, hissing at the scratches made on her bare arms. Behind her she heard a car door slam, heavy footsteps running and slipping on rocks and mud.

Shit, she didn't have much time. Thankful for the noise made by the wind and the occasional passing car a few yards away, up on the highway, she fought her way through the brambles and jerked free into a patch of clear land. Well, almost clear. She slithered around in an assortment of trash—Styrofoam and paper and empty plastic cups—tossed out from cars speeding by toward San Francisco. Helen winced as her foot twisted under her. She'd stepped deep into God knows what discarded fast-food frenzy left to rot by the roadside. This could only slow her down. And damn it, she could already feel her ankle swelling. She tried to put her weight on the foot and almost yelled out with the pain. With a grunt she dragged herself across the dark field, willing herself to ignore the searing pain that shot up through her leg.

Too late. He had her before she got to the next set of shrubs. She couldn't stifle a cry as he wrenched her backwards in his grip, putting pressure on her twisted ankle. His hands slipped as Helen struggled against him, but he got a better grasp and yanked her closer. "Fucking bitch, I oughta shoot you right here!" He pulled her upright, close to his body. Helen's face was a few inches from his own. He'd lost his baseball cap somewhere. She could smell his stale cigarette breath as he let go of her and slapped her, hard. Then slapped her again.

As he was gearing up for another blow Helen lifted her injured foot and with a final burst of energy shoved her knee into his crotch, leaning hard against him and careful to put her weight on her good leg. In the dull light she couldn't see his face clearly but she could hear his sharp intake of breath as he staggered backwards. She fell with him, her weight pressing on him. They landed with a crash onto—what the hell was it? Something long and hard and with a sharp edge. She felt it slice into her palm with a clean clear pain. She pulled her hand out of the muck. It was some kind of broken length of metal. He was still trying to catch his breath when she reared back and placed the sharp edge against his throat. She felt him grow still beneath her.

"Drop the gun, asshole. I said drop it!" She listened for it, heard the clunk of the gun to her left. She shifted the piece of metal to her right hand and found the gun, its safety still off. She tossed the metal away and kept the gun resting between his eyes. "I'm going to get up now. I'll tell you when you can move. If I pick up on so much as a twist your brains are going to get mixed in with all this shit here. Do you understand me?"

She took his silence for compliance and took her time standing up, making sure she was steady on her feet. Her ankle still hurt like hell but she could move. With the gun in her hand, loaded and ready to go, she could face the pain.

"Sit up. Do it."

He pushed himself up in the darkness. Helen caught a glimpse of his white shirt, his pale white face. The rain had stopped and she could actually hear him swallow. Underneath the stench of rotted food Helen smelled something foul and familiar. He'd wet himself, or shit himself, or both.

"Jesus," she whispered. She'd have to sit with that all the way into the police station? As if some kind of answer were waiting for her in the darkness Helen took her gaze off him for a moment and glanced to the highway. It loomed up over a rise just a few yards to her right. Nothing had passed by for quite a while, but getting out of here alive depended on either getting up there or taking over his car and—

And what? Driving into the police station with this poor bastard, screaming about how he'd threatened her? God knew if he was employed by the Giorgi family he'd be covered. They wouldn't take the risk. He'd have a lawyer get him out safely before anyone could say a word. And what the hell would they make of her? Coming in with some crazy story about the Giorgis, a highly respected family with important connections. Face it, she told herself, that's all you are. Crazy. Manny and his pals would love for you to show up like this, weapon in hand, yelling like a psycho with your fucking conspiracy theories.

She could take the gun, leave him there. That might work. But of course he'd find his way back to safety and then it was still a done deal that she'd get hauled in. It was his word against hers that she'd been attacked by him in her own apartment. The last thing she wanted, with her record, was to get tangled up with cops. No witnesses to that, and she hadn't gone to the police with the information. Maggie hadn't seen her attacker, either. How were they going to regard it all, especially since she'd said nothing to them when Maggie was in the hospital? She could still see Jordan's face as he took in the bruises and took in the fact that she wasn't going to talk about them.

The thoughts raced through her mind as she stood staring down at him. She didn't even know the guy's name. "Who are you?" She aimed the gun at his crotch. "Your name. Now."

"Jimmy, it's Jimmy," he yelled out. "Just—just put the gun down, okay? I'll tell you whatever you want."

"Jimmy. Your last name Giorgi?"

"What? Hell, no, I'm not family. I'm the hired help."

"Hired to do what, Jimmy?" She knelt down in the mud and trash, shoving her hair out of her eyes with a trembling hand. That half-sandwich was a long time ago. She didn't know how much longer she could keep it up. "To kill Alice, then kill me?"

"Crazy bitch," he muttered. She didn't catch the rest of it.

"What did you say?" She prodded him with the gun and he jerked away with a high-pitched yelp. "Speak up, Jimmy, I might not leave you out here in the rain."

"I said I didn't kill anybody! It wasn't me!" he yelled, his voice cracking as if he was about to cry. "Fuck, I didn't do it!"

"You didn't go after Maggie? Or my cat?"

He met that with silence. Finally she heard him sniveling. "Look, okay, I know I shouldn't have said all that. I know it. But I swear to you, all I did was follow you around."

"And break into my apartment and threaten me." She poked

him again with the gun. "And beat up Maggie and cut an animal open. Yeah, you're as pure as the driven snow."

"I didn't hurt no fucking cat. And I didn't do anything to that preacher, I swear! I got over there to talk to her—"

"Talk to her." Helen snorted. "Right, you talked to her with your fists. Got the Giorgis to call the FBI on her. You had a really good talk, I guess."

"What the fuck—" He leaned up on his arms. Helen could see him trembling with fear as his face loomed up out of the darkness. "I didn't do a fucking thing to your girlfriend! It wasn't me!"

This was wasting time. Helen couldn't take the cold, or the pain in her ankle, much longer. She watched Jimmy's eyes as she stood up carefully, trying not to wince as a new wave of pain moved up through her leg. "Get up, Jimmy. Get the fuck up, I said."

"Okay, okay. Jesus." He struggled for a few moments with the debris, then heaved himself to a standing position, wiping mud from his face and hands. "Ah, shit!"

"What now?"

"I think I cut myself on something. Shit!" He leaned over, face crumpling in pain. Helen watched, took a step back. Jimmy held his side and toppled down. "Give me a minute, okay?"

She tried not to look at the stain spread across his ass from when his bowels gave way, tried to keep focused on his hands. A burst of rain blew across her face and she blinked hard, making sure both hands were on the gun. A moment was all it took for Jimmy to grab a heavy metal pipe from the debris and bring it swinging across her twisted ankle.

Helen went down with a shout of pain, still holding the gun. With her good leg she kicked hard and high, connecting with Jimmy's face. He yelled out something, dropped the metal and put both hands to his face. "You broke my nose, you fucking bitch!" he hollered. "Jesus!"

She staggered to her feet. "Yeah, you keep praying. Come on, Jimmy, we're going. Now."

"Is that right? Where you gonna take me, huh? They already

think you killed that other cunt." Pain and desperation had apparently done its work with Jimmy. He stood there, angry and unafraid, his face swollen and bloody. "Ah, fuck, that hurts!" He wiped blood from his face. "Who'd believe you, bitch? The cops? Your pretty little preacher friend?"

Helen gritted her teeth. She didn't feel anything—no pain, no cold, no anger or fear. All she could feel was the gun in her hands. Like she was standing in a block of ice, so calm and cool and familiar that it felt like home.

Jimmy took her silence and stillness as an advantage. He staggered across the garbage closer to her. "You try to tell the cops I did anything, you show up with me all beat up, you with a gun in your hand—you think they'll do anything to me? They'll lock you up faster than you can say dyke, you stupid bitch." His hands moved—he was holding something. "I'm gonna enjoy watching that happen. I'm sick of watching you and all the other old dykes. Goddamn fucking cunts. All I been doing is watching. Now it's my turn to get something done."

Helen shrugged out of her frozen stance just enough to see he'd gone for the metal pipe again. She didn't fire until he lifted it up for another swing. Jimmy let his arm drop, still holding the pipe. He stared down at the blood spreading across his chest with astonishment. Staggering back he tried to talk but came up only with gurgles and sputters.

Helen fired again. A second dark stain seeped across his belly and she heard him grunt out a heavy wet sigh. His legs twitched, rustling against the heap of trash he'd fallen across. With slow strides Helen walked across the trash, back through the bushes, toward Jimmy's car. Another downpour began and cold rain hit her face.

A few feet away she heard a strange sound—something like a groan—almost drowned out by the rain.

She stopped, sat in the mud in the darkness, the gun in her lap, waiting for him to die.

Chapter Twenty

The sun shone with a hard brilliant light. It glimmered on the rainwater still pooled on the cement walks of the garden. Helen smoked, turning her face up to the light. In the three weeks since her overnight stay in the hospital she'd taken up cigarettes on a regular basis again. Maybe it was just the hospital rules about smoking that had made her want to go into challenge mode—she'd be damned if anyone told her what to do. Or not to do.

One good long drag left. She breathed in deep and looked around. This was the first time she'd seen the church's rock garden. It was tucked into a narrow plot of land behind the church. Helen didn't know the different ivies and ferns that draped gracefully over the stones but they appeared to be thriving. It was almost April. Maybe some of these plants would have flowers soon. A stone archway leading from the street marked the entrance. At the far end was another stone structure, something etched on a large block between two pillars. Helen ground the butt under her heel and walked along the garden's length to take a look.

A labyrinth, she saw, circles and lines in an intricate pattern. She moved in closer, following the lines with her eyes until she got lost in its complexity. She began to trace a path along the lines, savoring the feel of cool hard grit beneath her fingers. She'd reached the center when she heard heavy footsteps behind her.

"You didn't want to stay inside for the service?"

Helen shrugged and started to trace the slow meandering pathway out. "That's the early service going on now. The second one starts in a couple of hours." She turned around to face the intruder in the garden. "I'll probably sit in on that one. Maggie's sermons tend to get better the second time around, I've noticed."

"Mind if I sit down?" He didn't wait for an answer, easing his bulk onto a stone bench as he spoke. ""My knees aren't what they used to be."

"That's what happens when you get old." Helen finished tracing the circuit of the labyrinth's paths and moved to sit on a bench facing him. "Me, I think it'll be my hearing that goes first."

"Might be a blessing." Dominic Giorgi took a pack of cigarettes from his expensively tailored jacket pocket and offered her one.

Helen hesitated, then took one. His were bound to be a lot better than anything she could afford. As he dug in another pocket for his lighter she studied his fat puffy features. Yes, maybe a faint likeness to Jenny, around the eyes and mouth. His eyes were wide-set like his daughter's, but so hidden in folds of flesh that she wasn't sure what color they were. The hand that held out the lighter shook slightly, sunlight glinting off the thick gold rings with each tremble. He leaned back as she savored the taste, the feel of the cigarette, settling in with a heavy sigh. Giorgi's girth strained at the buttons of his jacket. He settled his hands on his knees—resting them or hiding the tremor? Helen regarded him through the smoke. He looked like a statue of Buddha, bald and heavy and solemn. Appropriate for the garden, perhaps.

He coughed, looking down and away from her steady gaze. "Shall we come to the point, Ms. Black?"

"What point would that be, Mr. Giorgi?" Mighty civilized of

us, Helen thought. She itched to look around and see if he'd brought company with him—another Jimmy, maybe—but she'd be damned if she showed him anything but boredom. "You're the one who came to see me. I'm just going to church today."

To her surprise a rumbling noise burbled out of him. He was laughing. "I understand you have a—connection, shall we say—to the minister here."

"Magdalen Evans. The woman you had beat up. The same woman you made sure got investigated by the FBI. Yeah, we have a connection. And it's none of your business." So much for being bored. She casually dropped the half-smoked cigarette onto the pavement and ground it beneath her heel.

"Relax, Helen—may I call you Helen? I feel we know each other now." He pulled out a silk handkerchief and wiped his brow. She noticed he was sweating in rivers, despite the cool air, and his skin was as pale and pasty as dough. She took a moment while he got his breath to glance behind her. No one else was there, just the two of them sitting in this lovely garden having a quiet conversation. He coughed, a short hard bark, into the handkerchief and started to breathe again. "Sorry, Helen. The doctors keep telling me I'll be fine."

No, you won't. "That's nice. What are you doing here?"

"I came to ask about Janetta. If you would tell me where she is." He tucked the handkerchief away and Helen saw a smile fold over his swollen face. "I could certainly make it worth your while."

"And if I don't tell you, there will be another visit from someone like Jimmy, right?"

"Oh, that—" He grimaced and gave a dismissive wave. "I certainly never asked Jimmy to do anything to anyone. All he was supposed to do was observe and report back to me." Giorgi looked at her expectantly, grimaced again when she didn't respond. "You can't seriously believe a man in my position would employ killers? Or be in cahoots with the FBI over something as insignificant as this little enterprise?" He glanced around the garden, his gaze resting at last on the peeling walls of the chapel. "Reverend Evans is probably a very nice person, but I can't imagine her efforts here will ever come to anything. I'm sure she will need a little help, getting all those wonderful social programs off the ground."

"First you want to buy me, now to buy yourself a church." Helen smiled and shook her head. "Jenny was right, that's all you care about."

She hid her alarm as his face went from white to red. "I assure you," he said in a carefully controlled voice, "I have my daughter's best interests at heart. You don't understand."

"Actually, I think I do." Helen got up. A long rectangular box, built low to the ground, held three stones and a bamboo rake. Helen picked up the rake and began to swirl the forks through the sand. "And despite what you may think, I have no idea where your daughter is right now."

"You were seen going into that abandoned building last week, after you got out of the hospital. You have been looking for her." She moved around the sand tray so she could see his face. It had gone back to pasty white and his breathing was easier. "Trust me, Helen. I must find her."

Helen shook her head and rested the rake against a wall. She stared down at the pattern she'd made. "She's not there now. She's long gone. I have no idea where she's gone. So it doesn't matter how many thugs you hire to follow me. I can't help you."

He sighed and stared at the ground. "The man, Job—we found him on the street yesterday. He doesn't know what happened to her, either."

"Too bad."

Another painful laugh. "Is that really what you think? Too bad? Don't bullshit me, Helen. I've been fed lies by better than you. You're glad she got away."

"No, I'm not." She picked up the rake again, smoothed out the lines and circles she'd just drawn. "If I knew where she was I'd tell you."

"Why?" All the harsh anger had drained from his voice. She

glanced up to find him staring at her curiously. "After all she told you about me—about the Giorgi family—why would you want me to find her?"

"Because I know she lied to me." There—a long clean line in the sand, from stone to stone to stone. Precise and straight, no faltering or fumbling. Helen lifted the rake and met Giorgi's stare directly. "She probably should be locked up someplace safe, where she can get some real help. Where she won't be allowed to hurt anyone else."

Again the odd grimace that might be a smile. "You know, then."

"That she killed Alice? Yes. Or at least that she watched her die, wouldn't call for help." Helen rested the rake on the wall and went back to the bench. Giorgi's face was blank now, resembling the carved Buddha. "I wouldn't hesitate to hand her over to you."

"Even though you think I care only for money?"

"Doesn't matter. You'd keep her someplace safe to protect the Giorgi name." Helen heard sounds coming from the chapel. The service would be over soon, and she'd have to go inside. Maggie would expect it. "Do you have another cigarette? I could use it before church starts up again."

"By all means. Although of course the doctors blame these"—he gestured with the pack of cigarettes—"for my condition. Tell me how you knew."

Helen took a couple of drags before answering. "She talked about the phone, lying next to Alice's head. About Alice trying to call for help during her final moments. Jenny—sorry, Janetta—wouldn't have known that unless she'd been there. During Alice's final moments."

"Jimmy and I went to see Alice, you know?"

"Yeah, I found that out."

He closed his eyes again. "The bartender, I suppose? We have been foolish. Careless." The massive head shook slowly. "I was desperate to find her, you see. When we located Alice—well, I thought I could get her to tell me."

“But she wouldn’t. Not for any price.”

“No. Do you understand that, Helen? Not having a price? I must say, in my experience everyone can be bought and sold.”

“You should broaden your horizons, then.” Her gaze flickered to the chapel. Giorgi caught the movement. “Yeah, like Maggie, inside. She can’t be bought.”

“Well, possibly. Perhaps her price just hasn’t been named yet.”

Helen’s blood ran cold. Giorgi continued to sit, still and silent as one of the rocks in the garden. “I think you and your family and the hired help have done more than enough to Maggie. Back off her.”

“Or what? You’ll see I meet the same end as Jimmy?” A chuckle rumbled in his chest, shaking his shoulders.

Helen smiled through the smoke. She planned to finish this cigarette. “I have no idea what you’re talking about.”

“Oh, come now! You were in Napa that day, your car was towed from the highway less than a mile from where his body was found.”

Damn, these were good cigarettes. Helen let the butt fall to the ground with a sigh of regret. Too bad they were out of her price range. “The police already talked to me. They can’t prove a damn thing. Jimmy O’Hara had a record as long as that rake. God knows what finally caught up with him that night.”

“I think it was you that caught up with him.” He leaned forward. Helen could smell his aftershave, the scent of peppermints, some other odd smell underneath it all. What the hell was that? Familiar but she couldn’t identify it. “I think you shot him and left him to die. No different from Janetta, watching that old woman die.”

“Me? I was out on the road, looking for help. It’s amazing, Mr. Giorgi, but there still are helpful people out there. Like the old couple, the Masons, who gave me a lift back to Napa when they saw me sitting in a car that wouldn’t start.”

“And the police bought it?” He shook his head. “I find that hard to believe. You have a record, too. A bad one. Worse than Jimmy’s ever was.”

"Depends how you define 'bad,' I guess. In any event, there was nothing they could say or do. Your employee was found dead, the weapon beside him, and the rain fucked up the scene. I'd be more worried about the police connecting Jimmy to you, frankly. Especially since Jimmy probably left his prints all over Alice's apartment that first little visit the two of you made."

"I may have been foolish to hire Jimmy, but do you really think I'd leave any trace of his working for me? You're smarter than that, Helen." With a sigh he stood up. "Well, whoever it was that got rid of Jimmy O'Hara did everyone a big favor. I should never have taken him on in the first place. A real asshole. And stupid, too."

He moved slowly toward the archway, stiff jerky motions as if his body hurt. Helen got a good look at his profile. From that angle, his puffy face looked gray and drawn, the eyes full of pain. One ringed hand strayed briefly to his side, holding in the hurt. Helen knew suddenly what the smell was, that odd scent beneath the cologne and mint. She wondered what his doctors had really told him. If maybe, underneath the money and power, Giorgi wanted to see his daughter one more time.

He turned at the archway, facing her again, his composure back. "A word of advice, Helen."

"What's that?"

"I can tell—I can feel it, really—that you've crossed some kind of boundary in all this. You've left behind a line you had clearly marked for yourself." He rested a hand on the archway and took a deep breath. Helen suppressed the urge to get up and help him. Let the bastard stand there and sweat it, she thought, aware that her inner response was a cover for worry. No, for fear.

But he was still talking. "Take it from someone who knows, Helen. From someone who's crossed more lines in his life than you'll ever know about." He pushed himself away from the stone wall and stared hard at her. "Once you cross one line you're more ready to cross the next one. Then one day there are no more lines left and you're alone with your own life. With everything you've done and said that you swore like hell you'd never do or say. And you'll have experienced them all."

She could barely see his face in the shadows but she thought he smiled as he spoke. "And then what?" she asked, hoping her voice came across as angry and defiant.

"Why, then, Helen, all you'll have left is that knowledge. In fact, nothing else may seem real. Tell me, does your new lover"—he jerked his head back toward the church—"know what you've done? What lines you've crossed?" The chuckle came back when she stayed silent. "I thought as much. Then you've already started."

She watched him walk off, a big black bulk moving out into the sunshine on the street. A few minutes later she saw a black car with opaque windows crawl toward Broadway.

Helen was sitting on a bench staring at the labyrinth carving when Maggie, robed and smiling, came out to the garden. "Don't you want some coffee? There's doughnuts and cookies at the welcome table. Someone brought in cake, too." She held out her hand, offering Helen a piece of chocolate cake. "Tastes homemade."

"No, thanks. Jan should be here any minute."

Maggie stood next to the bench, looking out over the garden. "You sure you want to do an interview here? It's not very private. Anyone could walk in. Like I just did."

"I know. No, this is fine." Helen stared absently down the narrow pathway, toward the pillars at the end of the garden, taking in the rock-lined path and the way the sun played on the damp grass. "It feels good here. Safe."

"Do you know where she's going to send the story?" Maggie's face was neutral, merely curious, as she licked chocolate from her fingers.

"Not yet. Jan thinks it could make her career, something like this. One of the big glossies might want it. This was just the first part of a series." And the contract Helen had made her sign ensured Helen would get a nice chunk of change out of the deal—if and when such a deal took place.

"All names changed to protect the innocent, I hope."

The innocent. Who were they, exactly?

"There won't be much left if we don't get in there."

Helen smiled, her gaze fixed on the labyrinth. "I'll join you in a minute. Have you ever walked a labyrinth, Maggie? The whole thing, I mean."

Maggie sat down next to her. Helen heard the rustle of her long robe. Today she wore a length of rainbow-striped fabric over a green surplice. Was that the right word, surplice? Maybe she'd get it right one day. "There's one just like this in San Francisco. At Grace Cathedral. It's copied from an ancient labyrinth at Chartres." Maggie placed a hand lightly on Helen's back. "Why? Do you want to go sometime? It's quite an experience."

Helen leaned into Maggie. She felt good. Solid. Real. Enduring. As enduring as the stone in this garden? "Maybe one day. Right now I have more than enough mazes in my life."

"No, not a maze. Mazes are meant to be lost in, Helen. Look, let me show you." Maggie got up, leading her by the hand to the plinth where the labyrinth was carved. Her fingers followed the same path Helen had just traced. "Mazes were designed to trap people, to give them no way out. A labyrinth"—her fingertip traveled slowly to the center, paused there—"is designed to get you to the center, then go back out again. You can't get lost in it, if you just follow it, let it take its path."

Helen put her hand over Maggie's, let Maggie guide them both back to the edge of the carved circle. "Right back out where you started, then."

"Yes. Back to the same place."

"So what's the deal? What changes, if you end up where you began?"

Maggie hugged her tight for a moment, released her gently. "Hopefully, you've changed. Because of the journey." She sighed. "Gotta go. You coming?"

"Yeah." Helen followed her back to the church.

About the Author

Born in Japan in 1957, Pat Welch has lived and worked in the San Francisco area since 1986. She began publishing the Helen Black mystery series with Naiad Press in 1990, moving to Bella Books in 1999. Her first Helen Black mystery with Bella Books, *Moving Targets*, was nominated for a Lambda Literary Award. When she isn't writing she likes to read, listen to bluegrass music and hang out with her wonderful partner, Angelique.

Publications from

BELLA BOOKS, INC.

The best in contemporary lesbian fiction

P.O. Box 10543, Tallahassee, FL 32302

Phone: 800-729-4992

www.bellabooks.com

CALL OF THE DARK: EROTIC LESBIAN TALES OF THE SUPERNATURAL edited by Therese Szymanski—from Bella After Dark. 320 pp. 1-59493-040-6 $14.95

A TIME TO CAST AWAY A Helen Black Mystery by Pat Welch. 240 pp. Helen stops by Alice's apartment—only to find the woman dead . . . 1-59493-036-8 $12.95

DESERT OF THE HEART by Jane Rule. 224 pp. The book that launched the most popular lesbian movie of all time is back. 1-1-59493-035-X $12.95

THE NEXT WORLD by Ursula Steck. 240 pp. Anna's friend Mido is threatened and eventually disappears . . . 1-59493-024-4 $12.95

CALL SHOTGUN by Jaime Clevenger. 240 pp. Kelly gets pulled back into the world of private investigation . . . 1-59493-016-3 $12.95

52 PICKUP by Bonnie J. Morris and E.B. Casey. 240 pp. 52 hot, romantic tales—one for every Saturday night of the year. 1-59493-026-0 $12.95

GOLD FEVER by Lyn Denison. 240 pp. Kate's first love, Ashley, returns to their home town, where Kate now lives . . . 1-1-59493-039-2 $12.95

RISKY INVESTMENT by Beth Moore. 240 pp. Lynn's best friend and roommate needs her to pretend Chris is his fiancé. But nothing is ever easy. 1-59493-019-8 $12.95

HUNTER'S WAY by Gerri Hill. 240 pp. Homicide detective Tori Hunter is forced to team up with the hot-tempered Samantha Kennedy. 1-59493-018-X $12.95

CAR POOL by Karin Kallmaker. 240 pp. Soft shoulders, merging traffic and slippery when wet . . . Anthea and Shay find love in the car pool. 1-59493-013-9 $12.95

NO SISTER OF MINE by Jeanne G'Fellers. 240 pp. Telepathic women fight to coexist with a patriarchal society that wishes their eradication. ISBN 1-59493-017-1 $12.95

ON THE WINGS OF LOVE by Megan Carter. 240 pp. Stacie's reporting career is on the rocks. She has to interview bestselling author Cheryl, or else! ISBN 1-59493-027-9 $12.95

WICKED GOOD TIME by Diana Tremain Braund. 224 pp. Does Christina need Miki as a protector . . . or want her as a lover? ISBN 1-59493-031-7 $12.95

THOSE WHO WAIT by Peggy J. Herring. 240 pp. Two brilliant sisters—in love with the same woman! ISBN 1-59493-032-5 $12.95

ABBY'S PASSION by Jackie Calhoun. 240 pp. Abby's bipolar sister helps turn her world upside down, so she must decide what's most important. ISBN 1-59493-014-7 $12.95

PICTURE PERFECT by Jane Vollbrecht. 240 pp. Kate is reintroduced to Casey, the daughter of an old friend. Can they withstand Kate's career? ISBN 1-59493-015-5 $12.95

PAPERBACK ROMANCE by Karin Kallmaker. 240 pp. Carolyn falls for tall, dark and . . . female . . . in this classic lesbian romance. ISBN 1-59493-033-3 $12.95

DAWN OF CHANGE by Gerri Hill. 240 pp. Susan ran away to find peace in remote Kings Canyon—then she met Shawn . . . ISBN 1-59493-011-2 $12.95

DOWN THE RABBIT HOLE by Lynne Jamneck. 240 pp. Is a killer holding a grudge against FBI Agent Samantha Skellar? ISBN 1-59493-012-0 $12.95

SEASONS OF THE HEART by Jackie Calhoun. 240 pp. Overwhelmed, Sara saw only one way out—leaving . . . ISBN 1-59493-030-9 $12.95

TURNING THE TABLES by Jessica Thomas. 240 pp. The 2nd Alex Peres Mystery. *From ghosties and ghoulies and long leggity beasties . . .* ISBN 1-59493-009-0 $12.95

FOR EVERY SEASON by Frankie Jones. 240 pp. Andi, who is investigating a 65-year-old murder, meets Janice, a charming district attorney . . . ISBN 1-59493-010-4 $12.95

LOVE ON THE LINE by Laura DeHart Young. 240 pp. Kay leaves a younger woman behind to go on a mission to Alaska . . . will she regret it? ISBN 1-59493-008-2 $12.95

UNDER THE SOUTHERN CROSS by Claire McNab. 200 pp. Lee, an American travel agent, goes down under and meets Australian Alex, and the sparks fly under the Southern Cross. ISBN 1-59493-029-5 $12.95

SUGAR by Karin Kallmaker. 240 pp. Three women want sugar from Sugar, who can't make up her mind. ISBN 1-59493-001-5 $12.95

FALL GUY by Claire McNab. 200 pp. 16th Detective Inspector Carol Ashton Mystery. ISBN 1-59493-000-7 $12.95

ONE SUMMER NIGHT by Gerri Hill. 232 pp. Johanna swore to never fall in love again—but then she met the charming Kelly . . . ISBN 1-59493-007-4 $12.95

TALK OF THE TOWN TOO by Saxon Bennett. 181 pp. Second in the series about wild and fun loving friends. ISBN 1-931513-77-5 $12.95

LOVE SPEAKS HER NAME by Laura DeHart Young. 170 pp. Love and friendship, desire and intrigue, spark this exciting sequel to *Forever and the Night.* ISBN 1-59493-002-3 $12.95

TO HAVE AND TO HOLD by Peggy J. Herring. 184 pp. By finally letting down her defenses, will Dorian be opening herself to a devastating betrayal? ISBN 1-59493-005-8 $12.95

WILD THINGS by Karin Kallmaker. 228 pp. Dutiful daughter Faith has met the perfect man. There's just one problem: she's in love with his sister. ISBN 1-931513-64-3 $12.95

SHARED WINDS by Kenna White. 216 pp. Can Emma rebuild more than just Lanny's marina? ISBN 1-59493-006-6 $12.95

THE UNKNOWN MILE by Jaime Clevenger. 253 pp. Kelly's world is getting more and more complicated every moment. ISBN 1-931513-57-0 $12.95

TREASURED PAST by Linda Hill. 189 pp. A shared passion for antiques leads to love. ISBN 1-59493-003-1 $12.95

SIERRA CITY by Gerri Hill. 284 pp. Chris and Jesse cannot deny their growing attraction . . . ISBN 1-931513-98-8 $12.95

ALL THE WRONG PLACES by Karin Kallmaker. 174 pp. Sex and the single girl—Brandy is looking for love and usually she finds it. Karin Kallmaker's first *After Dark* erotic novel. ISBN 1-931513-76-7 $12.95

WHEN THE CORPSE LIES A Motor City Thriller by Therese Szymanski. 328 pp. Butch bad-girl Brett Higgins is used to waking up next to beautiful women she hardly knows. Problem is, this one's dead. ISBN 1-931513-74-0 $12.95

GUARDED HEARTS by Hannah Rickard. 240 pp. Someone's reminding Alyssa about her secret past, and then she becomes the suspect in a series of burglaries. ISBN 1-931513-99-6 $12.95

ONCE MORE WITH FEELING by Peggy J. Herring. 184 pp. Lighthearted, loving, romantic adventure. ISBN 1-931513-60-0 $12.95

TANGLED AND DARK A Brenda Strange Mystery by Patty G. Henderson. 240 pp. When investigating a local death, Brenda finds two possible killers—one diagnosed with Multiple Personality Disorder. ISBN 1-931513-75-9 $12.95

WHITE LACE AND PROMISES by Peggy J. Herring. 240 pp. Maxine and Betina realize sex may not be the most important thing in their lives. ISBN 1-931513-73-2 $12.95

UNFORGETTABLE by Karin Kallmaker. 288 pp. Can Rett find love with the cheerleader who broke her heart so many years ago? ISBN 1-931513-63-5 $12.95

HIGHER GROUND by Saxon Bennett. 280 pp. A delightfully complex reflection of the successful, high society lives of a small group of women. ISBN 1-931513-69-4 $12.95

LAST CALL A Detective Franco Mystery by Baxter Clare. 240 pp. Frank overlooks all else to try to solve a cold case of two murdered children . . . ISBN 1-931513-70-8 $12.95

ONCE UPON A DYKE: NEW EXPLOITS OF FAIRY-TALE LESBIANS by Karin Kallmaker, Julia Watts, Barbara Johnson & Therese Szymanski. 320 pp. You've never read fairy tales like these before! From Bella After Dark. ISBN 1-931513-71-6 $14.95

FINEST KIND OF LOVE by Diana Tremain Braund. 224 pp. Can Molly and Carolyn stop clashing long enough to see beyond their differences? ISBN 1-931513-68-6 $12.95

DREAM LOVER by Lyn Denison. 188 pp. A soft, sensuous, romantic fantasy. ISBN 1-931513-96-1 $12.95

NEVER SAY NEVER by Linda Hill. 224 pp. A classic love story . . . where rules aren't the only things broken. ISBN 1-931513-67-8 $12.95

PAINTED MOON by Karin Kallmaker. 214 pp. Stranded together in a snowbound cabin, Jackie and Leah's lives will never be the same. ISBN 1-931513-53-8 $12.95

WIZARD OF ISIS by Jean Stewart. 240 pp. Fifth in the exciting Isis series. ISBN 1-931513-71-4 $12.95

WOMAN IN THE MIRROR by Jackie Calhoun. 216 pp. Josey learns to love again, while her niece is learning to love women for the first time. ISBN 1-931513-78-3 $12.95

SUBSTITUTE FOR LOVE by Karin Kallmaker. 200 pp. When Holly and Reyna meet the combination adds up to pure passion. But what about tomorrow? ISBN 1-931513-62-7 $12.95

GULF BREEZE by Gerri Hill. 288 pp. Could Carly really be the woman Pat has always been searching for? ISBN 1-931513-97-X $12.95

THE TOMSTOWN INCIDENT by Penny Hayes. 184 pp. Caught between two worlds, Eloise must make a decision that will change her life forever. ISBN 1-931513-56-2 $12.95

MAKING UP FOR LOST TIME by Karin Kallmaker. 240 pp. Discover delicious recipes for romance by the undisputed mistress. ISBN 1-931513-61-9 $12.95

THE WAY LIFE SHOULD BE by Diana Tremain Braund. 173 pp. With which woman will Jennifer find the true meaning of love? ISBN 1-931513-66-X $12.95

BACK TO BASICS: A BUTCH/FEMME ANTHOLOGY edited by Therese Szymanski—from Bella After Dark. 324 pp. ISBN 1-931513-35-X $14.95

SURVIVAL OF LOVE by Frankie J. Jones. 236 pp. What will Jody do when she falls in love with her best friend's daughter? ISBN 1-931513-55-4 $12.95

LESSONS IN MURDER by Claire McNab. 184 pp. 1st Detective Inspector Carol Ashton Mystery. ISBN 1-931513-65-1 $12.95

DEATH BY DEATH by Claire McNab. 167 pp. 5th Denise Cleever Thriller. ISBN 1-931513-34-1 $12.95

CAUGHT IN THE NET by Jessica Thomas. 188 pp. A wickedly observant story of mystery, danger, and love in Provincetown. ISBN 1-931513-54-6 $12.95

DREAMS FOUND by Lyn Denison. Australian Riley embarks on a journey to meet her birth mother . . . and gains not just a family, but the love of her life. ISBN 1-931513-58-9 $12.95

A MOMENT'S INDISCRETION by Peggy J. Herring. 154 pp. Jackie is torn between her better judgment and the overwhelming attraction she feels for Valerie. ISBN 1-931513-59-7 $12.95

IN EVERY PORT by Karin Kallmaker. 224 pp. Jessica has a woman in every port. Will meeting Cat change all that? ISBN 1-931513-36-8 $12.95

TOUCHWOOD by Karin Kallmaker. 240 pp. Rayann loves Louisa. Louisa loves Rayann. Can the decades between their ages keep them apart? ISBN 1-931513-37-6 $12.95

WATERMARK by Karin Kallmaker. 248 pp. Teresa wants a future with a woman whose heart has been frozen by loss. Sequel to *Touchwood.* ISBN 1-931513-38-4 $12.95

EMBRACE IN MOTION by Karin Kallmaker. 240 pp. Has Sarah found lust or love? ISBN 1-931513-39-2 $12.95

ONE DEGREE OF SEPARATION by Karin Kallmaker. 232 pp. Sizzling small town romance between Marian, the town librarian, and the new girl from the big city. ISBN 1-931513-30-9 $12.95

CRY HAVOC A Detective Franco Mystery by Baxter Clare. 240 pp. A dead hustler with a headless rooster in his lap sends Lt. L.A. Franco headfirst against Mother Love. ISBN 1-931513931-7 $12.95

DISTANT THUNDER by Peggy J. Herring. 294 pp. Bankrobbing drifter Cordy awakens strange new feelings in Leo in this romantic tale set in the Old West. ISBN 1-931513-28-7 $12.95

COP OUT by Claire McNab. 216 pp. 4th Detective Inspector Carol Ashton Mystery. ISBN 1-931513-29-5 $12.95

BLOOD LINK by Claire McNab. 159 pp. 15th Detective Inspector Carol Ashton Mystery. Is Carol unwittingly playing into a deadly plan? ISBN 1-931513-27-9 $12.95

TALK OF THE TOWN by Saxon Bennett. 239 pp. With enough beer, barbecue and B.S., anything is possible! ISBN 1-931513-18-X $12.95

MAYBE NEXT TIME by Karin Kallmaker. 256 pp. Sabrina has everything she ever wanted—except Jorie. ISBN 1-931513-26-0 $12.95

WHEN GOOD GIRLS GO BAD: A Motor City Thriller by Therese Szymanski. 230 pp. Brett, Randi, and Allie join forces to stop a serial killer. ISBN 1-931513-11-2 $12.95

A DAY TOO LONG: A Helen Black Mystery by Pat Welch. 328 pp. This time Helen's fate is in her own hands. ISBN 1-931513-22-8 $12.95

THE RED LINE OF YARMALD by Diana Rivers. 256 pp. The Hadra's only hope lies in a magical red line . . . climactic sequel to *Clouds of War.* ISBN 1-931513-23-6 $12.95

OUTSIDE THE FLOCK by Jackie Calhoun. 224 pp. Jo embraces her new love and life. ISBN 1-931513-13-9 $12.95

LEGACY OF LOVE by Marianne K. Martin. 224 pp. Read the whole Sage Bristo story. ISBN 1-931513-15-5 $12.95

STREET RULES: A Detective Franco Mystery by Baxter Clare. 304 pp. Gritty, fast-paced mystery with compelling Detective L.A. Franco. ISBN 1-931513-14-7 $12.95

RECOGNITION FACTOR: 4th Denise Cleever Thriller by Claire McNab. 176 pp. Denise Cleever tracks a notorious terrorist to America. ISBN 1-931513-24-4 $12.95

NORA AND LIZ by Nancy Garden. 296 pp. Lesbian romance by the author of *Annie on My Mind.* ISBN 1931513-20-1 $12.95

MIDAS TOUCH by Frankie J. Jones. 208 pp. Sandra had everything but love. ISBN 1-931513-21-X $12.95

BEYOND ALL REASON by Peggy J. Herring. 240 pp. A romance hotter than Texas. ISBN 1-9513-25-2 $12.95

ACCIDENTAL MURDER: 14th Detective Inspector Carol Ashton Mystery by Claire McNab. 208 pp. Carol Ashton tracks an elusive killer. ISBN 1-931513-16-3 $12.95

SEEDS OF FIRE: Tunnel of Light Trilogy, Book 2 by Karin Kallmaker writing as Laura Adams. 274 pp. In Autumn's dreams no one is who they seem. ISBN 1-931513-19-8 $12.95

DRIFTING AT THE BOTTOM OF THE WORLD by Auden Bailey. 288 pp. Beautifully written first novel set in Antarctica. ISBN 1-931513-17-1 $12.95

CLOUDS OF WAR by Diana Rivers. 288 pp. Women unite to defend Zelindar! ISBN 1-931513-12-0 $12.95

DEATHS OF JOCASTA: 2nd Micky Knight Mystery by J.M. Redmann. 408 pp. Sexy and intriguing Lambda Literary Award–nominated mystery. ISBN 1-931513-10-4 $12.95

LOVE IN THE BALANCE by Marianne K. Martin. 256 pp. The classic lesbian love story, back in print! ISBN 1-931513-08-2 $12.95

THE COMFORT OF STRANGERS by Peggy J. Herring. 272 pp. Lela's work was her passion . . . until now. ISBN 1-931513-09-0 $12.95

WHEN EVIL CHANGES FACE: A Motor City Thriller by Therese Szymanski. 240 pp. Brett Higgins is back in another heart-pounding thriller. ISBN 0-9677753-3-7 $11.95

CHICKEN by Paula Martinac. 208 pp. Lynn finds that the only thing harder than being in a lesbian relationship is ending one. ISBN 1-931513-07-4 $11.95

TAMARACK CREEK by Jackie Calhoun. 208 pp. An intriguing story of love and danger. ISBN 1-931513-06-6 $11.95

DEATH BY THE RIVERSIDE: 1st Micky Knight Mystery by J.M. Redmann. 320 pp. Finally back in print, the book that launched the Lambda Literary Award–winning Micky Knight mystery series. ISBN 1-931513-05-8 $11.95

EIGHTH DAY: A Cassidy James Mystery by Kate Calloway. 272 pp. In the eighth installment of the Cassidy James mystery series, Cassidy goes undercover at a camp for troubled teens. ISBN 1-931513-04-X $11.95

MIRRORS by Marianne K. Martin. 208 pp. Jean Carson and Shayna Bradley fight for a future together. ISBN 1-931513-02-3 $11.95

THE ULTIMATE EXIT STRATEGY: A Virginia Kelly Mystery by Nikki Baker. 240 pp. The long-awaited return of the wickedly observant Virginia Kelly.
ISBN 1-931513-03-1 $11.95

FOREVER AND THE NIGHT by Laura DeHart Young. 224 pp. Desire and passion ignite the frozen Arctic in this exciting sequel to the classic romantic adventure *Love on the Line*.
ISBN 0-931513-00-7 $11.95

WINGED ISIS by Jean Stewart. 240 pp. The long-awaited sequel to *Warriors of Isis* and the fourth in the exciting Isis series. ISBN 1-931513-01-5 $11.95

ROOM FOR LOVE by Frankie J. Jones. 192 pp. Jo and Beth must overcome the past in order to have a future together. ISBN 0-9677753-9-6 $11.95

THE QUESTION OF SABOTAGE by Bonnie J. Morris. 144 pp. A charming, sexy tale of romance, intrigue, and coming of age. ISBN 0-9677753-8-8 $11.95

SLEIGHT OF HAND by Karin Kallmaker writing as Laura Adams. 256 pp. A journey of passion, heartbreak, and triumph that reunites two women for a final chance at their destiny. ISBN 0-9677753-7-X $11.95

MOVING TARGETS: A Helen Black Mystery by Pat Welch. 240 pp. Helen must decide if getting to the bottom of a mystery is worth hitting bottom. ISBN 0-9677753-6-1 $11.95

CALM BEFORE THE STORM by Peggy J. Herring. 208 pp. Colonel Robicheaux retires from the military and comes out of the closet. ISBN 0-9677753-1-0 $11.95

OFF SEASON by Jackie Calhoun. 208 pp. Pam threatens Jenny and Rita's fledgling relationship. ISBN 0-9677753-0-2 $11.95

BOLD COAST LOVE by Diana Tremain Braund. 208 pp. Jackie Claymont fights for her reputation and the right to love the woman she chooses. ISBN 0-9677753-2-9 $11.95

THE WILD ONE by Lyn Denison. 176 pp. Rachel never expected that Quinn's wild yearnings would change her life forever. ISBN 0-9677753-4-5 $11.95

SWEET FIRE by Saxon Bennett. 224 pp. Welcome to Heroy—the town with more lesbians per capita than any other place on the planet! ISBN 0-9677753-5-3 $11.95